Twin

Jennifer E. Kirk

To Bob
Thank you for your
generous support

[signature]

DS Press

Twinkle Little Star

978-0-9542455-5-9

First Published 2011

Published by DS Press

Bolton
BL7 9YA

Printed and bound in the UK by the
MPG Books Group, Bodmin and King's Lynn

Twinkle Little Star

To Emily and Tesrin

1

You didn't have to be a genius to figure out it was a hoax. Anybody with half a brain would have realised that. But Dezza still found himself staring at the screen with a mix of curiosity and anger. Over the next two hours he made himself a coffee, drank it, started to shave and gave up before the lather had even touched his face. Each thing he did could not shift the image of the message from his mind.

Dead men can't talk, he told himself. Dead men tell no tales. That's what the salvagers always said about the more unusual salvage jobs in the aftermath of accidents that no-one could quite figure out. In the game you ignored the human cost and got on with the pure unadulterated rigours of what was just a job.

But Tubs had been more than just someone he had known. Quite apart from a tour across the reaches of space aboard the tugship *Solitude*, Tubs had been someone he had truly opened up to and could almost say had been a friend. Those were few and far between these days.

The message had been from Tubs. Short, clear and to the point. The trouble was, Tubs was dead.

He flicked the screen back on and brought up the message again. Reading the words, he felt his stomach knot at the memories. *He really was dead, wasn't he?* The seeds of doubt were there; he almost wanted to believe that he had been mistaken all those years ago and that Tubs was still out there, somewhere.

He shook his head and scrunched the empty Styrofoam coffee cup. Dribbles of dark liquid stained his fingers as he threw the crumpled mess into the waist disposal chute. It had to be a hoax – someone's idea of a sick joke.

A name flicked into his mind and he reached for the screen controls. He had to call somebody, so he called the only person he thought he could talk it over with. He hadn't had reason to call, not since the tribunal. But sometimes the past likes to come back around and make an unwelcome courtesy call. *Needs must when the Devil shits on you and all that*, he thought.

Some telephone numbers etch themselves onto the consciousness. Like old girlfriends and that sweet sixteen-year-old he knew at school but never had the guts to ring and ask out. He had bribed her friend for that number. What a waste that had been, but the number was still there in his memory, just like this one.

The line clicked live and the phone rang at the other end. It wasn't the most modern way to make contact after all these years, but if truth were told, it was the only way he had. So he let it ring, counting those annoying buzzes off in his mind as they came.

Just fifteen rings, he told himself, *fifteen then we hang up, delete the message, and pretend this all never happened*. Fifteen rings to turn his back once more on the past.

It got to fourteen before the call was picked up at the other end. With a pang of regret Dezza wondered if he ought to have hung up before now. But it was too late; if he hung up now they would have his number and call him back.

"Hey. Who is this?" came a gruff voice; "It's three in the goddamn morning for Christ sakes!"

Despite the reasons for him calling, a grin flickered momentarily on Dezza's face.

"Toze, you military pen-pushing prick. It's Dezza."

A sigh drifted down the line. "Dezza? Shit. I should have known I recognised the number. Same shit holds though: why are you calling me at this hour?"

"I got a message. It's kind of weird." Suddenly he felt stupid for calling. Just how do you broach the subject that you think a ghost is sending you a message?

"Message? What kind of message?" said Toze, suddenly taking more of an interest.

Dezza felt there was something Toze was holding out on. Not sure what, he threw caution to the wind and went for broke. If you were going to say something that could book you a one way ticket to the loony bin, he figured, you might as well tell it first to someone who wasn't going to call the men with white coats.

"It says it's from Tubs," he blurted. There – it was out now. Let Toze make of that what he would.

There was a pause before the reply came. "Tubs you say?" Toze mulled the idea. Strangely he seemed to take it in his stride. No laughing, no questioning. There was just plain acceptance in his voice.

"You aren't surprised?" Dezza found himself asking. Well, it was a valid question, wasn't it?

"Sort of. Yes and no," was the reply. "If the message is what I think it is, then I got one just the same yesterday."

Dezza was taken aback. So Toze wasn't the hoaxer. "Who do you think sent them?" he asked.

"Who do you have in mind?" came the retort.

He thought for a moment then came clean. "Shit, Toze. I thought it was you."

Toze laughed. "You doubting son-of-a-bitch. Well, this time it wasn't. There are some things that make a man not want to turn it on its head and make a joke of it, and what I went through with you was one of those things."

"So if you didn't, then who did?"

"Tubs?"

"A dead man? Puh-*lease*."

"Tracker saw him again on the *Cerberus*. At least he said so, right before he died. And Tubs' body was gone from the elevator."

"We guessed that was the creature, not Tubs."

"But the message," said Dezza earnestly, "The one I got told me things that only he could ever have known; things that never even came up at the tribunal."

"Me too," said Toze grimly. He did not sound like a man who was making it up.

Dezza shook his head. How could the same shit happen to the same guy three times? It was like that damn Starliner was a bad penny that was always coming back for more. Except this time the *Cerberus* was definitely gone – they had both witnessed the meteorite storm pummel that old hulk into nothing. But then, the message never claimed otherwise.

"Listen. Stay where you are. I'll come on over," said Toze, "I haven't seen you since the tribunal, and I'd rather talk in person than over a telephone. You still live at the same dive?"

"Yeah."

"Good. See you in a couple of hours. Don't go running out on me."

Then before he could say anything else, the line clicked dead and the dialling tone buzzed angrily in Dezza's ear. He hung up and settled back to wait; he had nothing better to do.

*   *   *   *   *

Toze came around five-thirty in the morning. The sun was already beginning to creep over the horizon of the Earth, and night shifted to day below the orbiting city as the terminator tracked slowly around across northern Russia.

Dezza let him through the stained door to the apartment without a word and checked the empty corridor outside before he spoke.

"What did your message say?" he asked.

Toze shrugged. "On the face of it, I'd say pretty much the same as yours."

10

Dezza grunted an acknowledgement. He stepped over to the screen and flicked it on. "Come take a look and tell me."

Toze shuffled closer.

Dezza's fingers tapped on the touchpad and the text message came up into view. Toze said nothing as he read. Then he leant back and massaged his eyes briefly with the balls of his fists.

"Yeah. That's it."

"Well?"

Toze looked to him, fixing him with a look that could have boiled eggs at twenty paces. But Dezza was immune and didn't react, instead waiting patiently for the answer. Toze relaxed.

"A hoax," he said finally and threw himself down onto the sofa to brood.

Dezza shook his head. "That's what I thought at first. But some of the things in there are just impossible for someone pulling a fast one to know. How *did* they find out about the dead man in the drive chamber for a start? I certainly don't remember *that* coming up at the tribunal. Do you?"

Toze shook his head. "No." He paused. "But how can it be true? Ghosts don't exist. Do they?"

"I didn't think so until I stepped foot on the *Cerberus*. That thing is one huge floating ghost, and the bastard keeps coming back to haunt me."

"Then you're going to go?" asked Toze at last. "Go on the cruise and see if this all pans out? That's one expensive wild goose chase if it doesn't. And anyway – they left us out to dry at the tribunal. Why do we care anyway? Let the authorities deal with it and send some other bunch of suckers to mop up the mess."

Dezza crumpled back into his chair. "I don't know," he replied, deflated.

"Shit. I thought this was all over."

"It is. I mean, it was."

Toze looked him straight in the eye. "Jeez. All this really spooks you. Do me a favour, Dezza. Just one thing – delete that message. Delete it, and pretend it never existed." He got up from the chair. "I'll tell you now that someday you'll thank me for it."

Dezza nodded.

Toze looked over the room as if he was seeing it for the first time. "Nice place you have here."

"Quit the bullshit."

Toze laughed. "Still a tetchy sod after all these years. Well, it was a nice trip over. Good to catch up with old friends and all that. Remember Dezza: no-one gets any prizes for being a burning martyr. Delete that message and get on with your life."

"Yeah, I guess so," said Dezza half-heartedly. But the words sounded false, even to his own ears.

"You just look after yourself, and think about what I've said. I'll see myself out."

Dezza watched him go, and watched the back of the closed door for another hour after he had gone. All the time his mind burned over the message. Finally he groaned and pulled himself up from the chair. Maybe Toze was right. Maybe he should just get really drunk and just forget about this whole thing.

The screen hooked his attention from the corner of his eye and he groaned again. Some things just wouldn't leave him alone. Angrily he stormed to the device and pulled the plug.

With an angry beep of electronics the screen went blank. But still the image of the message burned brighter still in his mind's eye.

*   *   *   *   *

An hour later he had scraped a few clothes together into a carryall and was on his way. Toze could say all he wanted – and Dezza knew he would if he found out – but he knew he would regret it if he didn't go.

Within less than two hours he was at a shuttle port waiting for a connecting flight. It gave him time to think, so he headed to the bar to drown his conscience in cheap watered-down booze in case it talked him into going home.

Sometimes the bottom of a bottle is the best place to be.

2

He could have listened. Hell, there were lots of people he could have listened to. But right now the one that his subconscious was nagging him about was Toze. He had told him to forget it - just delete the message and carry on his life as if nothing had ever happened.

Yeah, sure. That was the easy way out – the coward's way. But Dezza had been running from the behemoth of the *Cerberus* and everything it represented for too long. Toze had not been there at the start. Toze had not been forced once already to go back and confront the demons. Dezza *had*. He remembered that moment, stepping off the dropship into the dust-coated, decayed environment of the *Cerberus*. That time he knew he really had not wanted to go, and still regretted going. But now it was beyond that. This was third time lucky. Maybe.

He shook his head at the direction his thoughts seemed determined to take him. No – it was not worth the effort of self-analysis. At least if this turned into an ordinary yet expensive cruise through the stars, he could tell himself that it wasn't a wild goose chase. People had been telling him for years that he was due a holiday, and he had never listened. Maybe now he could do just that.

Deep down though he knew his fears would not let him kick back, get some rest and enjoy the cruise. The cold sweat gnawed at his body under his already sticky clothes. This was going to be the holiday from hell that would at the very least remind him for decades to come why he never did holidays.

The intercom brought him out of his reverie with a start.

"This is the captain speaking. We are about to make our final approach in to the docking bay. In a moment you will be able to see out of the starboard side viewing ports the Starliner *Persia* which will be your home for the next two months. Please could passengers fasten their safety restraints: there may be a little gravitational inequality until we have docked. This is nothing to be alarmed about; it is normal as the fields from the shuttle and the Starliner merge with each other."

Dezza saw the motley mix of passengers all fumbling for their belts. He smirked – there was no such thing as 'gravitational inequality'. Many years flying salvage crews had taught him that it was just an excuse to cover up any rough docking procedures, like airline pilots of old used 'turbulence'.

"Excuse me sir."

He looked up into the face of the stewardess. She was attractive, though her makeup suggested she might be a few years older than she was trying to look.

"Everyone has to be strapped in for the final approach," she continued with a smile.

A part of him bubbled with anger at being talked down to, but he forced a smile in return and did as she told him. There was no time to kick up a fuss. They would only get security involved and bundle him back to Earth on the next shuttle. That would be one hell of an expensive trip into space and back.

She nodded and moved on down the aisle as soon as the belts clunked into place. He turned and watched her go. Her arse was tight in her pencil skirt, and he thought he could almost see the outline of stocking-tops and suspenders. He forced himself to turn back – best not let his imagination get carried away. He reached instead for the in-flight magazine and leafed through its uninspiring

14

articles on Martian resorts and wines of the Rhine region. These things were always the same; useless junk written by jobbing journalists that couldn't get any other work.

He stuffed it back into the magazine holder with disgust and looked to the viewing port. At least they had given him a seat with a window – not that the shuttle was that busy. The *Persia* had no doubt been in orbit taking on passengers all week, and he was just one of the last stragglers taking advantage of cheap last minute deals. Not that it was that cheap; it had taken just about all of his meagre savings to get this far.

The stars seemed so clear up here. Up above the Earth's hazy atmosphere it was like looking up at the night sky with cataracts removed. No wonder they say that once you went into space you would be hooked and always want to go back. No kidding. Maybe that was why so many retired Astros chose to live in the orbiting cities. That and real estate on Earth being too expensive for the masses to afford. Still, it worked out in the end.

The shuttle altered course and the stars whirled around with nauseating speed. He saw that some of the other passengers were getting queasy. It wasn't a sight that the human mind took to too easily, and more than one quietly reached for a sick bag.

Dezza was an old hand. It did not bother him one bit and he turned back to the port to watch for the first glimpse of the *Persia*. It had been a long time since the *Cerberus*, but he could still feel his heart racing. Would the sight bring back unwelcome memories? He could feel his heart almost in his throat as he strained against the restraints of his seat to catch a first glimpse.

*   *   *   *   *

The *Persia* was not what he was expecting. Where the *Cerberus* had looked like her construction had been inspired by early twentieth century ocean liners of the

15

golden age of ships, the *Persia* was an ugly affair. The first thing he saw was the antenna cluster reaching out into space ahead of the Starliner. The cluster seemed to go on forever, gently drifting by as the shuttle nosed on in closer. Then came the hull at last. White and clinical, it was the typical anti-radiation coated material of preference for passenger ships.

Dezza felt his face twist into an ironic laugh. *Space will make you impotent* they had said far too many times to count. In a way it was true, from the solar radiation. Shipping firms only cared about that when they wanted their fare-paying passengers to return happy and intact. Only the lowest of the low doing the grunt work on freight and salvage runs got to be slowly nuked by solar radiation.

Still, who cared? He hadn't slept with a woman for years. The last thing he ever wanted was kids. So much the better if a shipping company's desire for profits and contempt for its workers had microwaved his balls.

As the hull scrolled by he was surprised at just how clutter free it was. Craning his neck to see as much as he could through the plexi-glass he saw that the hull – from what little of it he could see – was long and almost cigar shaped. How Starliner design must have changed from the days of the *Cerberus*. He shook his head and closed his eyes. No, it was not a good time to remember that. He might have been sent on this wild goose chase by a message claiming to be from the past, but that didn't mean that he had to dwell on anything. This was a time for relaxing. Even so, he found himself struggling to banish the bad thoughts.

The message had spoken of the return of the entity from deep space and that it would enter another ship – the Starliner *Persia* if it was to be believed – and the story would run all over again. It claimed to be from Tubs, but Tubs was gone; Dezza knew that. Absorbed into the entity, the manifestations of Tubs seen on the return to

16

the *Cerberus* were more creature than the man he had known. And at any rate, why would he go to Dezza? Of course it did not make sense.

But he had been unable to remove the thoughts from his head regardless. After Toze had left his apartment he had deleted the message, just as he had said to do. But the thoughts and memories and fears were still there inside his head, plaguing him until he did something to appease them. So he had done some research of his own. It was not hard to discover that the *Persia* really existed. That proved absolutely nothing. Deep space cruises were big business and always had been. There were at any one time more than a dozen huge Starliners coming and going from Earth alone. People liked to feel that they were pioneers exploring a new frontier, and space travel had given them the ability to pretend they were. Although the luxury in a Starliner was far removed from what real explorers would have to endure – the public tended to conveniently ignore or be ignorant of that bit.

Of the entity aboard the *Cerberus* there was no mention and no parallels to draw. He had, of course, come across the transcripts of the tribunal. He found them hard to read, like a knife being plunged into his psyche as he had read the slant the media had put on it all. They had been sceptical, just as they had been the first time he had returned. As for West, he had kept as quiet as he could all the way though. The cheek of the man! He had come to Dezza for help when the *Cerberus* had returned but had not lifted a finger to exonerate him at the tribunal.

He shook the thoughts out of his head. No – it would not do to get into that downward spiral of bad thoughts again. He massaged his eyelids with the backs of his hands. Forcing himself to think of something else, he looked back out of the viewing port.

The shuttle was on the final approach now – Dezza did not know how far they had travelled whilst he had been lost in his thoughts; the white metal hull of the *Persia* was so vast that it now blocked out any trace of the stars. It was just an endless gently curving wall of white punctuated by viewing ports coated with a protective film that made it impossible to see through them.

Abruptly the white steel wall came to an end and a huge bay opened out into the ship. For a moment Dezza felt a wave of disorientation as his mind struggled to cope with the anomalies brought about by the generated gravity fields. Up here, down was just a relative term to whichever way your feet were pointing. Looking out of the port it felt suddenly as if he was being forced over onto his side. But it was a momentary feeling, and it passed quickly as the shuttle rolled and aligned itself with the *Persia*'s gravity field for the final descent into the docking bay.

*　　　*　　　*　　　*　　　*

The other passengers were quick to depart. Maybe the lure of the onboard entertainment and a couple of months of mind-bending rest, relaxation and pure unadulterated fun was too much for them to let wait a moment longer. Or maybe the subsidised duty free booze at more than a hundred bars scattered along the Starliner's decks – if the literature he had scanned through told the truth – was calling them. Whatever it was the last few stragglers had departed clutching at their meagre hand luggage.

Only Dezza held back as the questions circled inside his head. What the hell was he doing here?

"Is there a problem, sir?"

It was the same voice that oozed sex appeal that he had heard earlier in the flight. He turned and looked straight into the face of the stewardess.

"Well?" she asked with a smile as she looked him up and down, "You don't strike me as the usual senior citizen cruiser that we get around here."

18

She looked to his small military-style holdall. He looked too, and suddenly felt a little stupid standing there clutching the faded and worn relic from a freight hauling company of a decade ago that probably no longer existed in the tide of take-overs and corporate asset stripping.

"Hell," she added nonchalantly, "You look like the kind of guy who left to his own devices and a suitcase would do his packing in three minutes flat with a shovel." She looked him quizzically in the eye. "Competition prize or are you just skipping planet side for a couple of months until the Police lose interest?"

For a moment he wondered if she was serious. Then he caught the twinkle in her eye, and his hardened exterior melted and he could not help but share a laugh.

"Shit. Yeah. I guess it was one of those more last minute things. I guess I just wanted to have myself a holiday and I left it a little late to do the organising," he lied. Well, it was a half lie. Sort of.

She did not seem to be convinced by his answer, but she nodded and stood back and gestured to the open hatch.

"Whatever it is, maybe you want to get on and get to the fun."

It took a moment for him to gather his thoughts. Her words left him wondering whether she had been trying to hit on him.

"What are you waiting for? A gold-plated invitation to disembark? Get the hell off my shuttle."

He could feel the regrets inside his mind wash over him, and suddenly he felt that he didn't want to go through with this. Maybe it had been a mistake; he thought about turning around and heading on back to Earth. Toze would never leave him alone about this, if he ever found out. But he could live with it. Right now he just felt stupid.

"When is the shuttle going back?" he asked.

She looked surprised. "You done with cruising already?"

"No," he stuttered, "I changed my mind. When is the shuttle returning the space station?"

She laughed – loudly. "Hell, that's a good one! I've never heard that one before. Forget it, mystery man. This is *Persia*'s own shuttle. It's here to stay now for the duration of the trip. Now get the hell off it so I can get going. You're fouling my act."

"What do you mean?"

"What does it sound like I mean? I mean: this shuttle craft is going to be sticking to the big weiß one upstairs like a limpet until we get right back into orbit here in a couple of months time. You, my friend, are out of luck in that department. Still, you could just go and have a good time like everyone else is sure to. Strictly speaking, mystery man: get off my goddamn shuttle."

She flicked open the panel at the side of the hatch and keyed a code into the control panel behind. Aboard the shuttle the lights dimmed then flickered off. She ducked through the hatch into the brightness of the docking bay beyond.

"Are you coming?" she asked. Without waiting for a reply she walked off down the connecting tunnel.

Dezza watched her go, watching that tight skirt and tailored jacket on her and the perfect figure that they emphasised just right. He shivered; the air conditioning in the shuttle was off and he could feel the air cooling down fast.

"Hey! Wait up!" he called and ducked through the hatch clutching his holdall.

She turned a moment and smiled as she waited for him to catch up.

"I never even got your name," he panted breathlessly.

She seemed to consider his request a moment, as if she might not tell him. Maybe she would even report him and get him thrown off this Starliner right at the start for making passes at the staff. A part of him almost wanted it to happen; though now he wasn't quite so sure.

20

"Philipa," she said finally, "But you can call me Ma'am. Remember kiddo: don't try it on with the staff unless you really have something to offer them."

"I'm sorry."

She laughed. "Cool it. What did you think I was going to do? Bite your head off?"

"Not quite. I'm Dezza." He outstretched his hand to her.

You know, your face looks somewhat familiar." She thought for a moment, looking him up and down.

Dezza almost knew what was coming; he had had this a thousand times before. He could feel the sinking feeling that came with the recognition from the media surrounding the tribunal. It never seemed to end well: 'come meet the mad man from space who will tell you all about his trip to see ghosts'. It usually ended in tears.

"You went and found the *Cerberus*, didn't you?" she said at last, sounding more sombre than she had been. She looked him back in the eye. "Yeah. I never forget a face that's been in front of me so many times. Well, on the vid-screen at any rate. No need to look like you're going to explode or something. I'm not here to taunt you. If you ask me, it sounds like someone set you up to take a fall when you came back, regardless of what you said really happened out there." She took his hand and shook it.

"There. We're friends now. But don't think that means we're going out or anything," she scolded. "Now scoot and get yourself a fun old time."

She turned and began to climb the ramp off the loading bay into the underbelly of the Starliner. Not wishing to be left lost in the service areas he quickly hurried to keep up with her.

She was a quick walker and he found he had to go at a fair pace to keep with her. Inside the *Persia* it couldn't have been further from the *Cerberus*. It seemed that all shipping companies picked a theme and went with it for all the décor. Here, they had gone for a more Egyptian and Roman look, mixed together like the bastard offspring of Anthony and Cleopatra. Columns and hieroglyph motifs were in everything. There was no real order to anything, and it gave Dezza the impression that the designers had only seen Rome and Egypt in old Disney cartoons and some casino in Vegas rather than bothering to do proper research. Still, if it kept the average punter happy then maybe that was all they cared about.

Philipa seemed immune to it all, just hurrying past on her way to wherever. From the way she didn't speak, Dezza was left wondering whether he was just a hanger on in all of this. The silence between them was like a vacuum trying to suck the words from him to fill the void. *Just say something, anything* his mind screamed at him.

"How long have you been doing the Starliner cruises?" he found himself asking.

She shot him a look. So she did know he was there, walking with her.

"About ten years more than any of the other girls," she said, "I don't know why but it's the only job I've ever found that held my interest. Sure, I've had other jobs. But they lasted all of three months apiece. I can't abide office work, and I'm not qualified to do much else, apart from this. I tried it after trying just about everything else, and the job took a liking to me. The rest, they say, makes up the last ten years."

He nodded. "I know how a job can really appeal like that."

With a pang of regret he remembered the salvaging work. That had been similar to the feeling she had described. "No two days alike," he murmured.

"Yeah, something like that," she interrupted. Then she stopped dead in her tracks.

Dezza took another couple of steps before it clicked, and he stopped too.

"What's up?" he asked.

"Are you going to be following me like a lost puppy all afternoon, or is there somewhere I can show you the way to?"

He felt his cheeks begin to glow red in embarrassment. "Sorry."

"I may be unpleasant sometimes, but not all the time," Philipa sighed, "Show me your boarding pass and I'll show you where your cabin is."

Dezza took the crumpled papers from his pocket and handed them over. "Thanks," he mumbled.

*   *   *   *   *

It wasn't the fanciest of cabins by a long way. A man like Dezza was always on a budget, living from one meagre cheque to the next. Even at last minute pack-'em-in prices, he would be still paying for this trip in a year's time. He tried not to think about that too much.

There were two bunks set into the wall at one side, one above the other – though he would be the cabin's only occupant. A small door opened out into a shower and wash room with a toilet tucked claustrophobically into the corner. For a Starliner that was several miles long, he mused; they were pretty stingy on space. Still, it reminded him of his apartment on the orbital city. Home from home – for a sky-high price.

Unpacking didn't take long at all. Just shove the holdall into a cupboard and give it a kick so the door could close again. Dezza never was the domestic sort; not since his trainee days had he ever bothered with such niceties. Still, it was better than he could really afford.

He tested the mattress on the lower bunk with one hand then lowered himself onto it. If truth were known, he hadn't had a good night's rest for a long time. Maybe that was why he was cranky all the time. Still, now was as good a time as any to catch up on sleep. So he kicked off his trousers and threw them with his top to the cabin floor and wriggled under the crisp fresh sheets.

3

At first there was darkness. Then as his eyes adjusted, the darkness begin to reveal some of the shapes it had hidden and statues and imagery of ancient mythology began to ease themselves from the shadows, ghostly and still.

He gasped; this place was so familiar. It had haunted his dreams for years. Once it had been real; so real that it had etched its way into his consciousness and become a part of everything that he did.

He took a step forward, struggling in his mind to make the memories unfold and tell him with certainty where he was. This place was so familiar, yet the name would not reveal itself to him.

Dust rose up from his feet in slow-moving choking clouds. As he looked down it felt as if he was exploring underwater in some shipwreck that had lain undisturbed for decades filling with silt until his feet had disturbed it all.

Looking further down, he saw his feet illuminated clearly through the haze, and he realised that wherever he looked, a beam of light seemed to follow – a light connected to his head. He reached up, trying to feel it. His hands moved slowly in front of his eyes and for a moment his heart fluttered. They were clad in white, bulbous around the joints like a version of the Michelin man. Then he realised he was wearing gloves and attached to those gloves, when he looked, a suit that covered his whole body.

He tried to touch his face, but the gloves stopped short with a clunk. Moving them from left to right he felt through their material the smooth invisible barrier of face glass – a helmet. Then the memories began to come, and he remembered the days aboard the *Solitude* and the derelicts they had encountered.

They?

With a stab of horror he remembered Zoë and Tubs like it had been only yesterday. Were they here too? He looked around, and the ghostly been followed the movement of his head picking out antique furniture, decayed and dirtied by neglect. There was no-one with him. Behind him the beam illuminated the clinical white of the airlock of a craft docked on the other side of the hatch.

Another memory triggered, and he remembered the *Solitude* docked with the *Cerberus*.

"Zoë? Tubs?" he called out. The sounds were muffled and echoey within the helmet, but there was no answer.

He looked around again. Something caught the corner of his eye, and he felt his heart flutter. The image of Neptune stared back at him in the beam, with the same streak running across it that he had put there in the past.

Could do with the cleaning ladies up here – he could recall the words he had said as clear as if he had just spoken them. But – Zoë had been with him that day. Where was she now? Then he remembered the marines with Toze and Tracker and the return to the *Cerberus* all those years afterwards.

Zoë was gone, just a memory for him by then.

He felt the tear running down his cheek and reached up to wipe it. But the glove banged against the helmet visor and he realised he could not.

*　　　*　　　*　　　*　　　*

For some reason he went on, heading deeper into the *Cerberus*. He didn't know why. He did not remember the descent down the stairs and through the corridors that led to the atrium. One moment he was standing beside the picture of Neptune by the airlocks, the next he was there, looking up into the stars through the transparent canopy above with no real idea how he came to be there.

In front of him he saw the footprints in the dirt – one set leading down. That was strange – surely there ought to be more? Pushed by curiosity, he began to descend the stairs, taking each switchback in turn. The footsteps went down all the way to the bottom and he followed them until he found himself at the lowest floor looking out across the atrium over the stumpy hulks that had once been lush exotic vegetation, now nothing more than black skeletons.

He had thought that the footsteps in the dirt might have lead to the lifts – that was where they had gone, the first time they had been aboard the *Cerberus*. But they didn't. Instead they headed out across the atrium, in a dead straight line between the hulks until his light could not penetrate any further and they faded into the darkness.

So he followed them. Again, he did not know why. It was like something was pushing him on. He walked the width of the atrium and on into a corridor lined with tarnished gold and velvet that had once been maroon, but which now hung in dusty shards, ruined by the decades of neglect.

The footsteps ran up the middle, never deviating to one side or the other until at last they turned through ninety degrees and stopped as a single pair of feet marks in front of a door.

The more he looked, the stranger it seemed. They hadn't gone through – the door handle was still thick with dirt and tarnish, undisturbed for a long time. But they also hadn't gone anywhere else – only one set of marks had led down the corridor.

He moved until he was stood straight behind where the person who had left the trail might have stood, facing that door. He considered opening it, and going through. But they had not done that; why should he?

Who had they been? The imprints were smaller than his. Looking down he looked at them for more than a minute and wondered whether it had been Zoë. Then he shook his head. No – he knew what had happened to her. But the thoughts still haunted his mind, refusing to be banished.

An echo floated down the corridor coming from somewhere far away, and he turned towards the sound. His light showed a corridor stretching out until the beam could illuminate no further. Had he imagined that sound? He stood motionless, listening in case it came again, but it did not.

Looking back to the door he reached out to the handle as if to open it. Then he stopped – the noise had come again, only this time louder.

What the hell was that? He thought. He felt his heart rate increasing and made to call out to the others, before he realised again that this time he was alone aboard the Starliner.

There was a thump – deep and bass, like a rumble except it came just once. The pause seemed to go on forever in unexpected silence that sucked in the sounds even of his breathing like a vacuum. Then the thumping sound came again, this time closer. A tattered remnant of the décor fluttered to the ground beside him making his heart jump. He watched it fall to the floor followed by a stream of dust particles.

What had caused that? His heart was racing now, and he realised that he should have started back to the airlock. This was no place to be for a man on his own. Before he could move, the rumble came again. All the dust on the floor seemed to move in unison, and the footsteps in the dust began to fade as the dust rose off the deck and settled again like a liquid.

He didn't wait for it to come again; he turned and ran. Reaching the atrium he could hear it behind him, getting closer all the time. Already the air around him was becoming hazy in eddies of dust being blown ahead of whatever was coming. The atrium seemed larger than it

27

had before. How could it ever have been this big? He started to run, faster and faster, but his feet did not seem to want to respond. It felt like there was lead in his soles.

"Shit!" he exclaimed, "Not now!"

"Over here!"

The voice sounded like a whisper, despite the bass rumble from the corridor. He tried to move, and to his surprise found that he could again.

"This way," whispered the voice and he blindly followed.

The atrium became a corridor, and that corridor became another, and then another. He still heard the rumble of whatever was pursuing him, but instead of getting louder, it seemed to fade away until it was gone altogether.

At last he could run no more, as the sweat stuck the gossamer-fine material of his suit to him. He collapsed into a heap into the dirt on the floor, not caring anymore.

Here he saw that the decorations of this corridor were simpler and lacked the extravagance of the areas he had seen before. They looked like they were for crew rather than passengers.

"Over here!"

With a start he looked about him. The voice was the same as before, whispering, but somehow sounding as if it was right alongside him. There was nobody there, and the light from his suit torch stabbed into the darkness revealing nothing but the utilitarian corridor.

"Stop playing with me!" he screamed at the top of his lungs, "If you want to kill me then I'm here now. Just do it, damn you. Do it!"

"I might have an unpleasant streak in me, but I'm not a killer."

He saw the figure in the corner of his eye, and turned, his heart racing in his throat again. Where had they come from? There had been no-one there a moment ago.

In the beam of his torch he saw the perfect figure of Philipa, picked out in her pristine tailored stewardess' uniform. Crisp and clean, and not a trace of dirt on her despite the dereliction all around them both. To his surprise, the first thing he thought of was that she wasn't wearing a protective space suit.

"I don't need one, and neither do you," she said softly as if reading his thoughts.

Reaching up he undid the seals of his visor and lifted it, just as he had done in front of Zoë all those years ago in the atrium. He hesitated a moment, feeling the icy fingers of cold on his cheeks, but the air was breathable, just as it had been all those years ago.

"See," she said, as if she could read the doubts from his mind.

"Why are you here?" he asked.

She smiled. "Because you made me be here."

He frowned, not understanding.

She laughed. "Do you really think all this is real? Well, do you?" she scolded.

Shit. Even my own mind is against me he thought.

"I heard that," she said and wiggled her finger at him.

"Is nothing safe from you?"

"Just remember Tubs' message. You've got two weeks until the *Persia* passes the outer planets and hits deep space. Don't mess this one up."

Then, she was gone. Then everything around him was gone, and suddenly he was sitting upright in the gloom of his nice clean cabin aboard the *Persia* with the sheets stuck to the sweat on his body and nothing but the sound of the air conditioning for company.

He threw of the covered and swung himself onto the edge of the bunk. It had seemed so real. Looking at his watch he saw that he had been asleep for nearly ten hours.

"Must have needed the sleep," he muttered. Not that it mattered.

Flicking the bedside switch, the cabin was flooded with light and it was all as he had left it. He shook his head –

what had he been expecting? Dirt? Decay? A picture of Neptune with his glove print swiped across it?

"This is stupid," he muttered angrily.

Storming into the wash room, he threw the last of his clothes into a heap on the floor and stepped into the shower cubicle to clean up and wash away the sweat from the nightmare. At least he could still look presentable.

4

He wasn't expecting to see Philipa again any time soon. But today, it seemed he was destined to run into her some time or another. As it happened, she was there in the colossal auditorium that housed one of the Starliner's many restaurants in the queue just ahead of him waiting her turn for the buffet.

"We ought to stop meeting like this," he said. Well – it was the best thing he could think of saying. The thought occurred that whilst he had found her in his dreams, she might not have given him a second thought since they had walked from the shuttle. After one casual encounter, maybe she saw him merely as someone she had met, very briefly.

"Mr Booth, I do hope that you aren't going to be making a habit out of this," she said, turning to him without missing a beat.

She didn't seem surprised to see him even though on a Starliner encompassing more space than an average city centre; it stood to reason that they could have never met again. He got the feeling that she had been waiting for him to turn up ever since she had showed him the way to the cabin decks.

"Please," he said hastily, "call me Dezza; everyone else does."

"I will call you a nuisance if I so chose. And Mr Booth; you are very close to being that."

She shuffled forward with the queue leaving Dezza feeling that he had pushed on in where he was not wanted.

"Look," he said, trying another approach, "I just wanted to apologise for on the shuttle. I haven't been off-world in a long time, and it just sort of started to get to me a little. New situations and all that."

His words seemed to fade out. They felt as if they were corny and made up. All the time she just kept on moving, taking a plate and helping herself to salad and seafood from the buffet.

"Do you make a habit of stalking?" she said without looking up.

He got the impression that she was not really angry with him. It was more that she was testing him in a way.

"No." He thought of Tubs' message and the *Cerberus*. "Usually things make a habit of stalking me."

Now she seemed interested, though it was a fleeting glimpse in her body language that he picked up on. Otherwise, she hid her emotions well.

He decided to lay it all on her, and see what the reaction was. What the hell – if she brushed him off like a piece of dirt, then he hadn't lost anything. Sooner or later it usually came to that for him.

"I'm here because I've got a feeling that something bad is going to happen on this cruise."

There – he had said it. Suddenly he felt stupid and could feel his cheeks reddening up. Had he said too much?

She didn't react. Instead she just kept on helping herself to the buffet, took a napkin from a pile and some cutlery from the open drawer next to them, and moved on to the end of the tables.

For a moment he wondered if he had really said it or that she had heard him.

"You know Mr Booth," she said at last, licking her fingers from where they had caught the mayonnaise on the edge of her plate, "You'll look a lot less stupid if you go through a buffet queue with a plate and actually fetch yourself something to eat." Then she turned from him and walked off amongst the tables of eating passengers looking for a place to sit.

"Hey buddy," drawled an American voice behind him, "You're holding up the line."

He turned, still trying to marshal his thoughts. "What?"

"Are you going to get some chow, or are you going to stand there all day hogging the pasta bar, buddy?"

The old Dezza would have kicked off at even the thought of some fat, balding tourist in a loud shirt talking to him in that way. But he resisted the urge and grabbed a plate of tuna pasta before mumbling his apologies and heading off into the crowded tables looking for where Philipa had gone.

He had a gut feeling that he had blown it with her. Once again the patented Dezza lurching through life with one hand on the social life self-destruct button had worked its usual charm. At least this time no-one had slapped him straight across the face. Well, not yet though there was probably still time.

He found her in a corner, at a table that he guessed was her usual favourite spot to eat. Out of the way, the tables around it probably never got all that busy. At the same time she could see all the comings and goings to the auditorium restaurant – useful for spotting clingy passengers who she did not want anything more to do with than she had to, giving her more than enough time to clear out of sight.

Clingy passengers like Dezza – it was a thought to have in the back of his mind.

If she pulled that trick often, she didn't let on that she did now. Instead she watched him coming with his messily piled tuna pasta. She looked him up and down across a fork of daintily mounded salad.

"You are making a habit of this, aren't you?" she said.

He sat down, not waiting to be invited and pushed his plate to one side, the food already forgotten.

"Look, I'm sorry," he blurted, "I guess I came over as a bit of a weird type just now."

Her fork paused between plate and mouth as she considered her words. "Let me guess: it came to you in a flash that pulling out the old 'I've been to space and seen weird shit and now the weird shit is back for more' story wasn't making you any friends, so you thought you would come and turn on the good old fashioned charm. Well, mystery man, let's hear what the charm has to offer."

The fork reached its mark and she chewed thoughtfully, waiting for what he had to say. Dezza realised he had at least thirty seconds to say what he had to and salvage any credibility that he could. At the very least, maybe she wouldn't call in the Starliner's security and have him frog-marched off down to the med-unit.

"I've been really stressed out. You know about what went on in my past. All I'll say is that please consider that the media were gunning for me from the start – they wanted to make me out to look bad, and I didn't get a fair press because of that. Ever since then, things have been stressful."

Philipa swallowed and jabbed the fork back into the food on her plate. "Go on. Let's say I'm listening."

"Okay. I've been really stressed – anyone would be. So I got told I needed a break," he lied. It was a half lie of sorts.

"You missed out the interesting bit."

"The interesting bit?"

Philipa sighed. "What, is there an echo in here? The bit about coming here to save the world. Or at least: save the *Persia* from a fate worse than death."

"I never said it was a fate worse than death," Dezza said sulkily, picking up his own fork and prodding at his tuna pasta with disinterest.

"So blow me away with your theories. I'm all ears."

"I got a message. From someone who was on the *Solitude* with me – the tugship that found the *Cerberus*. It told me that if I didn't want to see it happen all over again I should do my best to change the course of this Starliner."

Philipa chuckled, obviously not won over by his explanation. He had to admit it that it sounded pretty lame when described out aloud. Why couldn't he just show her it all, the way he had seen it? But Dezza was beginning to doubt himself. Had it really been that convincing? Toze had already warned him – perhaps he should have taken more notice of him.

"Hold on," she said, stopping him from continuing, "I'm not stupid; I watched the news. You're the only one out of the *Solitude* crew who's still around. How could any of the others have sent you a message? A message from beyond the grave? P-*lease*, mystery man. You have to be trying harder to get one over on me." She made an exaggerated show of checking her watch. "And it's not even April the first yet; two months early."

Pushing away her plate, she stood up and tucked in her chair. "I have to go. It was fun to talk."

"No, wait," Dezza said hurriedly. He wished he could take back everything he had said to her about the message. It was too late for that now. "Okay, bad joke. I'm sorry. Maybe it was in bad taste."

Philipa looked at him hard, her mind mulling what he had said over. "Okay. Tell you what, Mr Booth. I get the impression you are throwing me curved balls galore. But I guess given what you've been through, I'm always going to view you as a bit of a strange guy. The media reports didn't do you any justice, and I can tell that at least a part of that must have been exaggerated – they always do. But if you want a bit of free advise, I suggest you keep your message to yourself and just try and kick back and enjoy the cruise."

Without waiting for a reply she turned and was gone.

Dezza fought the urge to follow. That would be like picking and picking at a cut until it just got bigger. *Quit whilst you're behind,* he told himself. If only he could have followed his own advice sooner.

*　　　*　　　*　　　*　　　*

Rest and relaxation - a mind-numbing prospect for someone who has something else that they know they should be doing. Dezza had not had the luxury of time to spend for longer than he could remember. At least, not since he had joined the elite of the deep space salvagers. Of course back then on the *Solitude* he had not desired any time away; he loved the job.

All that came to an end the day the *Solitude* docked with the derelict *Cerberus*.

He tried many things to hide those thoughts from his mind and their destructive circular thinking. For that purpose, the *Persia* was well provided for. He tried the gyms first. At least there he could try and forget his mind's ills and at the same time lose a few pounds that middle age and lack of a proper job had spread around him.

But everywhere he looked seemed to provide the primer for his thoughts to return into that destructive cycle that he had known for months and years since the tribunal. The more he thought, the angrier he got and the harder he pulled away on the weight trainers. Each time he became fatigued and drenched in sweat, he would rack up another weight to the tally and train some more. Maybe the other punters to the gym in their crisp white plimsolls and starched shorts in this season's fashions thought he was just a fanatical weight pusher? Let them think what they liked. As much as he tried, he couldn't think like they did. What he would give to be able to just be *normal* and have a nine until five job, two point four kids and all the bullshit that went along with that. If only he could just get into the drudgery of an everyday life and not be bothered by it all.

Another group entered the gym, and he found the time to lean breathlessly on the weight trainer as they went by – another group of fashion-fitness passengers. He had seen the type too often – all the latest fashion outfits and a token effort on a rowing machine for appearances. They came to the gym for nothing more than to socialise and above all, to be *seen* at the gym. That was all that seemed to matter for some people. It filled him with a mix of envy and disgust. They were the kind of drones who went in the pool and just got in everyone's way. Why bother going swimming, he fumed privately, if all you were going to do was stand around waist deep in water just talking and getting in the real swimmers' way?

The weight trainer suddenly felt loose, and before he could register what was happening, there was a massive crash and he shot forward, stumbling to the ground.

"Hey, dude? You okay?"

One of the fashion-fitness passengers was at his side, white plimsolls and over-zealous applied sports deodorant – the smell of health-freaks and Jocks all over. In a daze Dezza realised that he must have been pulling the weights so vigorously that the cable had snapped.

"Yeah, I'm good," he mumbled, though he did not feel it. Getting to his feet he saw flecks of light flitting in his vision and realised the room was spinning. How long had he been in here? Actually, he didn't know – maybe a long while.

"Hey buddy. Take it easy." A supervisor was at his side, shooing the crowd of onlookers away.

"Hey! Give this guy some room, will you?" he shouted. The crowd dispersed, though reluctantly.

It was probably the most interesting thing that had happened to them all day, Dezza thought, as the supervisor helped him to a bench and sat him down.

"You shouldn't push yourself so much. I've been watching you for most of the morning. You came in here and you worked that machine harder than anyone else

I've ever seen. And you didn't stop for a break. You should go easy on yourself – and the kit."

"Yeah, maybe," Dezza wheezed. It had been a harder workout than he had realised, pushed by his mind.

"Well, I suggest you get yourself a shower and take a break. There are no prizes for working yourself into an early grave. How are you feeling now?"

"A little better," Dezza sighed; though his mind still burned with thoughts.

"Good. As soon as you're ready, get yourself out of here. And I don't want to see you back any time today. Take it easy, pal."

Dezza nodded his thanks and staggered for the way out. Looking back at the weight trainer, it was clear he must have really given it some. A couple of the fitness-fashion crowd were there, looking over the bent frame. Right now all he had for them was contempt. Still boiling with mixed up emotions he turned his back on them all and stormed down the corridor.

*   *   *   *   *

It hadn't been Dezza's intention to end up in the engineering spaces. One turn had led to another on the way back from the gym, and anyway; he was too burned up inside to be thinking straight about anything around him. Before he realised his mistake, he was past the cabin decks and on into an unfamiliar corridor. It was quiet here; just the rattle of air conditioning and that tacky potpourri smell loved of all hotels the system over.

"Where the hell am I?" he murmured, stopping in the corridor and looking up its simple utilitarian design.

These weren't cabins. Looking on one of the nearby doors he read off a sign that told him they were cleaning and laundry stores.

He knew he would have to retrace his steps – he must have passed the opening onto the sleeping decks from the stairwell and gone down too many levels. The trouble was that he could not recollect anything of the walk here from the gym. When he wracked his memory, he could remember the gym and leaving after the weight trainer broke. But from then on it was a blur as he had been lost in his inner thoughts. There were snippets of memories of a corridor or moving aside to let a group of people past, but nothing he could really string together. Worse still, this level seemed deserted with no-one to ask for directions back.

How hard can it be? He thought. *There can't be many ways off this deck that don't lead back the way I came*.

Looking back and fore, he realised that to boot it all, he could not remember which direction he had been heading when he realised he was lost. All the doorways looked the same. So he picked a direction, and walked on hoping he had got it right.

The corridor ended at a right angle junction. He had hoped that there he would find the stairwell, but instead he found himself on another, longer corridor at ninety degrees. Had he come this way? He tried to think, but his mind refused to oblige him with the answers.

"Dammit!" he swore, to no-one but himself. He half hoped that a voice might chastise him for his outburst; someone he had not seen yet here in these endless corridors. But still there was nothing to reward his outburst except the steady rattle of air conditioning vents.

He trudged on looking for an elusive set of stairs that could take him up to the passenger decks. This place was beginning to unnerve him. It reminded Dezza just that little bit too much of the decks on the *Cerberus*. He tried the doors on a couple of the stores with trepidation. Each was unlocked, and each one opened out into a small bedding store.

They were almost exactly the same as the ones that he, Toze and Tracker had sheltered in when the *thing* had chased them on the *Cerberus*. He shut each door hurriedly, shaken by the memories that were getting all too vivid for his liking.

At the next door he was hesitant, but the panelling was different and this one had a small brass plate on that said it was for access and should be kept clear at all times. He tried the handle – it too was unlocked and opened with ease. Dezza didn't know what to expect; hoping that it might be an emergency stairwell. Instead it led into the next best thing – a freight elevator.

Scanning the panel he saw that it offered the ability to go only down. Still, anything was better than walking miles of endless and deserted corridors.

The buttons for the floor levels were marked. Some were stores and others were for linen. Another was marked 'hotel services' and he jabbed its button with some satisfaction. Hotel services meant the equipment running the air conditioning and all the other niceties that the passengers enjoyed on the decks above without a second thought for how they got there. That meant that there would be crew there – hopefully.

The lift did nothing. Instead a steady tone blipped to him angrily, until he realised that, of course, the door to the corridor was still open. Closing it the blipping stopped and the inner door finally slid shut. With a whirr of hidden machinery, the lift car began its descent and Dezza wondered with apprehension what might await him on the lower levels.

This had not been his plan. There were too many things that stirred suppressed memories. At the very least he might have to explain what the hell he was doing down here when he found one of the crew to direct him out. The truth of course was simple. But Dezza had become conditioned to being suspicious. No matter how many times he told himself that he was not going to get in trouble, he still had that schoolboy apprehension of trespassing in the headmaster's private garden.

The buttons on the panel lit up one by one with an agonising slowness. Then finally the last one glowed brighter and he felt the car rock to a halt. There was a long pause and he found himself wondering if the car had failed, leaving him stranded in the depths of the Starliner. But at last the panel blipped once and the glow of the button flickered as the inner door slid open. Behind it a second door slid too. After that was nothing but a darkened corridor, the first few feet picked out by the light from the lift car; but the rest was nothing but inky black.

Dezza jabbed frantically at the buttons on the control panel, but none would light up save for the one for this floor which stubbornly refused to change. He could feel the panic now as his heart thumped loudly in his ears, fuelled by the adrenaline.

"Hey! Can anyone hear me out there?" he yelled into the darkness. There was no reply and no echo. The darkness seemed to have a deadening effect on sound as if it were like a fog. If silence could be deafening, then this was it. It sucked in all sounds and made Dezza's head feel numbed. He strained his ears, but there was nothing to hear save for the pounding of his heart and the dry rasp of his breathing.

"Hello?" Still there was no answer.

He pressed the buttons again. He reeled away in shock as the lights in the car began to flicker.

"No! No! No!" he exclaimed in horror.

Then, before he could think what to do, the lights flickered and died and left him in the darkness.

*   *   *   *   *

The walls felt odd and clammy under his fingertips. He wasn't sure if there was moisture on them, but the temperature seemed to have taken a marked decline. There was no way of seeing though – Dezza could not even see his hand in front of his face.

He took another cautious step forward. Something caught a toe, and he found himself stumbling. But when he carefully slid his foot back to feel for what had tripped him, there was nothing there but the smooth floor.

This isn't right, he thought, *this is supposed to be hotel services. There should be people here, and equipment. Where the hell is everything?*

He felt for the wall again, and missed. Where he thought it was there was nothing. It took a moment for him to realise, and he nearly fell over, misjudging his balance in the inky darkness. It was so dark that his tortured mind began to invent things for him to see, just to fill in the darkness. First Dezza thought he saw a light - dim and far off in the distance. But when he turned his head from the side to side, it was always straight ahead, never moving. When he waved his hands in front of his face he realised it was a figment of his imagination, and it faded away. Other images followed, making him think there were people lurking just out of reach.

He kept searching for the walls of the corridor so that he might carefully follow them along, but whichever way he probed, there was nothing. Finally he dropped onto all fours and began crawling on the floor. The corridor hadn't been that wide – it couldn't be too hard to find the edge, could it?

Once or twice his hands brushed *something* in the dark. But each time there was nothing there when he felt again. Finally he could stand it no more.

"This is no joke! What the hell is going on?" he screamed at the top of his lungs.

The darkness absorbed the words, sucking them in like a vacuum. Then, suddenly, the light blinded him. It took a moment for his eyes to adjust. Shielding them with his hands, he peered out through his fingers. At first it was painful, but then his eyes adjusted, and he saw that he was in an engineering corridor not more than a dozen feet from the open doors of the lift. Looking around, he wondered how he could have groped around for so long in the darkness without touching anything.

"Hello Dezza."

The voice startled him making him fall flat to the floor and roll over in a start. That voice – it had sounded so – *familiar*.

"Over here."

He looked in the direction the voice had come from. In the corridor stood Tubs, in the same space suit he had worn that fateful day on the *Cerberus* – his very last day.

"Tubs?" stammered Dezza, the panic wild in his voice.

"Hello Dezza. I see you got my message. Nice trip?" His words sounded so normal; so calm; so *wrong*.

Dezza could say nothing. The words he wanted to say were there in his head, but they seemed to choke in his throat on the panic.

But you're dead! His mind screamed.

Tubs seemed to read his thoughts. A smile crossed his face – that stupid Scouse grin that Tubs always had when something was going his way. "A part of me only."

Struggling for breath, Dezza tried to scrabble back towards the lift, but the world was spinning and his head was feeling light. As a buzzing filled his ears, his last thoughts were that he was going to die and that the entity had finally caught up with him.

5

The air conditioning sounded awfully loud. *Why won't it shut up?* Dezza's mind kept saying. His head felt fuzzy, as if hung over, yet it was as if part of his mind was still drunk. What had he been doing? He struggled to remember. No – his mind wasn't playing ball with him right now. He tried to summon up more concentration, to fight through the block. What was his mind hiding from him? He knew there was something, but it was annoying him by flitting just out of grasp of his recollection. There was a feeling though that something bad had happened. He could not remember what, no matter how hard he forced his mind to concentrate.

He tried to open his eyes and sit up, but his head exploded into a wave of pain, throbbing like a migraine. He felt a soothing hand rest on him and push him back down.

"Take it easy, Mr Booth."

He didn't recognise the voice. A memory prodded him; something dark and foreboding, but it wouldn't quite reveal itself.

"I'm going to give you an injection, Mr Booth. It will help you sleep for a while," the voice came again, "Sharp scratch, Mr Booth."

Without waiting for an answer, there was a sharp sting somewhere in his arm, and the swirling pain and thoughts faded away into peace.

* * * * *

He awoke in a room that had a strange smell. He knew that smell – the smell of surgical spirit and iodine. His head still throbbed, but the pain was more manageable now and he could open his eyes carefully.

He saw a white room with the lights turned down low. There was a row of beds opposite, and when he looked to his left there were more beds there too. He seemed to be the only occupant. Something beeped steadily and softly at his side, and he saw that a machine with flashing lights had been wheeled to the side of his bed. A tangle of wires and tubes led from it down and under the bedclothes, and he warily followed them carefully with a hand, cautious of what he might find.

"Ah, Mr Booth. I see you are awake."

The voice startled him and his hand drew back from the tubes.

"Where am I?" he asked. His voice sounded weak and hoarse.

"Sickbay."

He heard a shuffling and realised that in the shadows beyond the machine there was a desk at which a nurse was sitting with a book propped open to read.

He struggled to recall what had happened. He remembered the beginning of the cruise. He remembered a few other things too, and the foreboding of the message that had pushed him to come. But there was something else fighting to break free in his mind. He shivered and felt his skin run cold.

"What happened?"

"You passed out," came the matter-of-fact response, as if passing out were a perfectly natural and regular occurrence.

"Tubs? What happened to Tubs?"

"Tubs?" The nurse laughed and carefully placed the book on the desk. "Mr Booth, do you not remember? The attendant of the gym reported that you seemed to have had yourself worked up over something. You overdid it, and the cleaning staff found you on the way back to your cabin."

But I was in the engineering spaces."

"That's impossible," she soothed. Her tone suggested that she was taking everything he was saying with a pinch of salt. She shuffled over and checked the screen on the beeping machine.

"Stress and anxiety can do some strange things to a person."

He struggled under the sheets, trying to throw them off. "I need to get out of here."

She rested a hand on him and pushed him back down. To his surprise he was weak, and could do nothing.

"Get some rest. You will feel better in the morning."

*   *   *   *   *

One of the cleaners had told Philipa about the previous night's gossip. One of the passengers had been found sprawled out cold in the lower sleeping deck. Looked like a heart attack, the cleaner had said, only the doctor had decided more likely a panic attack brought on by stress and over exertion. That at least tallied with what the gym supervisor had been talking about. One passenger working himself so hard that he had just about trashed the weight trainer.

It was more interesting than the usual staff room gossiping. But unlike the usual cases where it was just some faceless here-today-gone-tomorrow tourist, this one had a name that made Philipa's skin go cold. She almost knew it was him from the description of the 'ghost man' from the media reports some years back. When the name came, it only confirmed what her mind was telling her.

"Is he okay?" Philipa found herself asking, suddenly taking on a renewed interest in the story.

This was someone she had taken the time to get to know. Sure, he was a bit odd, but there was something about his insistence in everything he had confided in her that left her thinking there was a lot more to his story than at least the media had portrayed.

"I guess so," replied the cleaner, not picking up on Philipa's sudden interest, "They took him to the infirmary and the Doc reckons all he needs is a couple of days rest and a serious chill pill. When he came around, Emma said he was babbling about some long-dead buddy of his from the *Solitude* case back in '34."

"Total fruit-loop if you ask me," chimed in one of the porters who had been listening too, "They say he went mad in deep space. Can't say I'm surprised at anything except how he's held together this long – if he has. My guess is it's his first trip back into space. Maybe they just let him out of his padded cell."

The whole assembled crowd laughed, but Philipa was already gone, having slipped out moments before. No-one saw her go.

*   *   *   *   *

It wasn't far to the infirmary – just down a couple of decks then through a couple of corridors of administrative areas. She always hated it down here. With a passenger list of anywhere up to several thousand, and several hundred crew, the only times she had had business to be down here before were with passengers who had befallen accidents of one sort or another. Heart attacks and food poisoning were the main culprits, though if the company had its way, they were hushed up every time.

This time it was someone she knew, well sort of. It wasn't often that she took a shine to a passenger. Trust her luck to get attached to the real hard luck case. Having to find time at the end of the tour to go ashore and attend a funeral and answer a barrage of awkward questions from relatives – if there were any – wasn't something she wanted to experience.

She met Emma, the nurse, at the door. She could tell from Emma's face upon seeing her that she had not been expecting Dezza to have any visitors, much less someone who she knew from the staff.

"Philipa – What brings you here?" Emma looked her up and down. "No damage or scuffs, so I'm wondering why you might be wanting to see the ghost man?"

Philipa cringed at the term, but she tried not to show it. "How did you know I'd be here for Mr Booth?" she asked.

Emma winked. "It isn't hard, when he's the only guest."

She waved Philipa in to the anteroom of the infirmary. The walls were stacked from floor to ceiling with cupboards stashed with all types of boxes of drugs. All were safely under lock and key, just in case anyone got any bright ideas about getting high on illicitly obtained ship-issue morphine.

Emma leafed through some paperwork on the desk. "It's a weird one," she said without looking up, "Found on a cabin deck, but babbled on about someone called Tubs and being on the engineering decks when he first came around."

She looked up at Philipa. "Any of this sound like a news story you know?"

Philipa felt a shiver run through her. "He mentioned something when he first came aboard. Seemed adamant that he had had some kind of paranormal warning that the *Persia* was going to end up like that other Starliner he found."

"And what do you think?" asked Emma darkly. She left the question hanging in the air.

"I don't know what to believe," replied Philipa with a sigh.

Emma shrugged and dumped the paperwork back on the desk. "He's almost ready for discharge – no point in keeping loonies here any longer than I have to. It's nicer when I don't have any patients to look after, then I can kick back and read a book all day long on company time. Just the odd cases of asthma and space sickness to break the monotony."

"Can I see him?"

"Sure, no skin off my nose. But remember the unwritten rule: never fraternise with the passengers. They'll bring you nothing but trouble."

Philipa nodded and walked on through into the infirmary leaving Emma to pull up a chair and settle back into her book.

*   *   *   *   *

"Visiting time, Mr Booth."

The night had been long and restless, but it had passed at last. Sulking over the half-eaten remnants of toast,

Dezza was surprised to see a face that he thought he had long since scared away from him.

"Philipa! What the hell are you doing here?"

"I came to see how you were," she said glancing around the infirmary, "You seemed in a strange old state yesterday."

She sat carefully on the end of his bed. "Don't get any funny ideas. I don't usually make house calls."

"I never said anything," he protested, before he saw her smile.

"Let's say that you've made an impression on me, Mr Booth."

He frowned. "Look, the only people who call me that are social security and my Mother. And she's been dead since long before I pissed my life away down the tube. Everyone else calls me Dezza, or other things that they don't have the guts to say to my face."

"Dezza will do just fine," she said dryly.

He grunted. "So why did you come down here? Really?"

She shrugged. "Something about what you said. The media made you out to be a fantasy story teller, but yesterday you were quite compelling." She waggled a finger at him. "Don't take this as a vote of confidence in your story, but at the very least you did sound like you truly *believed* it had happened."

He felt his emotions draining away. Back to the same old cycle of talking about the *Cerberus* and all the bad luck that Starliner had brought.

"I don't want to talk about it," he sulked.

She regarded him carefully. For a moment nothing was said, then she stood up and smoothed down imaginary wrinkles in her skirt.

"Fine. Suit yourself," she snapped curtly, "They're going to get ready to discharge you this morning. I thought at least that you would appreciate someone helping you back to your cabin."

She turned to go, but he called out to stop her.

"Wait!"

She paused and looked back to him, waiting for what he had to say.

He knew it was a long shot, and a voice inside him screamed to just shut up and play along with the real world and not go telling any more to anyone. *Just play along and act nice*, the voice warned him, *and sooner or later they will all just leave you alone.*

"Where did they find me?" he asked, ignoring the screaming inner voice of reason.

She glanced to the nurse's station and the duplicate paperwork on the desk. "The lower sleeping cabin deck. You must have gone down one level below where your cabin is. The cleaning staff found you flat out on the carpet. They thought at first that it was a heart attack, but the doctor's said it was just an extreme reaction to stress."

"Not in the engineering decks?" he asked slowly.

She smiled. "I really don't think so, Dezza. For a start there's no way down into them from the passenger decks."

"You are sure?" he quizzed. There had to be a way. He had found it – hadn't he?

"I've only worked this Starliner for the last ten seasons. I think I know my way around," she said, her voice tinged now with annoyance.

Dezza knew he was pushing his luck, so he finally listened belatedly to the inner voice and said no more.

"Rest until they kick you out," she said, "I'll be waiting to make sure you get to your cabin this time."

He watched her leave, frightened again that he had pushed her away in trying to talk to her about too much.

"Philipa?"

She stopped in the doorway, silhouetted in the light from the anteroom beyond.

"I'm not mad," he said firmly.

She nodded and left without saying a word.

Feeling forlorn he settled back into the sheets, wondering what she really thought of him.

$*$ $*$ $*$ $*$ $*$

The nurse had removed the drip and pronounced that he was as well as he was ever going to be. All the time Philipa watched on silently from the doorway, arms folded and regarding him with a piercing look, as her mind seemed to burn at unanswered questions. He tried to ignore her, as the nurse fussed over paperwork and the usual array of useless forms to sign. He put his signature on them all without reading a single one. They would just get filed in a drawer somewhere until the next time they had a clear out. What did they matter? He was just eager to get the hell out of this place.

Finally the nurse told him he could get up. His clothes were in the bedside cabinet, she said. She would come back in a few minutes after filing the paperwork. Without waiting for a reply she disappeared with the bundle to the anteroom and Philipa followed her.

His clothes were just as he remembered them. someone had taken the effort to fold them neatly – probably the nurse – and they now smelt of surgical spirit with only a trace of the sweat from the gym. They weren't much, and it didn't take long to ditch the hospital gown and slip on the vest and the tracksuit bottoms. The deck shoes slid on comfortably, and it felt good to be back in his own clothes. He sat on the edge of the bed, rubbing at the sticky plaster that covered where the drip had been until the nurse returned.

"Okay, all clear."

A sheaf of paperwork was thrust into his hand; copies of what he had just signed.

"Now shoo," she fussed, waving him to the door, "And I don't want to see you back here any time soon. Take it easy – you're supposed to be on holiday for pity's sake."

Philipa was waiting in the anteroom, leaning on the edge of a cluttered desk.

"Come on then, mystery man," she sighed, "I'll take you back to your cabin."

*   *   *   *   *

Neither said anything on the walk; really there wasn't much to be said. Dezza got the feeling that she did think he was mad, despite his protests. Given the circumstances, he had to concede that even he would have been inclined to doubt himself if he had been in her position.

It was not far to the sleeping decks. On the way they passed the gym, and Dezza shuddered at the memory. It had been only just over a day, but it felt like an eternity away. It was like seeing that day through a fuzziness that obscured the clarity. Maybe he had been affected by the stress?

He noted that from the gym there were a number of twists and turns and junctions in the corridors before they got to the main stairwell. Try as he might, he could recall nothing of coming this way – he really must have been lost to his own thoughts. It was odd though that he couldn't remember much of them either.

They went down a couple of levels until they reached the one for Dezza's cabin. A wave of familiarity washed over him, and he stopped in the stairwell, peering over the banister rails.

"What's up?" asked Philipa.

"Just a hunch," he replied without looking up.

He could see right down to the bottom lobby – there was only another floor to go. Looking up he saw that the stairwell had to go up at least a dozen floors before it ended in a mock glass dome.

Philipa leant over, perhaps trying to see what had attracted his interest.

"What are you looking at?"

"There's only one level down from here."

"Yes," she said, clearly struggling to understand what he was thinking about, "That's where you were found."

He started for the stairs again before she could say anything else.

"Hey!" she called out, hurrying after him.

"Just one moment – please."

One floor down the stairs ended at an open lobby. He looked into the gloom beneath them, but there was nothing but a carpeted area that was being used to store a cleaning cart. There was no way to get any deeper into the Starliner here. Looking up and down the corridor that led off, he didn't recognise it as being the one he remembered.

"Where was I found?" he asked.

Down to the left, I think," she replied, uncertain. "Why?"

He started off down the corridor in the direction she had indicated forcing her to jog along after him.

"I want to see – just a hunch."

At the end of the corridor there was a junction with another corridor at right angles. Looking up and down he felt the adrenaline kick in with a flash of recognition.

"Just up there. On the left," Philipa said slowly. "Look, you aren't going to go crazy on me now are you?" she warned, "I'll have no hesitation in calling security if you do anything funny." Her hand stole for the concealed communicator in her jacket pocket, just in case.

"I'm fine, honest." He pleaded, hustling down the corridor to the point she had indicated.

This corridor was somewhat more utilitarian than the others had been – just as he remembered. So that much had not been a dream or a hallucination. Reading the brass plates on the doors he saw they were cleaning cupboards and bedding stores.

"One of these had a plate on saying it was to be kept clear at all times," he called out hurriedly, "That's the one I remember going through."

Philipa folded her arms in disapproval. "Well, I'm telling you now what I said in the infirmary: there is no freight lift."

Dezza ignored her lack of enthusiasm, and continued reading off the brass plates one by one. It seemed that she was going to be right, then he came to a set of wooden doors with a plate that said what he remembered.

"Here!" he called out triumphantly.

"You're making a big mistake," muttered Philipa, but she came over to see anyway.

He waited until she was there beside him. "Access only, to be kept clear at all times." He said aloud with an air of satisfaction.

To his surprise, she laughed.

"Here's your freight elevator, Dezza!"

Taking hold of the handle, she opened it and flung the door wide. Inside it was dark, but Dezza new immediately with a sinking heart that it wasn't what he had been expecting. Stepping forward he tested the reels of fire hoses with both hands, as if somehow they might open up and reveal a lift behind. He hammered on the wall with a fist, but it was solid. There was nothing here.

"I don't understand it," he said at last, crestfallen.

"They're all over the Starliner," she soothed at his side, "And they most certainly don't hide any secret lifts, or I would know about it."

She steered him out of the fire locker and shut the doors behind them. Confused at the difference reality had shown him over what his memories had insisted should be there, he let himself be shepherded back to the stairwell and up to his cabin. He didn't even protest as she used her master key to let them in and pushed him into the bunk and tucked the sheets around him.

"Just go to sleep," she fussed, "You'll appreciate the rest and be a better man for it."

He grunted an acknowledgement as she flicked out the light and retired to the corridor. For a moment he saw her outlined in the door, as if contemplating him, then the door closed and he heard her footsteps fading away.

Within a matter of minutes he was asleep in a sea of dreams that made no sense.

6

In the secluded gloom of the *Persia*'s bridge, Captain Ventura regarded the starscape through the Plexiglas with dreamy eyes. It was always like this on every tour. There was something about the stars that had appealed to him since he was a kid. In his memories, there were none that didn't somehow have an edge of wanting to go into space to them. Everything he had done in his life had been to get to this point in his career and it felt good to finally be here.

The other bridge crew generally left him to it. He had done more than a dozen tours, as captain of the *Persia* and it was now a familiar routine. In space, there wasn't day or night as on Earth. Here there was just ship's time, loosely based on the latitude of the solar docking station that all the Starliner's used. If it were not for the passengers, there would be no 'day' or 'night' aboard the Starliner, just like how it worked on the vast interplanetary freighters.

"Are we clear of the outer markers?" he asked.

There weren't many crewers on the bridge, just a steersman and a navigator. It didn't take many people to get a Starliner underway and keep her there – all the real work was done somewhere in windowless control rooms deep within the vessel.

"Aye sir," called the navigator, never looking up from the holographic display in front of his console.

Ventura turned and looked at the hologram for himself. He trusted the navigator, but it was procedure to make sure. In a sphere ten feet across, the tracks of the planets of the solar systems swept, joined by dotted lines, with a rendition of the Starliner at the centre of the sphere as a winking yellow dot surrounded by shimmering lines of text and readouts.

The dot that was the *Persia* was already a good distance from the furthest planet orbits. Out here they were clear of any objects that might be blundered into or sucked to the Rösenbridge when the powerful engines pushed the Starliner into the jump for the next solar system.

On smaller vessels the passengers and crew might have had to go into stasis for the journey, protected from the forces of physics by quo fields. But on Starliners the party never stopped and the time in the Rösenbridge was business as usual for those aboard, entertained by all that was on offer. Protected by a field that encompassed the entire ship, there was no risk of the usual disorientation and space sickness that could come from experiencing the Rösenbridge jump unprotected.

"Engage Rösenbridge countdown. Alert any nearby shipping," he ordered – merely a routine precaution, as the holographic display showed no other vessels within any distance.

Ventura always thought there should have been something more impressive to mark the start of the countdown. Perhaps a montage of powerful rock music and wailing klaxons would have been nice? He smiled – that was how you thought when you had watched one too many science fiction films. In the real world, electronics did their work without needing fanfare and mood to accompany them. There was no big deal; just a set of numbers shimmering in the air counting down towards zero.

"Notify all stations: prepare for jump."

"Aye, sir."

The navigator tapped at his console. That was all it took. As the counter reached zero there was a pause, then in slow motion the stars through the Plexiglas flickered and disappeared without ceremony or fuss.

They were in the Rösenbridge. Outside, only the faint tinged glow of the Starliner's navigation field gave away that they were moving as it rolled and undulated at its edges. It would be like this for nearly a week, before the Rösenbridge would disgorge its contents, and the Starliner would arrive at a star system many light years away. On board, down on the passenger decks, the parties would never stop in that time. There were some tourists who came aboard without any intention of stepping off until the Starliner arrived back at Earth and they were kicked off at the end of the cruise.

"Mister mate, you have the bridge."

He didn't wait for a reply; there was no need. The holographic sphere, shorn of its projections of the planets and their trajectories now that they were long gone, still glowed green, but with only a yellow blip and a few readouts at its centre. He walked straight through it instead of taking the time to walk around and felt the static buzz across him as the projector struggled to keep up with this new object so rudely entering into its field. He passed through and the buzzing ceased. The sphere wobbled behind him, and a band of static passed across it before it settled once more.

*   *   *   *   *

Ventura's cabin was not far behind the bridge. Ever since the almost forgotten seafaring days of mankind, the captain's cabin had always been within easy distance of the seat of his power. Many things had changed over centuries, and mankind had reached out for – and taken in – the stars. But aboard a Starliner the designers still seemed stuck with nautical traditions.

Once inside the door, Ventura aimed his cap at the stand on the other side and threw it gently. It was another ritual, and one he usually lost at. But tonight his cap bounced on the peg and stayed there; he was getting better. The jacket was quickly unbuttoned and followed the cap to the pegs, though he was rather more careful with it.

Kicking back in an armchair he swivelled the computer console towards him and keyed in his personal codes.

"Might as well see what paperwork they've been making for me," he muttered under his breath and reached out for the drawer where he kept his secret bottle of Glen Livet, oak-aged twelve years. Pouring a generous measure to a glass, he eased the bottle back into its place and settled in front of the console.

The air shivered and took on a blue tinge before text rolled above the projector. Dabbing at virtual buttons, he read the reports and sipped the liquor. It was all the usual bullshit. Cooks complaining that the plumbing was backing up and the cleaners complaining about over amorous couples making love into the mornings without a concern to put up 'do not disturb' signs for them to heed. He could not help but snigger at the thought of the prudish idiot on the cleaning team wandering in mid romantic moment. He glanced to the name of the man who had filed the report, though he knew in advance which trouble maker it would be, and was right. Nothing to be concerned about – that man always seemed to find something to moan about. One of these days he would file a complaint if there was *nobody* to walk in on unexpectedly. Still, the man probably got his kicks from something.

One report stuck out above the rest, and he brought up a second virtual terminal hovering in the air to cross-reference something that hung around at the back of his mind. A picture of a man and a news article came up, and he compared it with the details of the report and the passenger roster. Taking another sip from the glass before setting it down, he settled back into his chair with a smile.

"So we have the deep space trouble maker aboard," he said out loud, "I wondered what had happened to that old relic."

He keyed open a blank message and sent a memo to the security teams.

It read: *Any trouble with passenger Desmond Booth, take no hesitation to lock him in the security cells. I don't want that crazy man causing any more trouble than we have to put up with aboard ship. He gets his first stay in the infirmary for free – any further nonsense and he goes on ice for the tour.*

Reading through, Ventura keyed to send the message, then flicked off the console. He finished off the liquor and stood up. Taking the empty glass across to the sink, he put it in to be washed before turning to one of the lockers. He rummaged for a moment in a drawer inside until he found what he wanted.

It was only an old photo frame, with a faded picture of a military passing out parade on one side. On the other it held a family picture, with a proud looking marine in front of his parents and another man – a brother – Ventura.

"He might have lost you out there," he murmured without taking his eyes off the picture, "But I'll see to it he causes our family no more trouble, bro. For you"

He retrieved the glass and with the picture in one hand he poured another measure of the Glen Livet and raised the glass in mock toast. "Bobby 'Exbo' Ventura – you chose your path and we respected you for it."

Flicking the photo from the frame he slipped it carefully into an inside pocket and drained the glass dry.

7

Dezza didn't see Philipa for the rest of the week. It did not surprise him at first given that he had slept for most of the first day, though he eventually came to wonder if she was avoiding him. With a bitter regret, taking her down to the lower sleeping deck level might have been the one step too far to push her away. Maybe he ought to just take the advice that had been given and just enjoy the cruise. Even travelling last minute economy was going to dent his meagre finances for at least the next few years, whether or not Tubs' message prophesy bore true. Maybe there was no sense in squandering it all over a message from a dead man.

At the back of his mind that still bothered him. Had it been a dream? The longer it went, the more he could convince himself that maybe it had been. He could always put in a frequency call to Toze, to send a message to ask whether it had happened. But if it was a dream, what would that do? Another person to alienate and call him nuts.

So he threw himself to the tourist thing. At first there was the gym, but it soon went from a novelty to a chore to push the weights and watch the same old crowd of fat sweating tourists trying to impress their friends on the squash courts of the weight machines. In the end he could stand it no longer and left to see what else he could find aboard the Starliner.

In theory, there should have been something for everyone, including the hard to please like Dezza. Miles long and with a hundred decks in places, there was every conceivable amenity known to man and a few more besides. Finding a velodrome, he tried cycling. It had been a long time since he had ridden a bike. Casting his mind back there was a dim memory as a child riding a cast-off hand-me-down affair that had seen better days. There had been friends, and bike rides along gravel tracks up to the quarry that lay a mile away from his childhood home. They had been chased off numerous times by security, but wasn't that what children were supposed to get up to?

They say you never forget how to ride a bike. As they kitted Dezza out with a Lycra jump-suit, helmet and a bike that looked so lightweight that it was a far cry from that childhood bike, Dezza mused that they failed to mention you got to look like a moron when revisiting the sport. Middle age had not been kind, and the Lycra pinched nastily on the spread of years on the bottle. He did not remember any of this safety junk they insisted on him wearing now. Always kill joys trying to stamp all the fun out of everything.

Still, he persevered and actually quite liked riding the track, until boredom set in and he grew tired of dodging the tourists who seemed to meander up and down the slope without respect to the lanes painted on the floor.

And that was the problem – he hated people. It seemed to him that the world was filled with morons, all out to push his buttons and get in his way. The idiots were everywhere that he looked, and he distrusted them all. Had he always been like this? He trudged the ship's shopping malls without paying much attention to any of the shops he passed. To him it felt that he was in a bubble, like an alien walking amongst a different culture. Once there had been a fresh faced young man, heading into space with untamed optimism. He could not help but laugh at the naïveté of that younger version of him. Life had done its utmost in the years that had passed to grind all optimism and faith in others out of him.

He wandered on, half lost to his own reverie and ignored by others until he lost track of the distance he had covered, and the decks he had passed through. It didn't really matter – there was always a deck plan somewhere to consult to find a way back to his cabin when he grew tired. Days and nights meant nothing – he slept when he was tired and ate when he was hungry. On a Starliner, the fun never stopped – how he laughed at the term in his mind. Everything ran twenty-four hours, seven days a week here.

In a casino he sat amongst a crowd of tourists from Nevada who had come to ride the slots having exhausted every casino that Las Vegas and Reno had had to offer. In a way he could get on with these people, sitting amongst them feeding the one armed bandits and punching the buttons like battery hens eager to get their next food pellets. They had no real cares, and were a friendly and accepting bunch, if a little brash for his tastes in their mock country and western attire. It took all sorts to make a world turn, he mused.

When they grew bored of this casino, he moved with them to the next on the Starliners own grand version of the Las Vegas strip. He watched shows with burlesque dancers, cabaret acts and comedians, all whilst feeding the slots. But eventually he became bored, and when the Nevada gamblers moved on again, he did not go with them but headed away from the strip to pace the Starliner's decks alone once more.

In a small burger bar decorated to look like an American diner out of old nostalgic films, he ordered a cheeseburger and sat with teenagers eager to work their way through the menus and eat until they could eat no more. Dezza liked their carefree attitude, but could not keep pace with them burger for burger. They talked about music and groups that he had never heard of, but he liked the company for a while. He stayed with them until they could eat no more, then watched them head off for their cabins to sleep off or puke up what they had gorged on.

Once again he found himself alone slurping the last of a soda noisily through a straw and contemplating the long walk through the decks back to his cabin. He felt alone and isolated. It did not matter how many people he was meeting and getting to know in casual encounters, there was always an end to the association and they would leave with him knowing that they would have forgotten all about him by the following morning. He just could not connect with anyone.

That night he stopped at an English themed pub on the way back to his cabin and decided he would have just one slug of whiskey as a night-cap. He had almost completely avoided it up until now. In truth it had felt good to be off the bottle, at first. But as he slipped through amongst the crowds of tourists unable to find a person to relate to, he found those old desires of the comfort of the bottle creeping back in.

Just one; it wouldn't hurt. But for an alcoholic, there never was just one. It seemed like the glass never quite emptied itself. He was dimly aware of credit changing hands, and a friendly bartender hovering back and forth, but it was the warm golden liquid that was his true friend.

Several hours later through the comfortable haze, the bartender suggested he should complete his trip back to his cabin and get a good night's rest. Dezza did not argue – he could not remember how long ago he had got up. Some stewards helped him with directions and he moved slowly on his way.

*   *   *   *   *

There wasn't a clear moment when he realised he was lost again. One minute a steward was directing him and he knew he had to make two left turns for the lifts, the next he was on a promenade deck looking out into the icy vacuum of space through a clear dome of plexiglass. It was then that it struck him that in all the time he had been aboard the Starliner, he had never looked out of a porthole or even contemplated that he was in space again. So he stopped, and looked out into the darkness as if seeing it for the first time.

The vacuum of the Rösenbridge was odd to him. Every time he had travelled it before he had done so in stasis. The smaller merchant ships never went to the trouble of having a quo field generator large enough to cover the internal decks, so the crew generally just slept their way through interstellar travel.

Here the *Persia* carried on business as usual protected by the faint green glow of the navigation field. At first he thought the Rösenbridge was completely black, like being trapped in a room with no windows and no lights, but after a while it seemed to him that there were faint shapes out there.

The promenade ran for some length along the upper deck of the Starliner. Here and there were passages leading out at ninety degrees to completely clear observation spheres about thirty feet from the structure of the Starliner. Here a passenger could sit and watch space go by, in a view untainted by anything manmade.

It was late and there was no-one around so he had little trouble finding the first free observation dome. In truth it intrigued him to feel the feel of space-walking again. He had been there so many times wrapped in the protection of a space suit, floating off a derelict and with the best seat in the house to see the stars. Back then it had come to be an almost mundane activity whose beauty blended into insignificance by familiarity. It had been many years ago now and through the comfortable haze induced by the drink, Dezza suddenly had the urge to experience that true freedom of being out there floating in space once again.

The connecting tube felt cold and icy to the touch, but that didn't bother him. A sign at the entrance warned of gravity field fluctuations and as he crawled he felt the weird sensation of gravity dropping the further he moved from the bulk of the Starliner.

Weightless again after all these years! For his middle-aged frame it was a true liberation, and he could not help but smile as he propelled himself on to the end of the passage and into the clear sphere.

There was a transparent seat in the centre, and he eased himself easily into it, buoyed by the strangely low gravity. Now he could see the Rösenbridge dimension much more clearly. The green navigational field was thinner out here, away from the hull. If he strained his concentration he could still see its protective touch on the outside of the sphere.

The shapes that he thought he had seen faintly from the promenade were still subdued – he had thought that out here they would have more clarity. It was as if some of them were made up by his mind, to fill the blank canvas that was otherwise presented beyond the Plexiglas. He had heard stories of the effect happening to cavers marooned underground. If his mind had not still been fuzzy from the drink, he might have thought more about that. But he didn't. Instead he looked out in awe, as shapes seemed to flit and move. For a moment his mind made the shapes move one way, until he realised that it was completely the opposite direction to that which the Starliner would theoretically be moving. Then his mind made the images whirl in nauseating patterns before they moved on in the direction that his mind expected them now to go.

It was like watching clouds pass overhead on a summer afternoon – there was a vague memory of doing that as a child too. The shapes were given meaning by his mind. So he began to see shapes that a more sober mind should have told him was just his imagination. He saw ships, as if moving to hold station with the *Persia* but far enough away that they were difficult to make out. He tried to concentrate on them to bring them into focus, but his mind stubbornly made them morph from one thing to another. Slowly the ships turned into faces, and he saw with a bitter feeling of regret a likeness of Zoë formed from the merest suggestions in the dark.

"Zoë!" he called out before he could stop himself. Emotions welled inside and he cursed for letting himself get drawn into thinking of the past like that.

Then the images changed, and there appeared to be another ship. This time concentrating on it made it seem clearer, and he saw the shape of an elegant cigar shaped Starliner morph into clarity.

A shot of adrenaline pumped in his veins. As a cold sweat took hold across his body, he realised that he recognised that ship. Blinking, he tried to tell himself that it was just his imagination.

Look away and it will be gone when you look back he told his mind, but when he did look back it was not only there, but clearer too. Wide eyed with surprise, he thought he could actually see her riding lights blinking through the darkness, and the scattered effect of lights behind portholes.

"You aren't real!" he muttered, scrunching his eyes tightly shut. The image of the *Cerberus* was still there, as if burnt onto the inside of his eyelids.

Scrabbling around he launched himself out of the seat and fought to throw his bulk back down the passage. He felt the icy fingers of the vacuum clawing at him through the thin and almost unprotected tube. It was a feeling as if the *Cerberus* were reaching out to him, to take him back for its own just as it had done with the others.

With his heart pounding he tumbled back onto the promenade deck. He felt nauseous – probably the drink coupled with the shock he told himself. Trying to hold it back, he couldn't and vomited on the clean deck. Not daring to look back into view into the Rösenbridge, he instead ran straight for the exit and back into the warmth and safety of the inner corridors of the *Persia*.

Somehow he found his way back to his cabin and pounded into the washroom without even waiting for the light to reach full brightness. He stooped over the toilet bowl and vomited again. That made him feel better as the booze cleared from his stomach. Realising he was drenched in sweat, he stripped off and stepped into the shower.

It should have made him feel better, but it didn't all the time he could see the image of the *Cerberus* there on his mind every time he closed his eyes, taunting him and reminding him of the message from Tubs.

For several hours he fought off sleep with the bland coffee from the hospitality tray, until he could stave it off no longer and fell into yet another night of restless sleep.

*   *   *   *   *

Talk of Dezza and the gossip that everyone seemed to have on him was the hot topic of the staff rooms, for a while. But to Philipa's relief it soon died away into the usual background hubbub as everyone found something new to talk about. That was always the way on every tour – this week's hot stuff was next week's memories. There was always something new to talk about.

It was not as easy to forget Dezza though. The others seemed to find it easy enough, but she found herself pondering what he had really seen on the lower decks. He had been quite insistent and seemed to truly believe what he was saying.

Emma warned her off him quickly. "Too much trouble," she had said, "Steer clear of him or you will be sorry."

It was advice that for once she took, keeping clear of the decks where Dezza had been. The Starliner was huge, so it was not hard.

Captain Ventura's dislike of Dezza wasn't difficult to notice. When the gossip had been going around, it was a brave soul who brought it up in front of him. It was strange to see the man so riled by something that seemed so trivial. No-one dared to ask the captain why he disliked the man so much, but he would launch into a stream of insults laced with venom at the mention of the name.

The security teams let slip about the memo. In some ways it was pretty reasonable. No-one wanted a mad man roaming the ship, if Dezza truly was mad. Eventually the subject went away and talk moved on. But it always seemed to Philipa that inside Ventura's mind the rekindled memories still burned. He wasn't a man whom she knew especially well, despite having worked on the same ship for every tour of duty he had had with the company. Sometimes in the restaurants during evening meals and her days off she saw him from afar and wondered just what it was that smouldered inside him and made a professional man so against an individual that he had never met?

Her thoughts pulled up – had Ventura met Dezza before? It was a question she supposed that she ought to put to Dezza. But that would mean finding him, and Emma had been adamant that she should just leave him alone. Actually, when she thought about it more, Emma was right.

So she let the thoughts fade to the back of her mind and in time they did fade as she busied herself getting on with working another trip on the *Persia*.

8

It wasn't a big deal at first; just a few warning lights winking on a console that had a reputation for false alarms. Unlike the other occasions though, these didn't go out when the console was reset – the usual trick that seemed to appease the glitches in the electronics. Even worse, each time the panel came back on, the Christmas tree of lights had grown in number until the winking red lights could no longer be overlooked and ignored.

The crewmen on watch drew lots on who was going to be the unlucky one to have to call the chief engineer's cabin and get him out of bed to come and have a look at this. None of them relished the prospect and the fear of the chief's explosion when he was roused from the sleep that he so prized.

*   *   *   *   *

On the *Persia*'s bridge, warning lights blinked too, mirroring the console deep within the engineering decks. There was only a night watch on duty – normally any Starliner travelling the Rösenbridge did not need much attention to keep on her pre-programmed way. Lulled by boredom and the daydreaming it tended to bring on, neither navigators noticed the winking panel for some time, and then both were locked in worried conversation trying to work out how long it had gone unnoticed.

A quick call down to the engineering spaces confirmed that this was no electronics glitch, and it became the turn of the navigators to draw lots to see which of them would have to go and fetch the duty officer from his cabin.

It was the younger of the two who came up worst and had to go. He suspected that the other navigator had rigged the draw, but there was no time to argue, and anyway he would probably pull seniority of time served if he did. He didn't relish the thought of waking the duty officer. Making the most of the short walk down the corridor from the bridge, he formulated what he was going to say. He did not get as far as the cabin though. Luck was with him, of sorts, and he ran into captain Ventura, dressed in civvies on his way back from a game on the squash courts.

"Sir, may I have a word?" the navigator asked. It wasn't normal protocol to disturb the captain when he wasn't on watch, but given the captain was here anyway, it had to be better than rousing an irate duty officer instead.

"What's wrong?" asked Ventura. Perhaps he could tell from the navigator's tone that something unexpected had happened.

"We have warning lights coming up on the bridge. We've checked with engineering, and this is not a glitch." The navigator paused, trying to work out how to phrase this. "The Rösenbridge is becoming unstable – the *Persia*'s drive core is in danger of collapse."

"Show me." The captain hurriedly tossed his squash racket in through the door of his own cabin, and the two stalked to the bridge as fast as they could.

It was only a matter of time before the engines failed. Running hot, something had tripped the failsafe shut down and with it the power to stay within the Rösenbridge had disappeared. As the navigator and the captain came onto the bridge, the remaining navigator could say nothing before the view beyond the Plexiglas screens flickered, and a starscape returned.

"All stop!"

"Aye sir."

The captain frowned. "Call up the chief engineer and have him report. I want to know what the hell is going on."

"Aye sir."

*   *   *   *   *

No-one noticed when it first began to happen. The stars began to wink out and die ahead of the Starliner. Soon there was an area of space that seemed nothing more than a black void. One moment there had been stars, the next a patch of darkness that seemed to suck away any light, and the patch was growing.

Ventura leant closer to the Plexiglas, as if that might make the stars reappear.

"What the hell is that?" he asked.

Nobody answered. Everyone else on the bridge was peering too, unable to believe their eyes. At last a navigator had the wherewithal to check the holographic display. And yet, the hovering sphere above the projector showed nothing more than the yellow blip that was the *Persia* and a few lines of readout of little significance.

"Whatever that effect is, it isn't local," the navigator reported at last.

"But it does seem to be spreading," replied Ventura.

Just as he had said, the area of pitch black continued to spread, until most of the stars ahead of them were gone.

Looking out of the side Plexiglas screens, Ventura noted that the stars to the side and behind the Starliner were still there. Beads of sweat stood out on his forehead as he dashed back to the scopes.

"There's nothing there!" whined the navigator.

Ventura pushed the man aside. "Then you aren't reading this thing right."

But no matter how hard he adjusted the computer controls, the readouts still showed that there was nothing there for the sensors to read. He looked up from the scopes and back to the Plexiglas, as if in those few moments the stars would have winked back and the mystery would be gone. But the void remained.

The back of his mind screamed that it had to be a meteorite, thousands of miles across and rendered black only by the massive distance from any illuminating sun. If such a thing were out there, then the *Persia* was in great danger. No navigation field that could be generated could ever hope to deflect something of that size. A meteorite big enough to blot out the stars would shrug off a hit with the Starliner as if batting away a tiny mosquito.

"Something on the scope!" shouted a crewman.

Heads turned to look. The holographic sphere showed an intermittent haze that seemed to come and go.

"Magnify!"

The image folded in on itself then grew at an alarming speed until the cigar-shape of the *Persia* could just about be discerned. Alongside it the intermittent blip had become a pulsating glow of red. For precious seconds no-one said anything. But then, at last, a crewman looked to the Plexiglas, back to the scope and then out of the Plexiglas again. "What the hell is that?" he asked slowly.

No-one answered. Outside, the darkness of the stars had got bigger until almost none were left visible beyond the inky black void.

"An alarm went off, making Ventura and the others look to the holographic sphere with a start.

"Proximity alert!"

"But there's nothing there!" shouted a navigator.

"Scopes say there is – something. Just not exactly whole."

"Dust cloud? Débris field?" offered another.

Ventura looked out through the Plexiglas. "If we're lucky it will just be that."

The blackness began to grey and blur. In the glow from the Starliner's navigation lights, the darkness began to fog and at last there was something to be seen.

"Dust cloud by the looks of it," said the navigator at the scope, "Can't get a proper lock with the scanners." He looked up. "Let's hope there's no substance behind it."

"I hope you're right," muttered Ventura. Silently he wedged himself into a seat, ready for any impact if it came.

The fog rolled in. For a moment it looked like the Starliner was about to be consumed by a tidal wave of dust. It felt to Ventura as if the wave might lift up the *Persia* and toss her around like a twig in an ocean swell. But with a strange anticlimax, the wave just soundlessly washed over the bows and rolled on by without any noise.

The holographic sphere blipped red and a klaxon wailed.

"Warning. Warning. Collision alert. Warning. Collision alert," a computer voice purred with a voice that did not seem to fit the urgency of the moment.

"I've got a lock on something solid!"

"Distance?"

"Hard to tell – the dust is clouding the scans. It keeps appearing and disappearing."

"I want answers, not excuses!" scolded Ventura.

"Two hundred metres and closing," came the reply after a pause.

Ventura suspected the navigator had made his best guess rather than rely on sketchy readouts from a computer which did not seem able to deal with the dust cloud. Maybe it was something that the programmers had never thought a vessel in space might encounter.

"There's something there!" shouted a crewman, pointing out through the screen. All heads turned to see where he was pointing.

At first Ventura struggled to see anything through the hazy waves of dust. Then his eagle eyes saw the tiny object, rolling over and over and coming closer all the time.

"Take us to port. Twenty degrees."

"Collision course!"

"I know, dammit! Get us on a new course now!"

The bows of the Starliner seemed disinclined to move even after the commands were entered. The seconds ticked by, and all Ventura could do was watch with the others as the object came closer, all the time heading straight towards them.

Straining his eyes, Ventura tried to make out what it was. There was something about it – something strangely *human* in its shape. Then he realised that it was a lifepod. *What the hell is that doing out here?* He found himself wondering. The drive core failure had brought them out of the Rösenbridge a long way from any of the major shipping lanes.

Too late the bows of the *Persia* began to move, edging slowly around. For a moment it seemed that they might make it. It would have been very tight at the least. But at the last minute it became clear that it was going to graze the hull.

It hit the navigation field first, at an angle that arrested much of the lifepod's spin. With less than three metres to spare, it passed down the port side, getting closer all the time to the hull and spitting static in angry lashes between itself and the Starliner.

The lifepod did not look as if it touched, but the dull bass resonance of metal on metal rumbled beneath their feet. It was only a graze – probably sounding worse than it was. As it yawed past, he caught a glimpse of an angry silver streak along its underbelly where it had scraped the hull. The rest of the pod was matt with dirt and dust.

There were only a few seconds to see it before it passed beyond the bridge.

"A lifepod?" asked the navigator with incredulity, speaking the words that no doubt many of the others had voiced in their heads.

They all felt a second more muted bass groan as the lifepod grazed the Starliner's superstructure again further behind them.

"Do we go back and pick it up?" asked a crewman at last.

Ventura's thoughts whirled. Certainly interplanetary shipping law would dictate that they should check, in case there were survivors who needed rescuing. But there was something about the lifepod that nagged the back of Ventura's mind. He could not quite place what it was, but there had been something amiss about it.

"Where is it now?" he asked.

"It's…." the navigator stumbled on his words. For a moment the holographic sphere rippled with static as the view swivelled around several times as the man searched. Finally he looked up, bemused. "It seems to have disappeared."

"Any débris?"

"None."

It was true. As much as the holographic sphere zoomed in, there was nothing for it to pick up and show. Even the dust cloud had dissipated until it no longer showed up either. Outside the Plexiglas, the starscape had returned like it had never been away.

How could a lifepod just disappear like that? Ventura knew that he had seen it, and no-one else on the bridge was denying it had happened.

"Where the hell is it?" he said, more to himself than to anyone else.

The sphere rotated and flickered with static as the computer searched desperately for any signs of the object they had collided with. Its search appeared to be in vain.

A communications panel buzzed on a crewman's console and the man answered. No sooner had the first few words been spoken at the other end than he reeled around to Ventura.

"They've found it."

"Where?"

"Deck staff report it tangled in the antenna aerials close to the main airlock hatches. Must have snagged the guy wires and been drawn in."

So that was why the scans had failed to find it – as far as the computer was concerned, it had become part of the ship. The moment it had been snared in the aerials, it was inside the zone that the scanners could sweep.

"Despatch an engineering team to see what they can do."

*   *   *   *   *

The metallic impact had been faint, but years of training in a salvager could never be suppressed. A cold sweat ran over Dezza as his memory told him he had heard that sound before.

"Something hit us."

The noise came again, fainter but definitely a metallic grating somewhere on the Starliner's hull. He thought of the message that had made him come as he hurriedly dragged on his clothes and headed out of the cabin.

A few tourists lingered in the corridor, drawn from their cabins too at the unmistakable sounds.

"Hey, did you hear that?" asked an old lady, but Dezza was too preoccupied to answer. Running for the stairs he pushed past more aimless milling people. Most didn't know what to do – maybe they had just followed the others, looking to see what the commotion was that was drawing people towards the upper decks.

From several stewards sat grouped at a security post glued to their communication channels he gleaned that the *Persia* was no longer in the Rösenbridge. Other whispered conversations hinted that something in deep space had hit them on a collision course – some other ship? Like Chinese whispers, the stories seemed to have only grains of truth hidden in them. Following the crowds, the flow led up to the grand staircase. It was an area Dezza had so far tried to avoid. Seeing it on the deck plan, the name alone had reminded him so much of the great open atrium on the *Cerberus*. His fears made him hold back, but the rush of people was strong now. Maybe amongst other people he would not feel too bad, so reluctantly he let himself move on with the crowd.

Contrary to expectations, the grand staircase was far removed from the ancient Starliner. Arranged in concentric circles, tiers of stairs went up at all angles, flanked by Corinthian pillars and mock hieroglyphs and decked with purple velvet tapestries that depicted stylised sword-fighting legionaries. At the very top of the tiers of stairs, where the flow of people seemed to be gravitating, the ceiling opened out into a truly massive dome of clear Plexiglas that looked out on a broad and spectacular vista of the stars. Dezza didn't pay it much attention until he realised that the crowds around him were slowing and heads were turning upward. Following their gaze, a shiver ran down his spine as he realised that they were all looking up through the dome. Not at the stars but at the huge lifeless hulk that was tangled amongst gossamer fine wires that had been severed as the object had grazed the Starliner and become entangled.

There were a lot of people now in the grand staircase. To Dezza's annoyance they milled around, blocking the stairs and the corridors that led off them. With most heads craned upward, no-one seemed inclined to move or get out of the way. It took him several minutes to push through to the stairs and start to climb. There was something about the tangled craft that made him want to look closer. Perhaps it was the salvager's instinct kicking in after so many years' hiatus – know what you are dealing with. Or maybe it was just pure curiosity. Either way, he wanted a better look, and that meant getting past all these tourists acting like sheep to get to the top level.

It took a long time, and there were moments when ignorant passengers seemed dumb to his requests to let him past. On one occasion he had had to resist the urge to come to blows with one particular fat idiot who just looked stupidly at Dezza with an idiotic grin until Dezza shoved him out of the way. He heard the man fall and shout insults, but he didn't stay to listen to the man's outburst and left him to be quickly swallowed by the crowd.

On the top landing the crowds were thinner. Several stewards and a team of security staff were trying to usher passengers away, but were fighting a losing battle against the tide of curiosity. Dezza slipped past them easily enough, and found a space at the edge of the gallery that ran all the way around the dome where he could get a clear view.

He could see it clearer now and could see it was a small vessel. From the shape he knew it had to be a lifepod, but the design was old and archaic. There was a gouge running the length of one side where it had scraped the *Persia*'s hull. Angry and bright, the bare silver metal contrasted against the dulled dark grey of the rest of the pod that had been floating unloved in space for quite some time. Dezza looked for the markings that would indicate the vessel it was originally from and the shipping registration numbers, but if they were still there, layers of dust made them invisible.

"Hey buddy, would you step back now?"

A firm hand rested on his shoulder. He turned to look into the burly face of a security guard. Behind the man the top gallery was completely clear.

"Can't a guy get himself a look?" Dezza found himself murmuring, stalling for time. He looked back up to the pod, but the security guard was more insistent the second time.

"There's an easy way and a hard way to be leaving here today, sir," the guard said, his voice wavering under the stress of the moment. Clearly he had not been ready for this unexpected encounter in space and the interest that it had drawn from the passengers. "You can leave on your own legs, or I can help you with mine."

Dezza wriggled free of the man's grasp. "No, it's okay. I'm going," he protested.

Deciding that the guard wasn't joking, he beat a hurried retreat to the stairs. A row of stewards opened up to let him through, then closed ranks behind him. As Dezza went, he heard the staccato of hurried communicator traffic and knew that there was something else going on that the crew wasn't letting on to.

*   *   *   *   *

Space walks weren't the most common of activities for civilian crews. Sure, they happened sometimes and all the commercial vessels carried the equipment, but it wasn't something they did unless they had to.

With a lifepod tangled in the antennas, it was time to draw lots, and the chief had drawn the shortest one. He could have ordered someone else to go, but the chief had a philosophy that you only gained respect amongst your crew if you showed them that you were equally as prepared to do even the most loathsome tasks. So he had drawn lots with his men, and had lost. It was all part of the deal – live, work and play with the boys. They called you 'chief' and no other name, and you earned that respect. Gritting his teeth he cracked a joke to make the best of it, and stepped into the airlock to don the suit for the short trip outside.

He had practised getting into the suit many times before, but the material still felt stiff and unused – casting his mind back he could remember only one previous occasion when he had had to walk out into the vacuum of space, and that was a long time ago. Then it had been a simple check of an airlock panel that wouldn't cycle properly on the routine checks. Nothing more than a frayed wire behind a panel – a routine job that could have been done by following the pages of a textbook.

This was something different and a complete unknown. As he pulled on the helmet and checked the seals, he could not help but think that whilst the bravado and false confidence would keep him as chief in the eyes of his men, inside he was still timid old John.

The connections all came up green. Tapping the radio controls on his wrist, he was comforted by the buzz of static and the voice of David, his second in command.

"All clear chief. Telemetry is good."

"Roger that."

It was still all textbook stuff, but once that airlock opened, it was all new and unknown.

The floor vibrated under his feet as the pumps began their work to empty the air. For a moment he could hear the sound through the air, then as that became a vacuum it was just the vibration through the deck. Finally after what seemed like an excruciating length of time, the panel cycled to green, and the airlock hatched rolled silently open on the stars.

He was startled to hear a dry rasping noise. Then he realised it was the sound of his own breathing echoing within his helmet.

Shit, he thought, *I'm a real loose cannon if I can scare myself that easily*. He forced a smile as he stepped to the edge of the hatch and swung himself through. The Starliner's gravity generators ended at the lip and he felt the nauseous feeling of the sudden shift in his weight to almost nothing. He felt a little sick, and had to wait for the feeling to pass.

"You okay, chief?" a concerned voice buzzed in his ears.

"Yeah, fine," he reassured, "Just getting used to the weightlessness. Moving on now."

There was a ladder alongside the hatch. Taking a grip with his toes on the rungs, he unhooked the safety line from his belt and clipped it to the bar that ran up the side. At least then if he lost his grip he wouldn't risk floating off into space.

Leaning back, he tried to gauge the distance to the lifepod. It didn't look far, but he would have to find a way to climb part of the aerial assembly. The lifepod had come crashing through and the access ladder hung torn in the middle at a zigzag angle. Still, in weightlessness it should not be too hard, he told himself.

It still took more than ten minutes to reach the edge of the lifepod and he had to stop twice to catch his breath.

"Must be well out of shape," he muttered aloud.

Finally he reached the lifepod, and after a moment's hesitation reached out and touched it. A haze of silvery-grey dust rose up lazily and hovered in a small cloud. Rubbing with his glove, he frowned as the dust stuck readily to the nice clean white gloves. He would have to find a way of getting that off when he got back into the airlock.

Underneath the dust he could see that the hull of the lifepod might have once been painted a rich cream colour, though years in space had taken their toll.

"This is one big cleaning job," he said.

"Not our department, chief," buzzed the voice in his ears, startling him.

Silently he cursed himself for forgetting that the radio had been transmitting all the time. They must have heard the quip about being out of shape, though they had said nothing.

Putting on a brave face, he hauled himself up onto the hull of the lifepod. Somewhere there had to be an access hatch. With all of this dirt it was difficult to tell. As he moved around it, the plating underneath turned from dirty grey to shiny silver and it was bent and buckled. Here and there he could see the shape of the internal ribs of the craft, picked out in the gouge. The impact didn't seem to have compromised the pod's hull integrity. Tapping the hull with a gloved hand, he rested his helmet against the plating and listened. There was an echo, and it sounded to him that there was still pressure inside. Not bad for the number of years the pod must have been out in deep space.

"Still airtight," he announced for the boys on the radio.

"Look for an airlock."

"Way ahead of you," he chimed.

It was a long and laborious task to check up and down the pod. The accumulated dust muted any surface feature on the hull, and he had to brush the dust away with his gloves to be certain there was nothing he had missed. More than once the clouds that had been stirred up became so thick that he struggled to see further than a few feet. The first time it happened he went to blow the cloud away, then cursed loudly.

"What's up chief?" came David's concerned voice in his ear.

"I just did the most stupid thing – just blew to clear the dust."

There was a moment's silence; then the voice on the radio chuckled. "Misted up good?"

"Yeah. The fans are clearing it now. Jesus – I can't believe I fell for the oldest mistake in the book."

"It happens to us all, chief."

He made it sound so simplistic, but John still felt he should have known better. Eventually the suit's fans cleared the misting, and he continued more carefully sweeping the dust aside with his hands.

Eventually he found the hatch. Under the dust the edge of a tightly fitted seal appeared, and he followed it around, clearing methodically until the whole ellipse of the hatch was clear. Of course, that still left finding the panel to get it opened. He wasn't familiar with the pod's design for a start. Searching the actual hatch came up nothing. It took a couple of passes of the surrounding metalwork to turn up a flush fitted cover which with a little persuasion he was able to prise open.

"This thing hasn't seen any attention in more than a few years," he cursed, "I'd wager this thing has been lost out here for decades, maybe longer."

"Are you sure then that you're ready for what could be inside then, chief?"

John picked up on the note of concern in the voice, and paused with the panel still ajar. There could be anything inside the pod. Generally crew used them to abandon ship in case of severe emergencies. They were little more than a life raft to get a crew to a point of being rescued. He looked down at the filthy plating. This one had been adrift a long time. If there had been anyone inside, they could not have survived. The thought of finding what was left of them sent a shiver down his spine, but he didn't dare show a weakness over the radio to the rest of the team.

"We'll just have to take it slow then," he said at last.

"Just take it easy chief," came the reply, devoid of any jovial edge now, "Don't let anything scare you."

Easier said than done.

The panel stuck at halfway; not quite open far enough to get his hand inside and feel for the release. It took a lot of effort until finally the panel bent into a curve. *That's never going to close again*, he thought. But it did not matter – he was into the controls underneath.

He took out a panel tester from his tool belt and eased the probe into the exposed wires. The needle on the gauge didn't even waver – the pod was completely dead. He tried not to think about what would be inside. With no power meant life support inside would have failed long ago. Perhaps the pod had been jettisoned by mistake? It was a good thought to hang onto right now, even if it was unlikely.

With a grim realisation of the reality, he radioed in. "No power, not even residual. This pod's been out of it for a long time. I'm going to try and pull the manual release and get in that way. We might need some heavy tools." A thought occurred to him – a get-out clause. "If this thing is completely dead, why do we need to look inside?"

"You know the deal chief – interstellar rules. Even if it looks dead, we have to check just to make sure. At any rate, we have to pull the black box – if there is one. There'll be hell to pay if we don't at least go through the motions."

John silently cursed himself for not remembering the procedure. Whether he liked it or not it meant stepping inside. If he was lucky the pod would be empty; maybe a false launch? It was a thought to hold on to. Looking back to the panel he pulled the dead wiring aside looking for a manual release; all the pods had them. There wasn't much in here. Somehow dust had found its way in and had coated everything in the same dull grey that made it hard to make anything out. His gloves were now exactly the same colour and it took a while to find a protrusion which when he rubbed hard enough showed traces of red paint. Grasping hold, he braced himself against the pod's plating, and pulled.

It was stuck. Why did nothing ever go like in the textbooks? There was a pry-bar on his tool belt. Getting it out he wedged it as best he could, and applied his weight to that. It took a lot of effort and for a while he thought it was just going to break the pry-bar. But with a grating that he felt rather than heard, the handle moved. He wasn't quite ready for it and the prey-bar jolted loose from his grip. Before he could catch it, it cartwheeled past him and disappeared out into space.

"Damn!" he cursed.

"Problem?" the radio voice asked.

"Just lost the pry-bar, that's all. It's unlocked though."

Sure enough, the edge of the hatch was raised slightly. That was new – it had definitely been flush before. Still there was little he could get a purchase on. Working his fingers under the edge, he wished for the lost pry-bar, and heaved.

There was a puff of silver dust, and the hatch eased open enough for him to press his helmet face plate to the gap. Inside was black with darkness so he fumbled for the controls on his suit and turned on the helmet light.

He recoiled in shock, and screamed. Instantly the radio was alive with the chatter of panicked voices, but he heard none of it as he fought to pull himself away.

* * * * *

The panic of the chief caused a ripple of frenzy at the control station next to the airlock. Frantic attempts to call the man failed. For a few seconds there was a garbled scream and words that no-one could make out, then the line reverted to static and no amount of radio calls brought the chief back on the line. In the end one crewman took matters into his own hands as he saw the scene descend into a leaderless panic.

"I'll go out," he said calmly.

At first no-one seemed to hear him, so he repeated his offer again. Only then did the hubbub diminish and a sea of worried faces looked to him.

Tom was nothing more than a junior crewman on his first trip out interstellar. In the days of ocean travel, he might have been referred to as a cabin boy – he was only sixteen. But such derogatory names had died out long before mankind took to the stars. The sentiment of his lowly position however had not changed though.

"You think you can do it Tom?" demanded a burly engineer, his face red and confused.

Tom nodded. "I've done my training – I'm as qualified as anyone else to go out there."

"We shouldn't be sending a boy," someone muttered.

Tom rose up angrily. "I don't see anyone else offering to go, and sitting around here bitching about nothing isn't going to find the chief."

He stood defiantly, cheek to cheek with the burly engineer. Finally the old man was forced to back down – the boy had guts.

"Okay," he barked, "Suit up and find out what's going on."

Tom needed no second prompt. Fuelled by teenage optimism and adrenaline he was into his suit in record time before the airlock had cycled back to clear. Stepping in, he realised he felt no fear. Not that it surprised him. If he had asked the burly old engineer what he thought of his courage, the engineer would probably have replied that life had not yet knocked the courage out of the young boy. But Tom had never asked, and the engineer's opinions remained unspoken.

As soon as the airlock lights cycled to green and the hatch rolled open, Tom rolled himself out into space and onto the ladder. The change in gravity didn't bother him – no different from childhood funfair rides, and the adrenaline was still pumping.

A voice buzzed in his ears; the burly engineer he had squared up to, sounding louder than Tom remembered. It was most likely a trick of the helmet's headset.

"Okay kid. Keep your head clear. Whatever you do, clip your safety cable on before you do anything."

Tom smiled as he grappled with the clip and made sure it was as the engineer said. The man's voice was more sincere now – whatever he thought of the boy, he wasn't about to let him get himself injured, or worse over an easily overlooked bit of safety procedure.

"Got it."

"Good. Take a look where you're going and then take your time in getting there."

Tom tried to look up, but all he saw was the rim of the helmet visor. "I can't see anything," he said, exasperated.

"Lean back to look up," the engineer said patiently, "You have to learn to move within the constraints of the suit."

Leaning back Tom saw the pod for the first time. He looked to see the chief, but he could not see him. A cable stretched from the top of the safety rod showed that the chief had to be somewhere close by. Following the cable he saw that it stretched out to the pod then disappeared looped over the top. The chief was somewhere on the other side.

Taking the engineer's advice, he climbed hand over hand slowly. It didn't take him long to reach the aerial assembly. Unlike the chief, he was young and fit. Weightlessness was still a new experience and he nearly misjudged the push he needed to give himself to get across the broken ladder to the pod. His heart fluttered as he sailed past. Then the safety cable went tight and he silently thanked the engineer's advice. Pulling himself in on the cable, he reached the dusty hull of the pod and hooked himself on.

The chief's safety line was only a couple of feet away. He reached over and tested it – it was under tension, so something had to be at the other end. He gave it a tug, but it wouldn't move.

"Any sign, kid?" came the engineer's voice.

Tom shook his head; then realised no-one could see him. "No. His safety cable is here. I'm going to follow it until I find him."

It was easy to pull himself around the pod using the chief's cable as leverage. He could see where the older man had been, sweeping the dust away from the pod's dirty hull. In places there was still a haze of the dust in the air that the safety cable flicked it up as it flexed under him.

Reaching the other side he saw a hatch slightly ajar. He remembered the radio chatter and the chief saying he had got it open. There it was, with a gap no more than a few inches wide around its edge.

Confusing though, the safety cable ran as far as the opening and disappeared inside. Had the chief got in before he panicked? He tested the cable again, but it wouldn't budge. He could see it bouncing on the cable's rim. Maybe the chief had got it caught inside?

Inside the hatch was pitch black, darker than Tom had ever thought could be possible.

"I can't see anything here," he called out."

"Use the helmet light," came the engineer's calm response, "The controls are on your wrist."

Tom fumbled with the box on his suit. Finding the right one, a beam of light shone out and immediately illuminated a haze of dust that hovered just inside the hatch. It was hard to see anything inside; the chief must have disturbed all the dust that had clung to the edge of the hatch when he went in.

Tom stopped mid thought – how could the chief have got in? The hatch was still ajar only a few inches. Carefully he checked around the edge. There were marks where the chief had levered it open, but the dirt caked in the hinged side suggested it had never opened further.

"How the hell has the chief got through there?" he said aloud.

"What are you on about?" came the engineer's voice on the radio.

"The gap the chief went through. It's only a few inches wide at most."

"You sure? The chief hasn't been that slim in well over twenty years."

"Sure as anything, boss. His safety cable goes in around the edge. No other way it could have got in – they're clipped nice and tight on the suit, aren't they?"

"Yeah."

"Well, then he's in there. But the hatch hasn't been opened more than a few inches. What do I do?"

"Get it open and get in there."

Tom grumbled – it was easy for someone sat comfortably in the luxury of the Starliner to say that. Out here in zero gravity things were just a bit different.

He took the pry-bar from his tool belt and used it to lever the hatch open further. It was stiff and he had to stop a couple of times to rest weary arms. It did not help that the suit restricted his movements. Finally he had the hatch open wide enough that he could wriggle around it and climb into the dirty darkness of the pod. Out of habit he started going feet first, worrying that there might be no room to turn inside before he realised that in space there was no up and no down. There was nothing stopping him from drifting in forwards using his arms to guide him in.

The dust stubbornly refused to clear. There was no air and no gravity, so it hovered in the stillness no atmosphere. Once he had his upper torso through the hatch though, his helmet light seemed a little better. He could make out the edges of the airlock inside. There was a control panel – no lights on, and when he rubbed the buttons a layer of dust showed no-one had touched it in many years. Looking around he found the chief's safety line and tugged.

He hadn't expected it to move – it had felt well jammed from outside, but surprisingly the thin wire came to him easily enough. Something moved in the dust at its end.

"I think I've got him!" he announced breathlessly into the radio.

"Is he all right?" The reply buzzed a little with static – the structure of the pod was interfering with the signal.

In a rush the suited figure appeared in front of him from the dust. He grabbed hold and manhandled the chief around. Despite the zero gravity, it was hard to move him. Finally he grabbed an arm; it felt limp and, well odd. Tom didn't register at first what was wrong, then he realised it was bending unnaturally. Turning the helmet to face him, he saw the helmet visor was cracked. Looking into the face of the chief, he recoiled in shock.

"Shit!"

"What the hell's wrong?" buzzed the frantic reply.

"The chief. He's dead."

"Dead? How?"

"I don't know. Looks like he's been...er..." his words faltered; it was difficult to know what to say.

"Spit it out Tom."

Tom swallowed; his mouth felt dry. "Crushed?"

"How?"

"I don't know."

He heard the muffled sound on the radio of the engineer consulting the others. Then his voice came back on the line.

"Get him back here as best you can."

*   *   *   *   *

It was not hard for Dezza to find his way to what was going on. Every security guard and steward he passed had radios buzzing loudly, spewing tantalising titbits to anyone listening. Just listen discretely and follow the information, using the frequent deck plans to find his way.

He had not thought about Philipa in all that was going on, but to his surprise he ran into her passing along an upper corridor. Working with two other stewardesses she was trying to keep passengers moving and stop them from getting access to a stairwell. It was a losing battle against the determination of the inquisitive tourists to find out what was going on.

She stopped when she saw him, radio in hand mid way through receiving a garbled message. He saw the pleading look in her eyes.

"Dezza!"

Relief was clear in her voice. Maybe she was glad to see a friendly face in the sea of passengers all trying to bully their way past? He wasn't sure.

"What the hell is going on?" he demanded.

"It's all hit the fan," she recounted breathlessly, "They went out to check what we hit, and now all hell has broken loose."

He remembered the frantic messages he had overheard across radio channels.

"It's just space junk? Isn't it? That's what it looked like?"

"I don't know," she pleaded, "They just told us to keep people away whilst they sorted out the problem."

He realised there was something he had missed. "What problem?"

"The guy they sent out. He's dead," she hissed as quietly as she could so no other passengers would overhear.

More people pushed past. With a chilling knot of fear balling in his stomach, Dezza remembered the message from Tubs – the omen that unless he could do something, the *Persia* would be doomed.

"Take me there," he demanded, grabbing her by the arm.

She wriggled indignantly, working herself loose. "What the hell are you doing?"

He looked her in the eye. "I need to know if it is what I told you about."

She was unconvinced. "Stop that," she snapped sullenly, "You were warned before that the captain is gunning for you. I don't know why, but he's been looking for an excuse to put you under lock and key since the day you ended up in the infirmary and he found out that you were aboard."

"I don't care." He took her arm, pulling her towards the stairwell.

She held back, stubbornly pulling against him. "He will care."

Dezza stopped and a part of his mind screamed to listen to her, but behind it all was the memory of Tubs and the urgency of the eerie message burnt into his consciousness. He made his decision. "I have to know."

She nodded, perhaps realising that he was never going to stop pushing if she tried to refuse. "Come with me."

*   *   *   *   *

Tucking the radio into her jacket pocket, she led him into the stairwell and they climbed amongst the eager tourists. At the top they left for a side corridor and she led him to a concealed door that they slipped through. Inside was another corridor, quiet and bare. He realised that she had taken him into the service areas reserved for staff.

"It's quicker, and the security on the top of the main way have been ordered to not let anyone through. There will be a crush and it will take ages to get to the front and argue our way past."

Dezza said nothing, hurrying to keep up. There were several junctions in the service corridors, but Philipa knew her way and they never faltered. Finally she led him to a doorway and they slipped though back out into a main corridor. There were no passengers here, though he could hear the sounds of quite a few arguing with

90

somewhere close by. There were crew though, gathered around a series of airlocks. As they approached, a medical crew hurried up the corridor to join the group.

"What's happening?" asked Dezza breathlessly.

A burly engineer glanced to him disapprovingly. "I thought passengers were to be kept away?" he demanded.

Philipa slipped forward. "He's with me."

The engineer grunted, clearly not approving, but he decided not to push the matter further.

"The chief went out to take a look. Somehow he got inside the pod and something happened – we aren't quite sure what. The boy's bringing him back in now." Ignoring Dezza, he turned back to the airlock.

Dezza pushed up as close as he could, peering through the armoured glass into the lock's interior. It was hard to see much, and the engineer kept trying to push him out of the way, but he caught a glimpse of two suited men. At least, one was moving and the other hung limp until he was dragged into the gravity of the airlock where he fell like a sack of sand to the floor.

It felt like an age before the 'boy' as the engineer kept on calling him got the airlock shut and set it to cycle. At last the control panel winked to green, and the hatch slid open emitting a pungent smell of ozone.

Several crew men leapt in, lugging the fallen man out into the corridor. In the hubbub of activity, Dezza was pushed to the back of the crowd, but he saw enough to know that it did not look good for the man. The suit was filthy, covered in dust that stank of ozone. And the helmet visor was cracked, meaning that the man inside had been exposed to a vacuum. His limbs hung at odd angles with more bends than a man could possibly have joints.

Through the broken helmet visor, Dezza caught sight of the man's face, still contorted into a look of abject horror, even in death. With a shudder his skin ran cold as he remembered the expression – it had been the expression on Tubs' face when he had seen him in the lift on the *Cerberus*. Zoë said he had died of a heart attack, brought on by absolute terror. From the chief's expression, maybe the same had happened here, though the broken and crushed body suggested there had been something more.

It was happening all over again – the *Cerberus* and what it had held had found him for a second time.

"What the hell is he doing here!"

Dezza looked up – he recognised the voice, even though there were subtle changes to when he last heard it. He tried to fix his mind on the elusive memory that refused to quite come to the fore.

Marching towards him down the corridor was the angry faced captain Ventura, and he was looking directly at him.

The hubbub hushed around Dezza and he became aware that all attention was on him and the captain. Ventura walked straight up to him, squaring face to face.

"So, up to no good again I see. When will you learn that your ghost story shit isn't welcome around here?"

"I had nothing to do with it," Dezza replied indignantly.

"Bullshit." The captain looked to the dead man's body. Medics had begun removing the suit. Underneath the skin was bruised and crushed; bones broken in a great many places.

"I've seen this happen before," hissed Dezza, "On the *Cerberus* my crewmate died with the same expression on his face."

Ventura shot him a look that could have burned a hole in plate steel. "One more word," he said icily, malice dripping in his voice as he let the threat hang in the air.

Dezza thought of Tubs and the message. It was happening – the message had been right.

"You have to do something. Isolate everything."

"Why?"

"Once that thing gets into the ship's systems, there's no stopping it." He could hear his voice was rising. From the corner of his eye he saw the pained look on Philipa's face, though she did not dare say a thing. Too late he realised the warning she had given him before.

Ventura's voice went to a deathly calm. "Security chief?" he called, without taking his eyes off Dezza.

A man stepped forward from the crowd. "Sir?"

"Take Mr Booth to the security cells and make sure he is in no position to try and scare any of my passengers or crew."

"Yes sir."

The chief signalled to his men and two stepped over and grabbed Dezza by his arms.

He struggled, trying to break free, but the men were too strong for him.

"You're making a mistake, captain!" Dezza called out.

"No, Mr Booth," Ventura said calmly, turning his back on the struggle, "I believe that *you* just made your last mistake of this voyage."

*   *   *   *   *

There was no use in struggling; the security men made sure of that. They were not the talkative types either, and anyway Dezza was in no mood to say anything. Inside he felt the twist of emotions brought about by seeing the dead man. It had brought it all back and made the message warning so chilling. Yet the captain was not interested in hearing what Dezza had to say of the omen. Given the negative spin the media had put on the whole thing it was hardly surprising. Yet Ventura had shown there was more venom to his dislike of Dezza. Philipa had warned him of that, but it wasn't until the encounter at the airlock that he had truly realised the depths to which Ventura despised him.

He had been looking for his excuse to send Dezza to the security cells, Philipa had warned him. Well, he had found his excuse and taken it. Frog-marched with no option of getting away the security escort were going to make sure that the captain's orders were carried out to the letter. Even if he were to wriggle free and run for it, where would he go? They would easily track him down and he knew Ventura would use it as yet more excuse to put Dezza out of the way. It would makes things worse than they already were – if that was at all possible. So he let them take him down to the security cells, and stood impassively at the front desk as the two guards booked him in.

It was as if they had been expecting him all along. Dezza could not help but suspect that the paperwork had been on computer file for a while, just waiting for him to foul up and give Ventura the excuse he needed. Without a word the staff ticked the boxes then ushered him to a clinical white corridor.

Doors opened out on either side. Each one was open, revealing the same clinical white cells with nothing but a metal bunk and a chemical toilet. At the final door – as far as it got from the security desk he noted – they showed him in through the door. Stepping through he heard the hatch shut behind him, and turned to see the guard peering through a tiny grill at him.

"Make yourself comfortable, Mr Booth," the man said politely but firmly in a manner that suggested replies were not welcome, "It's going to be a long trip."

The grill snapped shut, and he was left on his own in the cell with only a security camera on the wall behind a wire mesh for company. He smiled – no privacy. Even when he went to take a leak they could spy on him. Shaking his head he tested the spring on the bed's mattress and swung himself onto it.

If only he had listened to Philipa and been more cautious. He might have been ready for Ventura, and avoided giving him his excuse. But it was too late now.

9

The security chief bustled up to the door. There was a group of other men in security uniform already there, and a handful of wide-eyed and white-faced stewardesses. From beyond the cabin door the crash of furniture and the screams of a man were eerily loud.

"What's going on?" he demanded breathlessly.

"Disturbance in the honeymoon suite. One man has gone berserk. No-one is able to get through to him - he's just been thrashing around in there trashing the place."

The chief tried the door – it was locked.

"Did no-one think to spring the lock?" he demanded angrily.

"Tried chief. He's got it jammed on the inside real good."

"Is there someone else in there with him?"

"Just his fiancée as far as we know. At least, she's on the passenger manifest and no-one has seen her today so we're presuming she's in there with him."

From the other side of the door came a blood-curdling scream and a smash followed by a crackle of shorting electricity. The lights in the corridor flickered a moment then regained their brightness.

He nodded. "Break it down. I don't care how you do it, just get us in there before he tears the whole place apart."

A junior officer, wide-eyed with fear, stopped the security chief. "What's going on? There's disturbances reported all over the ship – it's like people are rioting all of a sudden."

He looked the man in the face, wanting to find an explanation that would reassure the young man, and soothe the fears. But in truth, there was no explanation.

"I wish I knew."

He signalled an engineer to cut the lock. Grim faced, all he could do was listen as the screams within the room reached a crescendo, turning into a chilling sound of pain. Sweat beaded on his face – this wasn't what he signed up for. Plain old Bob Smith hadn't wanted to be dealing with trouble. That was why he had signed up on the shipping lines. Nice and easy – tourists who had paid the equivalent of twice most people's average salaries to be on a cruise to the stars never were any trouble. They had paid far too much money to act like hooligans and get locked up on ice in the cells for the rest of the trip.

Until now.

The beam from the engineer's laser cutter lanced out, and Bob found himself having to shield his eyes from the glare. Damn that passenger! How the hell had he jammed the door, and why had he gone berserk? He wasn't the only one – they had three other reports coming in from across the ship. It was like madness had become a disease, and was spreading.

The smell of burning metal filled the air. It was a harsh, acrid smell that did not belong on the plush decks of a Starliner.

"This is weird."

He was pulled from his thoughts by the voice of the engineer. The cutting laser never stopped.

"What?"

"The lock's fused. Good and proper. Looks like someone took up welding, and decided to get in some practice right here on the inside of the room."

Bob's brow furrowed. "That's impossible!" he blurted. "Are you sure?"

"Sure as day," the man replied calmly over the roar of the flame, "I'd know that anywhere I saw it. I know it makes no sense, but I'm just saying what I'm seeing."

Bob tried to look, but the glare from the laser was much too bright. He had to take the engineer's word.

Another crash came from beyond the door. It sounded like something heavy was being thrown about. He racked his memory to remember what there was in these suites. Plenty of furniture, but most was too big and too heavy for one man to drag around, let alone swing about and send it crashing.

"Nearly through," announced the engineer.

The flame died, and the engineer inserted a pry-bar into the glowing gash in the door. With a flick he levered away at the hot metal. Another security man leant his weight against the door, and it visibly moved, though still would not quite yield.

"Get some weight onto it," Bob yelled, pulling out his stun stick as he spoke, ready for the charge into the room.

The door buckled and gave a little. At once the screams from inside went up an octave. They didn't sound human any longer. A blinding flash came from behind the door, silhouetting the edges as if a bolt of thunder had struck behind. The men recoiled in horror and Bob did too.

"What the hell was that?" shouted the engineer over the noise, but his voice was almost lost to the piercing shriek and the moan of displaced air.

The door buckled outwards in front of them, like it had been made of nothing more than tinfoil. The lights in the corridor flickered and buzzed and static discharge filled the air with a hazy blue light.

Then, as suddenly as it had started, the sounds were gone, and Bob found himself looking out from where he had been cowering as a gentle mist of steam rose from the deck and walls that were warm to the touch. He edged towards the door, his heart in his mouth; what they had seen had not been anything one berserk man could do. One by one the others edged forward too, the same unspoken thoughts etched to their expressions.

"Let's get that door down," Bob whispered. He was taken aback to find how loud his voice sounded after the barrage of noise that had been so deafening.

The door was hot to the touch. There was a smell of blistering paint, and he had to use the base of his stun stick to push back on the metal. Weakened by the torment, the door slid open, bent almost double by the forces that had hit it from the room.

Inside was a scene of total destruction. Where there once had been the finest of décor and furniture, now there was only scorched ruins. Char marks ran over every surface, and a pall of smoke still hung in the air. The lights had failed so Bob flicked on his own torch. Several of the other men did the same, and torch beams stabbed out across the room.

"This isn't normal," one of the men whispered.

"Just look around, see what you can find," ordered Bob.

The men nodded, reluctantly stepping over débris to head deeper into what had once been a suite of the plushest rooms on the Starliner.

Bob shone his torch over the walls. Paint had blistered and peeled in the heat and remnants of decorations hung as tattered and burnt shards. At the edge of the beam, markings zigzagged crazily over the wall, gouged deep into the metal and singed black. Some of the gashes still smoked gently.

He signalled over the engineer. "What do you make of this?"

The engineer played his beam over the markings, following them across the walls and up over the ceiling.

"It's like nothing I've ever seen."

"Do you think one man in a rage could do all this?"

The engineer thought a moment. "Not likely. This is something else."

"Chief!" The hissed voice from the next room made them both turn. Bob hurried through the charred doorway. In the next room, the destruction was as complete in the first. Two of the security men stood, their torch beams pointing across through the light smoke to the corner, where a human shape huddled.

Bob stepped closer, keeping his stun stick at the ready.

"Sir?" he called out. The huddled shape didn't respond.

He cleared his throat and tried again, a little louder. "Sir? Can you hear me?"

It was never clear what happened next. In the blink of an eye the figure appeared to stand up. But the way it did it was unnatural, and almost indescribable. The figure folded in on itself, and with a high pitched shriek, the matter seemed to dissolve into a ghostly cloud of nothing more than crackling static. The cloud rose towards the ceiling, swirling and pulsating. Bob wanted to run, and maybe so did his men. But they were rooted to the spot with fear.

The cloud of energy grew, until it hit the ceiling and mushroomed out. For a moment it seemed that there was a face in the cloud – one minute it was not there, the next it was. Afterwards, no-one could remember exactly how it had appeared, but it had.

With a blood curdling scream, the *thing* moved as if it might attack, then in a swirl and a crackle of static, the energy cloud seemed to fold back in on itself. It found an electrical socket and like water, just poured itself in. There was a hiss and then the noise was no more, and the *thing* was gone.

Torch beams stabbed over the corner where it had been.

"Did you see that?" stammered the engineer.

"I think we all did," replied Bob slowly, stepping cautiously to the corner of the room.

There was a smell of ozone lingering in the air. Noticing the walls were streaked in something wet, he dabbed a finger in the ooze and sniffed it before recoiling in realisation at what it was.

"Blood."

"There's more over here, chief."

He looked to where another of the men had pointed their torch. Slowly it dawned on him that blood streaked the floor, walls and ceiling. Moreover, here and there, were the undeniable remnants of torn and shattered human flesh.

Bob reached for his radio, and with a trembling hand took several attempts before he could key in the right code.

"Security here. We've attended the disturbance on the honeymoon deck." His voice faltered. "I think we've got one hell of a problem."

The radio buzzed before a matter-of-fact voice came across. "What the hell are you talking about?"

"I think," said Bob, choosing his words carefully, "We have some kind of ghost aboard. And it is not the kind that stops at just rearranging the furniture."

"What? What happened? Are you winding us up?" demanded the voice, its tone more angry now.

"I'm telling you, we've seen something up here that none of us ever want to see again."

The junior officer came up to him; more wide-eyed and white faced than ever before. The man looked him in the eye.

"Tell me that didn't happen, chief. Tell me that none of this happened."

"I wish I could."

He looked around the wrecked rooms. "Get this place sealed off. I want no-one coming in or out." He looked back to the power socket that the *thing* had seemed to pour itself into. "Hey, engineer?" he called out.

The man hurried back over. "Yes?"

"Where does that go?" He pointed to the socket.

The engineer thought for a moment. "Into the ship's power grid."

*   *   *   *   *

David stared long and hard at the video image of the stranded lifepod. If it had been up to him, he would have left it where it was and head back into the Rösenbridge letting it take its chances. It had claimed one life already – the chief. Why risk more men on something that was clearly dead? If it broke free in the Rösenbridge, who was going to shed a tear over a useless piece of space garbage?

But it was not to be that simple, and he knew it. On the video screen there was nothing to see but the dirty grey pod. But the engineers had broken the news of a somewhat different story. On collision with the antenna aerials, the pod had chewed up more than at first glance. They had told him, with some degree of earnest, that with the pod where it was, the aerials were useless, and the Starliner was all but cut off from the outside world. Grounding across several banks of cables, it had rendered every interstellar communication channel silent and useless.

In short, the engineer had explained, it had to be moved. Just cut it free and shove it off into space with a jet pack had been his suggestion, but of course some damn fool had vetoed that right away. Despite there being no chance of survivors, some prissy little officer had decided that they had to follow procedure to the letter and retrieve the lifepod's black box. Up against academy pen pushers like that, it seemed there was little use in arguing about further jeopardy to the men. That, of course, meant another space walk with a crew that was not used to such work.

The chief's body had been removed by the medical orderlies, leaving a skeleton crew from engineering at the airlock to decide what the next move was going to be. Without the chief, it fell to David to call the shots. It was time to be strong – the men looked up to someone that could rise out of chaos and try and bring some order.

Well, David was not about to take any more risks than he absolutely had to even if the prissy officer was going to have it their way. Taking the boy Tom to one side, he looked the kid in the eye.

"You did good today, kid. Think you can manage another space walk?"

Tom smiled back, his face a lop-sided grin. Only the young could ever look danger in the face, and come up hungry for seconds.

"Sure, boss."

The kid was still in his suit, smeared in the dust from the pod. He dashed to the airlock, ready to go, but David held him back.

"Not so fast, kid. I'm coming with you this time."

He watched the kid from the corner of his eye as he pulled a suit from the rack and went through the suiting up procedures. Tom seemed impatient to go, but he waited until David stood beside him checking the connections for his helmet. Catching site of the reflection of himself in the visor of Tom's helmet, he saw that his suit was brilliant white by comparison. Well, a space walk with all that dirt encrusted on the pod would quickly change that.

The airlock cycled to green. He checked the radio channel, and heard the welcome buzz and replies back that told him that both Tom and the rest of the team on the Starliner could hear him. Then with deliberate care, he swung himself out onto the ladder, clipped on his safety line and gestured for Tom to do the same.

It took a while to reach the base of the antenna. Twice Tom seemed eager to rush ahead, but each time David held him back and calmly told him over the radio that they had to take their time. Rushing, he pointed out, was how men got themselves hurt in space. Reluctantly Tom seemed to take heed, but he could tell the kid was eager to get back into the pod and get the job done.

It amazed him that the kid could still be that enthusiastic after finding the chief's body. Still, he was still young and life had yet to beat the optimism out of him. He would learn the hard way in time.

Getting across the bent ladder section was easy with two of them. David went first, then told Tom to just haul himself across using the safety line as a guide. Once he had arrived by his side, David started to survey the scene.

The chief's safety cable hung limp in the vacuum, freed by Tom before when he had brought the body back. Coiling it in, he tucked it around the aerial cables and pulled it taunt with a simple knot.

"We don't want to find our own lines tangled in that on the way back," he told the kid.

Then, when he was satisfied, he followed the marks in the dust of the pod's hull with Tom close behind.

"Just over the other side," said Tom breathlessly.

David leant back to take a look, and saw the outline of the hatch, still open to space.

"I see it kid."

They pulled themselves around the pod's hull, helping each other over the gritty metal. Just as he had expected, David's suit went from a pristine white to a grubby grey.

"This dust is awful," he groaned as another cloud kicked up from under his gloves.

"It's worse inside," hissed Tom's voice over the radio.

"We'll have to manage when we get in," he replied with a grim tone. Secretly he cursed the officer who had ordered them out here. How easy to sit in an office and make decisions at will without ever actually going and having to do the hard work. It would have been a different story if the officer had had to come out here, he wagered.

The hatch was almost fully open when they reached its edge. David fumbled with the controls for his suit, and the helmet light stabbed out revealing the pall of dust hanging inside.

"I'll go in first," he said, and lowered himself head first into the gloom.

The beam picked out snatches of dull panels amongst a sea of floating fine dust. Eventually after a little scrabbling he reached the inner door and ran his glove around its edge.

"Strange," he murmured.

A second beam of light stabbed through the dust behind him indicating Tom was making his way in.

"What is it, boss?"

"Looks like this hatch has been opened recently. How far in did you go?"

"Just the airlock like we are now, boss. This is where the chief got to. I just pulled him out and came on back."

David leant in closer until his helmet visor was almost resting on the metal. Most of the inner hatch was coated with the fine dust that flaked away under his glove. But around the edges, a pattern in the deposits showed that it must have been opened then closed again. Maybe that accounted for the amount of dust that had been kicked up in the airlock chamber?

"We have to go in, kid. The power's long dead, so it's a case of cracking it open on manual."

"What about the pressure?" asked Tom.

He wrapped his knuckles against the hatch. Of course, floating in the vacuum there was no sound except the vibration back through his suit. He rested his helmet against the metal and tapped again. He heard the rap, but to his surprise, there was no echo that might have signalled pressure on the other side.

"Hey, didn't the chief say this thing was still airtight?"

The radio buzzed, and the voice of the team leader aboard the Starliner came back on the line.

"Yeah, that's right. Still airtight – I remember him saying."

David weighed up the evidence for a moment. "Well, she isn't now."

"Could the pressure have blown when the outer hatch was opened?" asked Tom.

He shrugged inside his suit. "Maybe. But the inner door is sealed. Looks like it has been opened recently. Maybe the chief did make it in, and the pressure blow slammed it shut? I don't know."

"Do we open it?" asked Tom.

David felt for around the hatch until he found the manual release lever. "The officers at the top want the black box, so that's where we're going."

The lever was stiff. Probably seized with a combination of dust and any lubricant that it had once had vaporising into the vacuum. He got both hands around it and braced himself against the panelling.

"Stand back, kid," he warned, then pulled as hard as he could.

The lever moved, slowly, and he felt the jarring vibration come through his hands and his feet into the suit. Testing the inner hatch, he felt it move under his touch. His hunch had been right – there was zero air pressure left in the pod.

"We're in," he said, turning to Tom, then flashed his helmet light into the widening gap.

Inside was blacker than obsidian, but the helmet line shone through showing there was almost no dust inside. Propelling himself inside, he turned and waved Tom through too.

"This place gives me the creeps," whispered Tom.

"Me too," he admitted. "Look around and see what you can find. The sooner we get what they want then the sooner we can get out of this tomb."

It was difficult to see much of the lifepod's interior in the torch lights. Here and there he saw seats and straps, but they were empty and unoccupied. He breathed a sigh of relief. It had not been something he had wanted to say in front of the boy, in case it made him freak out, but a part of him had been worried that the pod would have been full – a real tomb of escapees.

"Looks like its empty," came Tom's voice.

David didn't answer – his helmet light had picked up strange marks on the inside of the pod's hull. He rubbed his gloved hand across them, and felt the texture. Several lines of parallel scrape marks ran around the inside of the hatch that they had entered through.

"What have you got boss?"

Tom's light played over the marks, and in the light of two beams David saw that the marks went all over the inside of the pod.

"Scrapes."

Tom rubbed one with his glove too. "Looks like…. Nah – too stupid."

"What?" demanded David.

Tom feigned a laugh. "No boss. Just some crazy idea. Forget it."

"Spit it out," he insisted.

"Well," the boy began hesitantly; "I was going to say that they look like claw marks. But that's just weird."

David looked closely at the marks. Yes – Tom was right; they really did look like claws might have made them. But gouged into pressure-sealed metal? That was the part he struggled to find an explanation for. And what kind of animal must it have been to do that?

"If there was an animal in here that did that, it'll be long dead," he reassured, "But we ought to look."

Tom's helmet nodded in agreement.

He headed to the front of the pod. Somewhere at this end would be the controls, and that should yield the black box whilst the boy checked the back of the pod for signs of what had made those marks. He was not sure that he actually wanted to know. The only consolation would be that in an airless and powerless lifepod, it would be long past being able to add a few extra claw marks to these two new visitors.

He found the controls for the pod, along with two chairs fitted out with safety restraints. The restraints were shredded, and he held up a length of the strap to the light. The material was strong in itself, but had physically been torn rather than deteriorated with age. He shone the torch over the chairs' padding and saw that that too had been gouged. The marks were old and dulled by a thin layer of dust and oxidation – whatever had done it had done so long ago.

Looking over the panel he flicked a few switches, but just as he had expected the power was completely dead. In front of the control panels, set into the curve of the pod's hull, two Plexiglas screens should have looked out into space. But fine scratches misted the inner surface. On the outside the same dust from space that covered the rest of the hull had coated the screens making them completely opaque.

Putting the scratches and the damage out of his mind, he felt around in the central console beneath the panel. Lifepod design wouldn't have changed much over the decades – just a few extra gimmicks, but the fundamentals ought to stay the same. He was rewarded as his fingers found a panel clip and opened a drawer that revealed a large orange box. There was a name stencilled to it, but he couldn't quite read it. Taking hold of the handle on its end, he pulled, but it wouldn't budge. Something had it jammed from behind.

"Hey boss, over here!"

Tom's eager voice over the radio made his heart jump – he hadn't been ready for that.

"Take it easy, kid."

"I got an occupant."

It took a moment for Tom's words to register. The black box was forgotten, for now, as he made his way back through the pod to where Tom's light illuminated a compartment in the pod's rear.

As soon as he saw the body lying there, he felt his hackles go up. Tom hadn't realised the significance of the grubby suit coated in a soft sheen of grey around the gloves and boots, but he did. There was no mistaking the design of suits used on the *Persia*.

He pushed Tom aside and struggled to free the body. Somehow it had got wedged under a partition face down.

"What's up?" came Tom's worried voice.

"Help me roll it over."

It took both of them a few minutes to get the body free and finally roll the helmet up into view. It took a few moments for the truth to register through the shock. Then Tom spoke, slowly and uncertain.

"But how can he be here if I brought him back inside?"

David stared at the face of John – the chief to his men. The face was waxen in death, but there was still no mistaking him.

"Something's wrong here. Something's very wrong," he muttered. "What the hell is going on?"

"We've just seen them take the chief's body down to the morgue."

"Well, here he is. There can't be two of him."

He tapped the controls on his wrist to open a channel to the team at the airlock. Static buzzed in his ear and he winced.

"Come in? Come in?"

Still nothing but static. He looked at Tom and signalled for him to try his radio. Once again there was nothing but a buzz of static.

"Shit, must by the hull of this heap of junk screening the signal. We need to get back outside." He moved back towards the airlock.

Tom hung back. "What about the body? And the black box?"

He hesitated a moment. "Bring the body. someone else who gives a shit about it can come for the box."

He helped the boy drag the body to the airlock and out into the dust. Outside with better light he took another look at the chief's face through the helmet visor – there was no mistaking a face he had worked with for more than four years. Tom made another call on his radio, but static buzzed in their ears again.

"What are they doing in there," he grumbled.

Between them they took the body and worked it back along the outside of the pod. Once they got to the aerial,

108

David unhooked the chief's safety cable and hooked it to the dead man's suit.

"Less chance of having him drift off."

Hauling the cable after them, he tried not to pay attention to the lifeless body, and the way it floated with limbs drifting up and down and the head nodding from side to side.

The outer airlock was still open, and the pair slipped inside dragging the body with them. As soon as it hit the gravity field it fell like a stone to the deck and lay there. As soon as Tom was in too, he opened the panel and keyed in for the hatch to shut and the airlock to cycle.

Nothing happened. He tried again but the hatch still refused to shut. Crossing the airlock he pressed his helmet visor to the armoured glass and tried to peer inside and get the attention of the crew. It was difficult to see much. Banging his fists on the door, he expected to feel the reply from the crew banged back in Morse code. Maybe there was a fault in the electronics? But no reply came. He turned to Tom, glad that the fresh-faced boy could not see the worried look that he almost certainly had on his face.

"Something is very wrong," were the only words he could find.

Tom looked down at the lifeless body. "How long before we end up like him?"

The calm in the boy's voice surprised him. But the words sent an icy shiver across his skin. Running on the suit's air packs, they had only a finite amount of time if they could not get access to the Starliner. He checked the wrist panel on his suit. There was time, but it would not last long.

"If no-one is answering, we ought to find another way in," Tom suggested.

David nodded; quietly pleased to find the boy was surprisingly good under pressure. Maybe he had underestimated him before now.

They left the body in the airlock – there was no sense in trying to take it with them. It would be safe for now, held in the gravity field. Climbing down the access ladder, David led them towards the upper promenade decks. Here, even if they could not find another working airlock, they would be able to attract the attention of people inside.

At the bottom of the ladder the superstructure of the Starliner opened out, and he tested the plating with his feet. There was a tiny amount of gravity here – just a leftover of the edge of the Starliner's internal generated field – but it would be enough to make walking easier. He had not looked forward to the idea that they might have had to float along at risk of losing a grip and disappearing into space.

Neither said a word as they struggled along. The gravity made it possible to walk, but not easy. The suits were cumbersome and it was hard to get enough purchase on the smooth metal of the plating to propel along.

More than once David looked over the edge of the narrow ledge that they were following. There were no safety rails out here and it was disconcerting to look out over an abyss that led to a vertical 'drop' – up and down were relative terms – that ended as a continuation of the stars. He knew there was little risk other than disorientation, but habit still kept him tight against the inner edge of the ledge. Behind him Tom did the same.

After twenty metres, the ledge opened out and was taken up by the curving dome of Plexiglas. There was a walkway along the front, made of Plexiglas too so as not to disturb the view for passengers inside on the promenade.

"Hold here," he ordered, waving the boy to a stop. He wasn't sure just how strong the Plexiglas walkway really was. The gravity was stronger here – he could feel the pull that made his legs feel surprisingly heavy and weary. It was strange how quickly the body adjusted to consider near weightlessness normal. He gave himself a moment to rest and to let his body get used to having more weight again.

Looking down he could see the promenade deck through the Plexiglas. In the centre of his view, the clear material reflected back a ghostly image of himself, distorted to twice his normal height by the curve like he was looking into a fairground mirror. Strangely the promenade was empty and the lights were intermittent with most of the fittings dark.

He frowned – that wasn't right. There should be lots of passengers here, taking the view. The whole promenade had a foreboding look to it. As far as he could see to where the curved Plexiglas faded into the distance, there was nobody there.

"Nobody home," he growled. He had been banking on there being passengers to see them.

The plating beneath their feet vibrated and a groan rumbled through their suits.

"What was that?" squealed Tom.

David looked to the boy. Through his helmet visor he saw the kid's face ashen and fearful. He wanted to be able to give him an answer and to reassure him. Kids like that always looked up on the more senior crew – he too had once been there. At sixteen years old, everyone thought the senior staff knew what they were doing. He did not want to have to break the kid's illusion and admit that he knew just as little, and to boot was just as scared too.

"We have to look for another way in ourselves," he said, glossing over the question.

"We could try the keel," Tom suggested, "If we can get down there, I know there are emergency hatches dotted all along the bilge plates."

David nodded in approval. The kid was right – and every single one of those hatches had to be manually workable in case of the need to evacuate the machinery spaces after an accident. That was enshrined in interstellar law, and he knew the company took that almost as seriously as they took profits.

"How much air have you got?" he asked, glancing at his own gauges.

"Less than a fifth," was the reply.

He grunted, tapping his own gauge. It showed just under a fifth. Given the boy had already been out on a space walk once in his suit, he must be going through the air faster. He cursed himself for being out of shape. They would have to take it easy on the climb.

They back tracked to the long ladder again and clipped on their safety cables to overcome the sudden lack in gravity. He led the way, and showed Tom how to descend quickly by keeping his legs clear and pushing down arm over arm. It made his shoulders ache like someone was pulling them out of their sockets, but it was certainly easier than trying to use every single rung.

*   *   *   *   *

The emergency hatchways weren't ever intended for comfort, and certainly not for more than one person. Squeezing inside, David tried to ignore the warning blip on his suit's control pad indicating that the air was almost out. He tried not to think about the stark truth that if there was a problem with the airlock cycle, then there was no more time to find another.

Pulling the boy, they cleared the outer door and rolled it back into its runners. Checking over the control panel in the weakening light from his helmet light – the power pack was failing – he found the controls and prayed that they would work. Flicking the control lever to the manual override position he was rewarded with the flicker of lights across the tiny panel, and he breathed a sigh of relief; it was going to work. The suit's air warning squealed in his ears – it had come not before time.

The sound of pumps working filled the tiny chamber. At last he was able to reach up and flip open the helmet's visor. The air smelt metallic and cold, but it was better than being left with the exhausted remains of his suit's own supply.

Tom did the same. His suit's supply had lasted better, but was not far behind. Already the lights on the wrist control panel were blinking.

"That was close," David panted.

Reaching around he unlocked the inner door and waited as the pressures equalised with a hiss of air. Kicking the door fully open, he wriggled out of the tiny chamber and rolled onto the grilled catwalk beyond.

It took a moment to get orientated after the long time on the space walk. Unclipping the cumbersome helmet he lifted it from the suit and placed it beside him. There was a harsh smell of ozone in the air. Sniffing his glove gingerly he realised it was the dust from the lifepod reacting on contact with the Starliner's atmosphere. Unclipping the wrist ring he removed the gloves and massaged his face with a sweaty hand. It felt good to be free of the constraints of the suit.

Tom followed his lead, ditching his gloves and helmet. "What now?" he asked at last.

"Find out what's going on. We found John's body still in the pod, so I'd say the first thing is to find who the heck you brought in."

He saw Tom shudder at the mental image of the chief's broken body.

"But I saw his face," he said, "When they took his helmet off, it was definitely him."

"If it was, who was in the lifepod?"

Tom had no answer.

Ditching the last of the dirty space suits behind them, they stretched weary muscles and took their bearings.

10

Philipa watched from a distance as the body of the chief was mounted on a stretcher and taken by the medical staff. Ventura had watched too, with a grim expression on his face; she could not work him out. From the day he had learnt that Dezza had been aboard, he had taken an instant dislike to him.

She watched him share only a few solemn words with the other crew. She wanted to try and find a way to get the captain to rethink packing Dezza off to the security cells. Hesitating with nerves, the moment never quite felt right to broach the subject. Finally he made to leave and she realised with a sinking heart that she had lost the chance. In one last-ditch effort, feeling that she owed Dezza at least one try, she hurried after him as he left for the lifts.

"Captain," she called, "Can I talk to you?"

"I'm not in the mood," he snapped sulkily, jabbing at the call buttons.

As the doors began to close, she had to follow if she was ever going to help Dezza. She slipped through the gap and tumbled into the car beside Ventura. He looked down disapprovingly.

"I told you that I'm not in the mood," he growled.

The lift car rocked as it began the descent. He sighed, and his expression softened.

"Okay. I'm sorry. You just caught me at a bad time. What do you want?"

Finally she spat it out. "It's about Mr. Booth."

She saw the way the look in his eyes changed at the mention of the name. It was like a storm cloud had rolled over him. His forehead bulged as he spat out his reply. "That man deserves all he gets. He is nothing but trouble."

"He had nothing to do with that man's death," she said, holding her ground.

"I don't care," raged Ventura, turning to stab at the lift's buttons as if that might somehow make the car arrive faster.

"Why don't you care? You might be the captain of this Starliner, but that does not give you the right to have people thrown in a cell on a whim. Are you running a ship or a police state?"

Once the words were out, she regretted having spoken them. At any moment she expected the captain to whirl about and have her sent to join Dezza for the rest of the journey.

For nearly a minute he did not speak, leaning against the lift control panel. Then he began to shake. She thought it was rage and flinched at the thought of what she might have brought upon herself. But slowly it dawned on her that he was actually crying.

With timid steps she edged to his side, debating whether she should comfort him, or press a button for a random floor to leave him in peace. Gingerly she put an arm on his shoulder.

"Captain?" she asked softly.

He turned, red-faced with tears running down his cheeks. "You want to know why that man is trouble?" he asked in a voice that betrayed none of the emotion she could see in his face. He reached inside his jacket and took out a photograph. Passing it across to her, he rubbed his cheeks clear with the back of a hand.

Philipa took it in nervous hands. It was warm to her touch and showed a family picture. One of the men she recognised as a younger version of Ventura. The two people behind were clearly his parents, and with them all was the smart dressed soldier in his parade best uniform. She didn't understand, and looked back to Ventura.

"That's my brother," he said in a calm voice. "Never the sharpest tool in the drawer, but all he wanted to be was in the military and go into space. The last time that dream came true for him, he had the misfortune to be on the trip with Mr Booth, going back to his fabled ghost ship. He never came back."

She handed the picture back, realising its significance. "You blame Mr Booth for the death of your brother?"

"Who wouldn't, under the circumstances. I find it odd that almost everyone who accompanied him on two trips is now dead. They said after the first time he came back that he had something to do with the death of one of his own crew."

"Media hype," she blurted.

Ventura shrugged her words off. "There is no smoke without fire and I don't care. That man is trouble, and you would be better off not getting yourself attached with him."

She rose up indignantly at the suggestion. But the lift car rocked to a halt before she could say anything, and the captain stepped out and was gone before there was anything she could do. There would be no use in following – the captain had made up his mind and given his personal connection. As the lift doors slid back shut she jabbed at the buttons for another floor and considered the fact that she would have been better off never meeting Dezza at all.

There never was the time to reflect on it. The lift car dropped a few feet before the lights flickered. She looked up at the dying panels. Carefully she pressed the button again. There was no response. Looking down at it she saw all the lights on it were now off. Pressing the emergency button yielded no response.

"Hey! Can anyone hear me?" she called out.

A faint sound echoed from above the car. It sounded like it could be a voice, so she shouted again. Her words were cut off by a metallic groan from above and the car dropped suddenly then stopped, knocking her to the floor.

"This is not good," she whispered under her breath. The car moved underneath as she slowly eased herself up.

"Hey! Anyone up there?"

116

A groan of cable under extreme tension came as the only reply.

"Shit!"

She tried to reassure herself, that there were plenty of safety devices that would stop the car from being able to free fall even if the cables broke, but the reassurances rang false against her own fears. Glancing up at the ceiling, it was not worth the chance of waiting around to find out whether all that safety stuff really would work if put to the test.

There was a hatch in the roof and she stretched out trying to reach it. She was tall, but it was still out of reach. A handrail ran around the inside of the car and bracing herself against the corner she eased herself up on it. Her skirt was too tight to give her full freedom of movement, so she rolled it up.

"You hussy," she muttered to keep her spirits up, "Showing off your stocking tops. Good job no-one's around to see."

The car rocked again and she froze to the corner, heart racing. Gradually the rocking slowed and stopped, but an ominous creaking came from above and didn't stop.

"Philipa, dear," she whispered, "Haul some arse and get yourself the heck out of here."

The handrail let her get just high enough to touch the handle of the hatch before she nearly slipped. Steadying herself she stretched out and tried again. This time she found her mark, and with a tight grip on the handle eased herself up onto the handrail.

The car rocked again, but she ignored it – too close to be cautious now. The hatch was stubborn at first, refusing to move. She heaved as much as she dared against it, and was rewarded to feel it lift up beneath her fingertips. A shower of dust fluttered from above and she shut her eyes, waiting for it to stop.

The creaking was louder now, echoing through the open hatch. Pushing it up as far as it would go, she lost touch with it and felt her heart jump as the metal banged down unseen above the car. Grasping the sides, she said a silent prayer and let her feet slip from the handrail as she hauled herself up. Buttons popped on her jacket, though it did not concern her. After a few seconds of swinging half in, half out of the hatch, she rolled herself out onto the top of the car.

It was dark in the lift shaft. The light that shone through the open hatch picked out the metal runners that surrounded the car. There was a cable in the centre, attached through a complex locking mechanism; it gave off a steady hum and vibrated like it was being plucked somewhere far above.

She called out again, hoping that someone might here her better now she was out of the car. Above the hum of the cable she thought she heard something, but it was hard to be certain that it was not just an echo of her own cries.

The car dropped without warning, and for a brief moment it felt as if her stomach was in her throat. The cable juddered and a rending sound shrieked from above. Flung to the floor, it took her a moment to orientate herself again. There was no telling how many more times it would do that before it gave altogether.

There was a box structure above the car and it left a gap between steel girders around six feet tall. It had been twisted in the fall, and looking closer she saw that it was holding most of the strain of the lift's weight on metal brakes. Two of them were bent and no longer holding whilst the remaining two were ticking under the strain of the load.

Frantically she crawled her way under the box structure, trying to put out of her mind the fact that if the car dropped again that she could be sliced in half by the beams. She felt the metal move as she crawled; it made her wriggle faster. Getting clear, she grabbed hold of the support structure within the lift shaft. Levering her legs clear, she breathed a sigh of relief.

There was no warning as the brakes parted company. Two cracks like gunfire echoed in the shaft, then with a roar the lift that she had just escaped from disappeared from view down the shaft, though she could hear its noise fading for some time as it fell.

"Give me your hand!"

The voice startled her, and she nearly lost her grip on the steel.

"I'm here to help!"

She saw a figure moving in the darkness, reaching out to her from a maintenance walkway that ran tight against the shaft's side beyond the steel beams. She recognised the voice.

"Captain Ventura?"

"Yes. No time for chat, the counterweights are on their way up and you are on their tracks. If you don't take my hand and let me help you, they'll slice you in two."

Above the sound of his voice she realised she could hear the steady rumble of something coming closer up the shaft. The metal beneath her body began to vibrate and hum, and her heart leapt.

Reaching out she felt his fingers and grasped hold.

"Now your other hand!" he shouted.

She realised her grasp was so tight on the steel that her knuckles were white.

"I'm scared," she called out.

"You can do it," he reassured, grasping her hand tightly, "Jump!"

Scrunching her eyes shut, she let go of the beam and swung towards him. She felt his other hand grab tight, then her feet slipped from the beam as he pulled. The roaring became overwhelming and she felt the air move around her, then it began to fade and she opened her eyes to find herself tangled in Ventura's arms on the grubby metal grill of the walkway.

"I heard you calling," he said, no longer having to shout as the rumble died into the distance.

"The power failed and the car began to drop," she said, her voice breathless and her heart still racing.

"It did in the corridor too."

A roll of thunder echoed up through the lift shaft as the car reached the bottom. Right now, Philipa reflected, she could have still been in that.

"Is there a way out of here?" she asked.

He pointed to a red metal ladder that led up from the end of the walkway. "I'm afraid you'll have to climb."

She glanced back over the edge. "It can't be worse than anything else I've had to do so far today."

*   *   *   *   *

The corridor was filled with a layer of dust that had settled gently over every inch of the walls, floor and furnishings. Everywhere she placed her hand or a foot it left prints to show where she had been. Most of the lights in the corridor were not working, and only an intermittent few around the lift area were still on.

"This is new," he said slowly.

"Where has it come from?"

"I don't know."

A bass rumble reverberated through the floor and walls, and the dust upon the floor shimmered and danced, erasing their footsteps almost immediately. From the walls and furnishings fell a gentle rain of the particles.

"What," she whispered, "was that?"

The rumble intensified and a mist of dust rose off the floor and began to ripple and move, drawn by the vibrations.

They started to step away from the direction it came from. The noise grew, and the dust began to move in a steady flow, engulfing them in a mist. Then the noise changed and became a banshee-like wail that sounded so close it sent shivers running down Philipa's spine. The remaining lights in the corridor began to flicker and promptly died, plunging them into darkness.

Stumbling blindly, she thrashed her arms out, searching for Ventura. Panicked, she did not want to be alone. She shouted, but even yelling at the top of her lungs she could hardly hear herself. Worse still, the dust made her gag every time she inhaled and she could feel her eyes streaming down her cheeks.

At last her fingers brushed against his and she grabbed his arm tightly. She heard his voice at her ear as he pulled her closer.

"Keep with me!"

Then he moved off, dragging her in the darkness behind him.

Somewhere behind them a bright glare lit the corridor like a photographic flash. Turning, she caught sight of a face in the receding glow seeming to edge along in her footsteps. The fear boiled over inside her and she screamed. The light faded, but the image of that *thing* still burned itself in her mind. Quickening her pace, she nearly tripped over Ventura's heels.

Another flash filled the corridor, though this time she did not dare to look. Scrunching her eyes tightly shut, she felt Ventura pull her to one side, then the sound of a doorway being slammed shut was followed by the wailing shriek sounding muted and further away.

"You can open your eyes now," Ventura panted breathlessly somewhere nearby.

Cautiously she looked. They were in a stairwell whose lights still shone brightly. Behind them was the door from the corridor, safely closed but with a pall of dust still drifting in front of it.

"I saw it!" she spluttered, "I saw the thing."

He pulled her close and comforted her.

"Hey, hey. Relax."

She looked him square in the eye. "Don't treat me as the 'little woman' who goes to pieces at a little stress," she scolded angrily, "I know what I saw. It was the creature Dezza told me about."

She saw him flinch at the mention of the name and remembered the photo.

"What killed your brother wasn't Dezza, but that *thing* that just chased us. It killed the engineer too, and it's going to kill others."

"I don't want to hear any more of these ghost stories," he stormed.

Exasperated, she threw her arms up in the air. "Get with the programme. Did you not see that back there?" she demanded.

"I don't know what I saw."

It was clear that he was determined not to let it seem that Dezza was right, but Philipa was too angry to care about the consequences.

"Dezza fought this thing before. He told me he only came on this cruise because he knew this was going to happen."

"How did he know," he snapped, "Did it ever occur to you to ask that?"

"A message he received from one of those who found the derelict with him."

"A message he received from a dead person?" the captain protested, incredulous, "Please. Just listen to yourself. Everyone from his first trip out to find this derelict is dead, and only one came back off his second trip."

"Fine," she snapped, arms folded, "Believe what you want, but I'm going to find Dezza and find a way out of this."

She turned her back on him and started down the stairs.

"You're making a big mistake," he called out angrily over the banister.

She didn't care what he thought anymore. She owed it to Dezza to believe him and help him now his warnings were slowly turning out to be true.

*   *   *   *   *

The medical staff did not stay long; they never did. One dead body, nothing more they could do, so they left it on the table like no more than a hunk of meat, cracked their jokes, and left.

It did not bother Zeb – he had not taken the job for the company. Every Starliner had a morgue, in case of heart attacks, accidents and natural causes. It was an easy enough job to get paid a salary for nothing more than babysitting the chill room and working his way through a shit-load of dime novels.

The deceased they had brought in was not anyone he had known. Long ago Zeb had figured that if you were going to work in the morgue, it was best not to get to know anyone too well in case they turned up dead. It was a pretty pessimistic approach to take, but he did not care. Just keep the dime novels coming along with the pay cheques.

He set to work sliding the body onto the main table. Most of the clothes had already been removed, leaving just undergarments. Zeb left these in place, as he meticulously recorded the details on his little palm pad for the computer records. Next he scanned for the bio tag – implanted in everybody to record such details as blood type, next of kin and a host of other bits and pieces of mindless information that would otherwise just clutter up wallets, according to the governments.

It made identifying bodies a whole lot easier too. Usually the tag was implanted in the left shoulder. Taking the scanner from his instrument trolley, he ran it over the body, ignoring the puffy bruising that looked purple and angry.

The scanner didn't blip and read off anything. He ran it over the area again, then tried the other shoulder in case this guy's surgeon had been bored the day the tag was planted.

Nothing registered to the scanner. He knew the thing was working; he had spent part of the previous day playing with it on himself. Just to make sure he ran it over his own left shoulder, and heard it ping as it retrieved his personal data. Nothing wrong with the equipment then, he thought, and ran it over the body.

He considered the possibility that the crush injuries in the body might have destroyed the tag, but he dismissed the idea, as the scanner should at least be able to tell the presence of the tag, even if there was an error in reading it.

"I'm going to give you a thorough scan, buddy," he said for the benefit of himself rather than the corpse.

Kicking off the brakes on the table's wheels, he pushed it across to the partition wall. There was a small alcove here and the table fitted neatly into it.

Pulling up a roller chair, he settled at the adjacent console and brought up the scanner readouts of the body in the alcove. Static rumbled on the screen, and he tapped the keys for a while, suspecting a system error. That was until the diagnostic programme returned no problems – the scanner was working fine.

Leaning around the edge of the partition, he glanced to the body. Definitely still there, lain out like a hunk of meat.

He keyed the commands again and watched as the system did its scan. Once again the static rumbled on the screen, preventing any meaningful images to be displayed.

"You are one tough cookie," he murmured.

"I know."

The voice at his ear made him fall from the chair in shock. Sprawling on the floor he looked wildly around the room. There, stood by the upturned chair, was the man who he swore had been dead.

"Is this some kind of joke?" he stammered, "Did the boys put you up to this."

"Goodbye."

He opened his mouth to speak. But before he could, the lights and electronics in the room flickered and died. All that Zeb could ever know was the brief moment of confusion before the blinding light; and then, nothing.

11

For most of the morning – or was it afternoon? It had been hard to judge the passage of time – Dezza had made do to count the cracks and scrapes in the paint of the cell. It was an oppressive environment, clearly largely unused in all the time that the Starliner had graced the stars. Every Starliner had to have one though, used as a drunk-tank for the occasional passenger who took the twenty-four hour, seven day a week drinking to an extreme; there would always be one or two. He glanced across to the chemical toilet, and considered that it at least had probably seen more than its fair share of heads down the pan.

There was no graffiti, even along the edges of the bed where any occupant might be expected to spend long times. In a surge of rebellion, Dezza thought about adding some, but they had taken from him any objects that could be considered remotely sharp – not that he had had much on him to take. That put paid to that idea, explaining at the same time why there was no graffiti. He tried his fingernails, but the paint was too hard. Giving up, he settled back to get as comfortable as he could on the bed.

It was not easy. The bed had been designed with strength and to have no removable parts that could be used as weapons, rather than for getting good rest. It was hard and not particularly yielding and whichever side he lay on he could feel the hard mattress quickly make his joints ache. Finally he settled to lying flat on his back. The pillow had a miserable thickness, but by folding it in half it made a reasonable enough rest for his head. Closing his eyes he lay listening to the buzz of air conditioning and finally drifted off to sleep.

*   *   *   *   *

He woke to the crackle of electrics shorting. At first he leant over, reaching for an imaginary alarm clock to snap off its alarm with a satisfying click. Only instead his arm brushed against the cool hard steel of a wall.

"What the?" he mumbled, rubbing the corners of his eyes.

He looked around, taking in the cold utilitarian starkness of the cell. Immediately the reason he was here came flooding back, and he sighed, settling onto the hard mattress.

"Oh."

Where was that sound coming from? Flicking off the wafer thin cover, he slipped from the bed and wriggled his feet into his deck shoes. At least they had not taken them away from him; he did not relish padding around in bare feet on the cold steel floor.

The lights in the cell were fine, but when he pressed his face to the grill in the door it was clear that the lights in the outside corridor were blinking on and off in rhythm to the shorting noises.

"Hey!"

There was no answer.

"Hey!" he called again, this time louder. Still no response.

He felt across the wall to the tiny call switch on the wall. The echo of the buzzer echoed back down the corridor. The seconds dragged by into minutes and still nobody came. So, the bastards were ignoring him. Maybe Ventura had ordered them to make his life unpleasant?

He shouted again until he was hoarse. Once or twice he thought he heard another noise, like the sound of heavy sacking being dragged across a floor. But each time the crackling obscured the noise and he was not entirely certain what he was hearing. Eventually he grew tired of standing at the grill and retired back to the bed, unable to think of anything else to do.

*   *   *   *   *

He woke with a start, confused by the passage of time. The lights in the cell were still on, but the flickering and crackling from the corridor outside had stopped. Slipping from the bed, Dezza pulled himself up to the grate trying to see as much as he could. Infuriatingly the grill obscured all but a small view of the immediate corridor.

He tried calling a few times, in case someone might hear him this time, but as before there was no answer. His stomach began to rumble, telling him that it had been a long while since he had had anything to eat.

"Hey! I'm getting hungry in here," he called angrily. Were they just going to let him starve?

He looked for his watch before he realised that they had taken it off him. There was no accurate way to know how much time had passed since they had brought him down to the cells.

Remembering the camera high in the corner of the cell, he stood on the bed and waved his arms wildly at it. Was the operator asleep on the job? Not for the first time the thought that the captain might have ordered them to undertake the bare minimum for Dezza. In the end he returned to the bed and sat down on the edge of the bed, dejected by the lack of response and he began to consider Philipa's warning that the captain had something against him.

It would be pretty unusual for a man of his standing to have such a grudge without ever meeting him. Sure, the media reports had not been favourable, but that did not explain the man's actions entirely. Racking his memory, he tried to think if at any time he might have run into him before, but he drew a blank. Normally he was pretty good at remembering faces; if still a little hazy on the names, but Ventura's face was not one he recognised from anything other than seeing him at a distance around the ship.

A sound from the corridor brought him from his thoughts and he listened intently, unsure of what he had heard or whether he had heard anything at all. Was his mind so desperate for human contact now that it would make up things to hear?

Standing up again, he tiptoed across to the door and listened at the grill. The corridor was pretty quiet now. Thinking back, he recalled that the security consoles had been right at the end of it. If there were anyone on duty, they would have to be sitting very quietly indeed to not be heard.

That sound came again. When he concentrated it sounded like people talking far away. A feeling of loneliness washed over him, and he found himself calling wildly.

The voices stopped, and for more than a minute he thought that his shouts had done nothing but perhaps alerted the guards that he could hear them. Maybe they really were running some kind of deprivation treatment?

The voices came again, closer this time, and there was no mistaking that this was not a trick by the guards. One of the voices he knew, and they were calling out his name.

"Philipa!" he called back.

He heard footsteps in the corridor that stopped with a sharp intake of breath. The grill frustrated any attempts to see.

"Philipa, what's up? What's going on?"

Philipa came into view, white faced and subdued.

Dezza was taken aback. She was filthy, and her uniform was covered in marks of grease and dirt. Her hair looked tousled, and there was a small cut on her left cheek that oozed blood.

"Am I glad to see you," she said; her face broke into a lop-sided smile.

"I was rather inclined to say the same to you. What's happened?"

She fumbled with a bunch of keys and began trying them in turn in the lock.

"Really, don't ask. All hell has broken loose. Your warning was right. I only wish you could have got more people to listen sooner."

He felt an icy shiver run the length of his body. "The message from Tubs? It was real?" he whispered.

She nodded. "Uh-huh. You can say that again."

He glanced to the wall, deep in thought as the keys continued to rattle one by one in the lock as she worked through the bunch.

A part of him had come to doubt the message. Hell, Toze had been adamant it was bullshit. In the time on the *Persia* a part of him had always warned that he was letting himself be led by memories of the past and what could be little more than a hoax. He had, after all, seen Tubs dead with his own eyes. Yet the message had spoken so convincingly about what could happen again. Maybe he believed it, because he knew from first hand just what the creature that had taken over the *Cerberus* was like.

But then, he had seen the *Cerberus* destroyed. How had the creature persisted at all? With a sinking feeling in the pit of his stomach, he realised that it meant that Tracker's sacrifice in the meteorite swarm had been for nothing.

The door swung open at last and Philipa burst in. "Are you going to stand there staring at the wall all day," she demanded, "We have to get out of here."

He blinked at the suddenness of her words, bringing him with a start from his thoughts. "Yeah. I guess."

Leaning forward she grabbed him. "Well come on then."

Out into the corridor, it was much as he remembered it except that there was a lingering smell of something in the air that he could not quite place. It had smelt of disinfectant and *clean* but now there was something else. He took a sniff. There was a trace of ozone, and a faintest of faint smells of burning hair.

"What the hell is that?" he asked.

Philipa tried to avoid his question, tugging his arm for him to follow, but he stuck his ground. "I want to know."

"The guards are dead," she blurted. "Electrocuted."

He remembered the electrical shorting noises and the flickering of the lights whilst he had been left alone in the cell. Now he realised that they had been more serious.

They came to the end of the security corridor. The smell was stronger here, and the security desk and console had been destroyed beyond all recognition. Twisted metal marked the spot, and even the flooring had buckled under an immense force that had been applied. Over the surfaces of what metal that was left ran black burn marks. There was no clue as to how exactly it could have happened, quite apart from how he had managed to not be woken by it when it happened.

On the floor to one side a man was crouching over two bodies, checking through the pockets of their uniforms before taking their jackets and draping them over the charred bodies. Dezza recognised him with a pang of fear.

"Captain."

The man seemed unimpressed to see Dezza, though he was not surprised.

130

"I guess I owe you at least a partial apology, Mr Booth," he began icily, "Your warning about this creature was correct."

Dezza was not sure what to make of it. He had apologised, though his body language said much more about open hostility. Dezza came on out and said what was on his mind.

"I can tell you do not like me captain. However, I believe it is at least only fair that you tell me why."

"Show him the photograph," said Philipa grimly.

Dezza glanced to her. "What photograph?"

Ventura reached inside his jacket. Producing a small picture he passed it across, and Dezza accepted it, staring at the picture closely. His shoulders sagged as he recognised two of the figures on it.

"It isn't how you think," he began, but the words just faded in the withering look from the captain. He passed the photograph back.

"Mr Booth. I lost a brother to your last trip out into deep space. Maybe only you and he will know what truly happened. However, just because I now find myself forced to work with you, does not mean I have to like you. As far as I am concerned, you took him into a hostile environment and left him to die. His death is still your fault."

"Boys, boys!" interrupted Philipa, pushing herself between them. "If any more testosterone leaks out of you two then I'm going to be in danger of understanding the off-side rule."

She looked to the dead bodies on the floor, covered by the jackets. A parboiled human hand peaked out from the edge of one of them in a stark reminder of the sight she had walked in on with Ventura. It was a sight that she most likely wanted to forget.

"We have to get out of here. I talked the captain into coming to get you, Dezza, because you have fought this thing before." She looked him firmly in the eye. "I want to get out of here alive, and it seems with a track record of two to nil, you are the best ticket we have to get out of here."

Her words were cut off short by a wailing scream and a groan that vibrated through the structure of the room around them.

Dezza looked in turn at Ventura and Philipa. "Um. You mentioned that I had a good track record on these things. What exactly is making you think that this is the same thing?"

The shrieking came again. This time louder and clearer. He saw the fear well up in Philipa's expression, and the normally cool and calm exterior that Ventura projected begin to waver.

"It chased us," said Ventura.

Dezza nodded and ushered them towards the door. "Then we need to get out of here, fast. It'll keep following you until it finds you."

They hurried into the outside corridor and began to run. "This way," panted Ventura, "We can lose it in the access levels."

Dezza was not so sure. Adrenaline surged through his body as he hurried down the corridor, and he could not help but feel a worry at the misplaced confidence that Philipa at least had placed in him. What if it was just pure fluke that he had survived before? On a balance of probabilities, here he was at a third encounter all out of luck.

Philipa stumbled, and he and Ventura stopped to help her up. Around them the lights began to flicker, and a light haze of dust shimmered above the floor.

"It's coming!" panted Philipa.

"Come on," urged Ventura, "We can't stop now."

"I can't run fast in this skirt!" she pleaded.

Ventura looked lost. "I'll carry you if I have to," he said, holding out his hand.

Dezza reached down and grasped hold of the hem of her skirt. "Hold still," he ordered.

"What are you doing?" she cried as he ripped the skirt. "Mr Booth!"

He stood up and rubbed the dust from his hands. "There. You can run now." He looked to Ventura before the man could protest. "We can't afford to be held back by anything."

Philipa waved a finger at Dezza. "Mr. Booth. At any other time I might slap you in the face, but I respect your judgement – for now. Just remember this: if you touch my clothes in that way without warning again, do not be surprised if you end up with my foot in your face."

They ran on, the dust around their feet growing thicker all the time. He remembered the *Cerberus* and the dust that had coated everything thickly there. They had wondered where it had come from, and there had been suspicions. It had always come with the creature, and even now it prompted a feeling of fear and dread within him. The *Cerberus* was gone, but the creature lived on.

The captain stopped at a doorway. It was marked with a panel that said it was for crew use only, and a palm scanner was set into the wall discretely beside it. Without stopping for breath Ventura pressed his hand to the panel and the door opened.

"It still works," he said hurriedly with relief, "Get in."

He ushered Philipa and Dezza through, then darted in himself.

Inside was an open area that led to a utilitarian switchback of stairs. The steps were of wire mesh, and looking through them Dezza realised with a start that there was very little between them and a drop a very long way down.

"Machinery ducts," Ventura explained, "They get used in port if any equipment needs craning in or out of the machine rooms and the air conditioning plants."

"Can we get anywhere in the ship through them?" Dezza asked.

"Sure. They go the full height of the Starliner, interspersed only by airtight seals in case of hull breach."

Dezza peered over the edge. A long line of yellow emergency lighting strips led away to what seemed like infinity. Looking up he saw that they must be immediately under one of the seals; the shaft was plugged with the outline of a massive hatch.

"Can we get through these seals?"

"Sure. There are personnel hatches at the side. As long as the security systems haven't locked everything down then we can get all the way to the bottom. We don't need to though, because all we have to do is get to the lifepods."

Ventura made towards the top of the stairs to climb down. Dezza saw Philipa begin to follow, but he hesitated.

"I thought a captain always stayed with his vessel? Aren't we going to destroy it?"

As soon as he said the words, he saw the same cloud of emotions descend across Ventura's face that he had seen before when the man had talked of his brother. Even before the captain said a word, Dezza knew it was going to be about Exbo's death.

"If you want to preach your brand of getting us all killed, then so be it. But you can go about it on your own. The communications are all dead – the lifepod that we hit coming out of the Rösenbridge put paid to that. The only way to stand a hope of sending out a distress and getting any survivors rescued is to use one of the transmitter beacons on the lifepods. Do not assume, Mr Booth, that I would just run away and leave the other survivors aboard this vessel to their fate."

"That thing hooked into the aerials was a lifepod?" Dezza interrupted, his hackles raised. He had known there was something about it the moment that he had clamped eyes on it. It had remained at the back of his mind until now.

The *Cerberus* had been shorn of her lifepods when he had first seen her. They had assumed the crew and passengers had tried to escape, but what if a part of the creature had escaped with one too?

"Yes," began Ventura slowly, not understanding.

The door behind them reverberated with an enormous crash that nearly sent all three leaping down the stairs. The creature had found them and was trying to break through. Around them all in unison the yellow emergency lights began to flicker.

"Run!" ordered Ventura.

Philipa followed him, with Dezza behind them both. He had seen the creature transmit itself through many things. All it took was one electrical conduit or even a radio signal left on, and it would find its way through.

The banging still echoed in the shaft, though the lights flickered less further down.

"Through here!" called the captain and pressed his palm against a reading plate by the door out to the next deck.

Only too late did Dezza realise. "No!" he screamed, but already the reader was scanning the captain's hand – and activating the same circuits that were connected to the one at the doorway the creature was trying to enter through. Immediately the banging from above stopped.

There was a crackle of light and Ventura fell to the ground in shock. Philipa reached forward to grab him, but hesitated when she saw the static humming in the air above the captain's body, stretching back in a ghostly white shadow towards the palm reader pad.

"What is that!" screamed Philipa, shielding her eyes from the glare.

Dezza could hardly hear her; the buzzing in the air was deafening. The white shape writhed and grew, as if it were trying to find form and search for the hand that had made it possible for it to enter the circuitry.

"It's the creature. It can travel between matter and energy when given the chance to. Ventura activated the scanner and gave it a portal to pour itself through. If we don't do something it will keep on coming."

Fumbling on the floor whilst shielding his own eyes from the intense glare, he felt Ventura's arm and grabbed hold to pull him free. Philipa helped and just in time they saw the ghostly static-fuelled limb stretching from the scanner gently caress the floor where the man had been, like it sensed that there had been fresh prey for it.

Dezza looked around frantically. The shaft was mostly bare except for the grilled walkways and stairs running along the edge. There were cables battened to the walls between the emergency lights and he grasped hold of the plastic conduit, testing its strength. It was not that firmly attached, and he was able to pull a section clear. Levering with his strength, he snagged enough of the covering so that it split, exposing the wires underneath.

"Stand back!" he ordered, and thrust the bared cable towards the base of the creature where it protruded from the scanner plate.

The bare wires touched, and a second flash bigger than the glow from the creature blinded him for a second. There was a wail and a scream, and a sound like wet leather. Then silence, and the shaft was quiet again as the echoes faded away.

The blue splotches in his vision faded and he saw that the creature had gone. The bared wires lay burning severed in the middle; the scanner plate had melted from the charge. One row of emergency lights stretching all the way down the shaft had gone out, but a second set still provided enough light to see in a muted yellow glow.

"You killed it?" asked Philipa quietly.

"No. Just wounded. It will be back, in time."

He knelt beside Ventura and felt for a pulse. He was relieved to feel the man move and groan beneath him – he was only shocked.

"Help me get him up," he said, hoisting Ventura's arm around his shoulder.

Philipa took the other side. Together they carefully helped him hobble back to the door.

The power jolt had fried the lock and fused the door shut. With a free hand Dezza tested it, but it was never going to open. They would have to keep heading down, and hope that there was another way out of the shaft.

12

The machinery spaces were eerie and echoed hollow to the sound of Tom and David's footsteps. Neither was certain whether there should have been people down here. But the passageways were well lit, consisting of piping runs in tunnels that stretched on into infinity. Occasional shafts led off vertically lined with bundles of cables thicker than a man's body and the most slender looking of ladders running alongside.

Up there, somewhere above them, were the main machinery decks and control rooms. There they hoped they could find people, and hopefully an explanation. David still fumed about the fact that they had been locked outside. Surely the rest of the team knew that their air was limited? He remembered the chief's body, the memory jarring a shiver that ran through him. He glanced to Tom. If he had not brought the body of the chief aboard, then whom had he brought? It certainly looked like the chief – David had had the best look of any as they had taken his helmet off and pronounced him dead.

The air here was hot and humid; it felt like a jungle amongst the pipes. Feeling the casing of some of the bundles carefully he was surprised to find that the metal was almost too hot to touch. At a vertical shaft, moisture dripped down the walls and dribbled through the grating of the walkway. A mist rose upwards from the heat and dampness.

"There must be something wrong in engineering," he said, "This isn't right."

"How do we get there?" Tom asked.

In all David's time aboard the *Persia* he had never been down to the lower levels. He wagered that normally only a small number of the maintenance crew ever came down here to the pipe runs that ran the length and breadth of the vessel.

"By my reckoning, most of this heat has to be coming from the main drive cores. If we follow the pipes, we ought to get to the radiator clusters that should be down here. From there it's an easy climb up to the drive cores. There should be people there at least."

It sounded so easy, but he knew that it was far from that. The boy took his word though – the naïveté of youth. How nice it would be to still be that easily reassured.

At the next junction in the pipe run they found a staircase that ran switchback up the shaft that opened out above. Here too steam and moisture were evident. What if something unforeseen had happened in the drive room? Maybe something very serious that might justify the airlocks becoming abandoned. What if an evacuation had been called? He shook the thoughts from his mind – no. With some effort he banished the train of thought from where it was leading him.

They took the staircase without sharing a word and climbed into the layer of mist. Soon it became difficult to breathe in the humid air. The air in his lungs burnt and stifled in the heat. Every breath was becoming an intense labour. Their climbing became slower until it felt to David like a mammoth trek up a huge mountain.

"How much further?" panted Tom breathlessly, the mere effort of forcing out a few words a great drain.

David had to stop before he could reply; it was too much for him to force his weary body to keep going and talk. "I don't know."

"Why is it so hot?"

"Cooling problems? I'm not sure – we'll find out soon," he reassured, but in truth he knew that he had as much knowledge of the lower depths of the ship as the boy did.

They climbed on again, listening to the twang of the stairs beneath their feet on every step. The rising steam drowned out any other noise so it appeared that they were in their own little cloud bubble insulated from the rest of the ship. When they could almost go no further, the stairs ended, and David saw the platform open out to the side of the shaft. There were banks of fans set behind grills in the ceiling, though none of them were turning. The steam drifted lazily through the platform level, and on into a larger room. The ceiling through here was higher, and there were banks of heat exchangers laid out across the floor. From where David and Tom stood, grilled walkways snaked out in a grid pattern around the exchangers, with humped bridges over piping and around large fans. The room was eerie in its quiet – nothing was running.

"Shouldn't they be spinning?" Tom wheezed.

"Yes. Something's wrong."

There were control panels set along the opposite wall, and David scrambled across the walkways to them. At the panels he inspected the controls, flicking switches with disgust. The panels were dead and the computer screens were blank.

"Offline," he said angrily, "There must be a power fault somewhere."

"Here?"

"No – upstairs in the drive room. That's where everything is routed from." He looked back over the silent plant room, "The heat suggests upstairs the core is working, but it won't be for long if there's no adequate cooling."

"What will happen then?"

David tried to find a way to keep the boy happy without telling him the naked truth. "It will eventually shut down," he said at last. The truth, he knew, was more likely to be far more severe. At the very least, radiation would spill out from the cores if they ruptured.

To one side of the dead panels there was a lift lobby with two freight lift cars. One of the cars was at this level with the doors half open, as if they had stopped in the middle of closing. David peeked inside, but the panels were dead. He squeezed through and felt the car rock on its runners. It was dark inside, but he managed to find the emergency locker and felt with his fingers until he found the standard issue torches that were in the emergency rack. He pulled out two and tossed one through the gap in the doors to Tom.

"Take this – we might find them useful."

Flicking his torch on he played it over the inside of the lift. To his surprise the interior was shredded and panels hung limp from the ceiling. When he shone the torch upwards he could see through the tattered structure to the darkness of the lift shaft above.

"What's happened in there?" asked Tom nervously as he peered through the gap in the doors.

"I don't know."

David felt the lift structure move slightly beneath him. Maybe now was not the best time to be stood in it. Whatever damage had been caused seemed to affect its structure. He turned to leave, but some marks caught in the edge of the torch's beam drew his attention.

"Just one moment," he called out, "There's something here I want to get a closer look at."

Leaning closer he saw that there were gouge marks in the panelling. Something on the outside had hit the lift repeatedly. Looking back across the rest of the inside, the patterns were repeated elsewhere. Running a finger across the metal, it was hard not to notice that they looked remarkably like claw marks. The marks that they had seen in the lifepod; they had been claw-like too. He shivered at the thought.

Something wet splashed on his cheek and he looked up. There was something leaking through the ceiling panels where they had bowed and distorted inwards. Another drip splashed down, narrowly missing him and landing on the floor. It had not been dripping when he had entered the lift. Testing the liquid on his cheek between finger and thumb, it felt warm. It was dark and a little viscous. The first thought was that it was hydraulic fluid from the lift, but it did not smell right. Testing it with the tip of his tongue he recoiled and spat several times to clear the taste.

"What's up?" asked Tom.

"It's blood," replied David calmly, looking back to the spreading patch on the ceiling, "There's something up there. I'm going to try and look."

Ignoring the rocking of the lift under his movements, he reached up and flipped open the access hatch in the ceiling. It too was bent and distorted, but with a little persuasion it lifted clear into the dark void of the shaft. He could feel the cooler air flowing down in a breeze.

Bracing himself between the walls in the corner he raised himself up level with hatch's opening and peered on through. The beam of his torch lit up the girder supports and the greased steel cables that held the car. There were other things too. A tattered scrap of clothing was wrapped tightly around the end of the steel cable. It was blood stained too and had been shredded with some force. The material was recognisable as a standard company issue engineer's boiler suit.

The beam picked out something else almost behind him. It was difficult to see without twisting and he was afraid of slipping. There was something there, immediately above where the liquid was now freely dripping into the car's interior. He saw the outline of more material, ripped and in tatters with dark stains soaking through. It looked like someone had dropped several pounds of steak over it. He began to wonder why anyone would throw all that steak into the shaft until his thoughts stopped abruptly, and he realised it was not steak. A fragment of bone protruded from the mess, with a scrap of skin that he recognised as a finger. On that finger was a bloodied wedding ring.

He dropped quickly back inside the lift car.

"What did you see?" pleaded Tom, already very nervous at having seen the pool of blood spreading.

"Nothing, kid," David reassured, but the words sounded so false. He did not want to startle the kid, but maybe it was too late for that.

He scrambled across the car towards the door. From above there was a groan and the sound of metal parting company.

Tom reached out to grab him. "Quick," he shouted, "It's all letting go."

He leapt for the gap between the doors as the floor began to slide away. The whole car tilted and jammed, and the gap began to close as it dropped.

He vaulted the last few feet and slid through the narrowing gap. The torch slipped from his grasp and fell back into the car, skidding away and playing its beam drunkenly across the floor. He rolled through just as the frame above let go in a roar and the lift dropped like a stone, taking its gory cargo with it.

Looking up at Tom he could not help but laugh even though he did not know why. The near brush with death made him feel such a mix of emotions inside. At least now there was no need to hide the minced body from the boy anymore.

A rumble echoed up the shaft then gradually faded away; nothing else was moving in there. David took Tom's torch and flashed it through the doors. The shaft was empty now except for two cables that swayed back and forth, no longer under any tension. He flicked the torch off to save the battery; they might need it later on, and he had lost the only other torch.

"There should be an emergency staircase off this level. I think we would be safer using stairs instead of lifts for the time being."

*   *   *   *   *

Most of the stairwell was in darkness. Some of the lights were still working, but only just. Most were dangling, held by only the remnants of the wiring conduits that dangled limply from where they had been shorn from their supports. It was difficult to see the cause of the collapse, but much of the stair structure had been bent and buckled and hung at precarious angles. Getting to the upper engineering decks looked like it was going to be harder than he had thought.

Some of the mess jammed in the shaft looked out of place. There were pieces of twisted yellow metal that looked like it all might have once been a vehicle. In the light of their one remaining torch he could see what looked like a rubber tyre that had been crushed flat under the weight. It was a battery-powered cart of the type used by engineers to carry tools and equipment. There were no indications of a driver though. The vehicle's fall had taken out much of the cabling and other structures. It was little wonder that most of the consoles had been dead. Somewhere amongst this tangle of débris probably ran the control circuits for the cooling systems. When the vehicle had fallen, it had tripped out all of the computers.

There was nowhere else to go but up. At first it was easy to get a purchase. The tangle at the bottom was well impacted and stable. Further up though the stair supports had been ripped away from the wall, and they were forced to climb slower and slower, testing each handhold carefully to see that it would support weight.

It took over an hour to make it up to the top level. At the top landing it was clear that the small vehicle that had caused so much destruction had been rammed at some speed through the protective barrier that was supposed to protect the stairwell. Angry-looking scrape marks across the walls on opposite sides showed the vehicle had bounced several times before pure chance had taken it into the stairs. The driver must have escaped uninjured, perhaps jumping free before the fall – there was no trace of him.

There was a communications console set into an alcove at the side of the corridor. Like the consoles on the level below it was dead and did not respond to attempts to activate it. Further along, the corridor opened out into maintenance workshops where vehicles similar to the one jammed in the stairwell shaft lay in neat rows plugged to their chargers. The lights were on and tools lay on the workbenches, but a search of the offices and stores turned up nobody. On one bench they found a book resting face down to mark a page and a cup of tea with greasy fingerprints on the handle that was stone cold. They were abandoned nonchalantly as if the owner had been called away on an errand that they had not expected to last more than a few minutes. Elsewhere they found evidence of everyday activity just discarded with no evidence of haste or emergency.

"The Marie Celeste," Tom murmured.

At a junction they found access points to the next level. Here the stairs were brightly lit and undamaged. There were elevator points too, with undamaged cars and panels that were still lit up and working, but they shunned them. It did not take long from here to reach levels that David recognised.

*　　　*　　　*　　　*　　　*

The hum of the cores was apparent before they reached the huge room in which they were housed. The toroidal structures glowed a steady purple. There were four that powered the heart of the *Persia* and every single one was at full load. It was little wonder that the heat was building up in the cooling plants.

A diagnostics terminal revealed that no breach had occurred; there was no radiation risk yet. However none of the main computer terminals would allow access. At every screen he was presented with an access-denied warning. He tried every trick he knew to get around the logins, but none work.

Before David could come up with another plan the air began to crackle with static. He darted to one side, but Tom did not move quickly enough and was surrounded by a haze that shimmered in the air.

"What the?"

David reached out to him and grabbed his arm. The haze buzzed around his own arm too, until he pulled Tom clear of the console. He could not help but laugh as the shimmering air, free of the obstruction of the boy, formed up into the flickering holographic image of a man.

The boy was shocked; he had not seen such a thing before, but an old hand like David knew at once what it was. Every vessel's computer had a hologram projection program built in. Few people cared for such things; they were creepy and unnerving. But they were there as an easy method of running diagnostics on computer systems. If all else failed, talking to a hologram was somewhat more straightforward for the average engineer than typing lines and lines of unfathomable machine code.

""Help hologram has activated," he said to Tom with a wink, "We must have triggered it."

"Help what?"

The boy was confused at the idea, but David moved to reassure him. "You'll see."

The haze formed into the outline of a man. He looked like the stereotypical image from a thousand government issue recordings on integration and diversity. With tanned skin and a short hair cut and smiling face, he was

145

nauseatingly box ticking in the demographic he seemed to have been programmed to represent. If a computer could be programmed to replicate a human accurately, then David had a suspicion that in some way the image of this perfect man would tick boxes for single mothers, teenagers, old people and more than a dozen different races, defying all physical possibilities.

Standing impassively the hologram's face broke into a smile. A programmer had probably thought they would make the image do such a thing, to put the user at ease. It failed miserably, and looked instead like the image was sneering at them both.

"I am the ship's computer real systems runtime basic input output protocol," the image babbled in a softly spoken voice, "State your need."

"What weird-ass bullshit is it saying?" Tom whispered.

"Probably English," David replied. He turned to the image and spoke, hesitant at first. "What is going on? Where are the crew?"

The hologram cocked his head to one side. It was a strange move that broke the illusion that he might be human. One minute his head was straight, the next it was leant to one side without any animation in between.

"Question not understood," the image spoke in its infuriating softly spoken voice.

"I guess it doesn't do English after all," Tom said quietly.

David ignored him. "Why are there no people in engineering?" he asked again, trying to make his question as simple as possible.

"Unknown."

"Unknown?" he demanded angrily, "What do you mean unknown? Give me some answers, dammit!"

He lashed out at the image, but his fist passed soundlessly through only serving to send a temporary ripple across the image that the hologram seemed unable or uninterested in acknowledging.

"Unknown."

David growled, but there was nothing to be gained from getting annoyed at the image. He wished that he knew how he could shut it down. It would probably be better just to ignore it.

"We need to find a way of overriding the computer," he told Tom.

"Unknown," chimed the hologram.

David ignored it, though he saw Tom was getting nervous of the image that watched them from cold and empty computer generated eyes.

"It's just a computer," he said, trying to put the boy at ease, "The computer doesn't understand what we're saying, so it keeps on churning out the only response it knows. Don't let it spook you, kid!"

Tom gingerly reached forward and pressed a finger into the image. Ripples spread out in concentric circles as the projector struggled to cope, but his finger passed into the shimmering coloured light without any resistance.

"I guess so," he said, though sounded unconvinced.

"Look, just hunt around for anything we can use to get the circuit breakers out." He glanced to the humming toroidal chambers, "We need to shut it down."

"Why?"

He stopped. It was an odd question to come from the hologram. "What's it to you?" he asked the hologram.

Tom looked scared.

A ripple of static passed through the image, and for a brief moment its eyes took on a different, darker look. Then the static distortion cleared and the hologram was back as it had been as if no change had happened.

David felt odd, as if he had just caught a glimpse of something else beyond the politically correct demographic ticking exterior of the computer programme. Suddenly he too was afraid and started to back away. Taking hold of Tom's arm he pulled the boy away. "Let's just leave the computer here. I think we would be best to leave, slowly and without fuss."

The image flickered again. As the static cleared, those eyes were back, like dark voids into another dimension. Peering out from behind this tanned and softly spoken exterior, they looked like something else was looking out through a mask of the politically correct man's face.

Tom looked at David. "But you said it was just a computer projection?" he began slowly.

The boy reached over and waved his hand through the holographic image.

"David shouted a warning, but it came too late. Tom's hand brushed the image, and static buzzed around his hand. Where there had been expanding images of distortion before, this time the image seemed to close in around the arm, feeding its way up until Tom seemed enveloped to the shoulder.

"Get back!" David pulled on the boy's arm.

"I can't!" the boy stuttered, shocked.

His feet slipped on the floor, as he was dragged closer into the centre of the projection. David's mind raced – a hologram was not supposed to be able to touch and interact in such a way with real objects.

"It won't let go!" Tom screamed.

Whatever had hold of the boy was too strong. The static buzzed angrily in the air, and the image kept coming until it consumed the boy. Tom's open mouth and fearful expression disappeared with a sickening liquid sound into the hologram.

Scrabbling back across the floor, he could not believe what he had just seen. The boy had been sucked into a hologram and then, against all physical possibilities, he had disappeared. The image was still rippling and unstable and he half expected Tom to fall out from the other side. Instead, the image settled down until the outline of the tanned skin man returned and stood impassively before the console as if nothing had ever happened.

"Tom?" he called.

The hologram cocked its head to one side. "Unknown."

"Unknown?" David screamed at it, "You just made the boy disappear, and all you can say is unknown?"

"Unknown."

Reeling around he grabbed a swivel chair and hurled it with all his strength at the hologram. A part of him expected it to be enveloped and ingested as the image had done with Tom, but the hologram rippled and buzzed and the chair passed through, hitting the console behind and tipped over onto the floor.

The hologram slanted its head to one side as if scrutinising the man who had just thrown an object through its space. David expected it to say something; to parrot off the same phrase of 'unknown' over and over again. But none came.

He did not dare step close to the projection in case it did the same to him. He circled around it, trying to find a way of explaining to himself what he had just seen. The hologram never moved, staring impassively ahead with its head cocked to the side. In a fit of rage he took a clipboard from a console and hurled it at the image. He was not sure why he did it; it was just the reaction of inner rage and frustration. Papers flew from the board, fluttering to the floor. The board sailed through the air and passed into the hologram just as the chair had.

Ripples spread out and the board clattered across the console behind and fell to the floor. This time the ripples in the image did not dissipate, but instead grew and enlarged until the whole figure of the man pulsated and grew.

Static added to the turmoil of the image, and then in a change that happened in a split second, the man was gone replaced with the figure of a woman. She was dressed in an archaic uniform that made her look like a leftover from another century.

The woman filled him with a feeling of unease. She turned and looked across the machine room as if seeing her surroundings for the very first time. Then she looked back to David, regarding him with piercing eyes that probed into the depths of his soul with their stare. He took an involuntary step backwards until he felt the cold steel of the bulkhead behind him. There was a fire axe in a case beside him and he fumbled for the clasps that held it with shaking hands.

The hologram saw his move and stopped for a moment, thinking. A wave of static crossed the image, and for a moment he saw the same eyes that he had seen before, like two portals to hell with a demon from beyond looking out at him. Then that look in her face passed and she was just an archaic woman again. But he never forgot the look of those eyes.

He managed to get the axe free and waved it in front of him. She took several steps forward slowly, moving across the room towards him as if curious about what it was that he was doing.

"Stay back," he ordered, brandishing the axe.

She ignored him and took another step.

"I said to stay back!" he said again.

She was almost upon him and he could feel the claustrophobic wall of the bulkhead behind him. There was nowhere to go except through the hologram. He swung the axe with all his strength at the woman, but it harmlessly passed through the image without any resistance, and he nearly lost a grip on it as it rebounded harmlessly off the bulkhead.

She stopped and blinked. A ripple of static edged through the image. No longer did her eyes appear to be demonic.

"Who are you?" she asked.

He swung the axe again. She blinked and took a step back as it passed through her image. He slipped around her and back towards the consoles.

She turned and looked at him with pleading eyes. "Who are you?" she repeated, "You are not who I expected."

"Just who were you expecting?" he hissed.

"I do not know," she conceded, seeming crestfallen.

"What's going on, David demanded, "First you are a man who made my partner disappear, now you're some woman with a fashion issue and a momentary lapse of memory."

She looked across the room past David to the toroidal structures, then she looked back with a darting expression on her simulated face. "Shut them down if you want to live."

He ran her words through his mind again. "What?"

"Shut them down if you want to live," she repeated, more firmly. Then the image rippled and she threw her head back as if to scream, but no scream came. Instead the image sagged, as if the woman was cowering to the floor. Before his eyes she was gone and the impassive man from before returned, regarding him with those same evil eyes.

David remembered her words though. He looked back to the consoles where reams of text scrolled on screens. The computer was out of his control; something was running programme after programme, and all the time the drive cores were humming under maximum load. Suddenly what he needed to do became clear to him and he raised his axe to strike.

"Stop," hissed the hologram in a flat voice.

David flinched, but only for a moment. The axe crashed down and the screen on the console shattered. He pulled the axe back out and raised it again.

The hologram lunged forward, changing as it went into a column of white that poured across the room. It wrapped itself around the head of the axe and he felt it torn from his grasp and saw it flung across the room. White swirled about him and he turned and ran. Something reached out and he felt the electric pinch of a shock riding through his arm and the feeling of burning. Then what had been the hologram screamed, and collapsed in on itself in a huge vortex of thrashing tendrils.

As fast as he could run he followed the corridors that led from the drive room. A hatch began to roll shut in front of him and he side-stepped to avoid it before it impacted the rim. Retracing his steps he was faced by another hatch rolling shut. Whatever that thing was it was trying to herd him and to force him to take a route that would lead him back to it. Deliberately he did not take the obvious way. Coming to an open hatch, he slipped through it just as it began to close. Beyond it there was a stairwell. An emergency klaxon sounded and he knew it to mean that the computer was shutting the airtight hatches that connected the machinery decks to those above.

Taking the steps several at a time he hurried up the switchback, half expecting to meet the creature at every turn, but instead he was faced only with a lowering wall of steel blast door. There was a gap a few feet high at its base and he ducked underneath, getting through with moments to spare before it sealed shut and the wail of klaxons faded to nothing more than a background hum beyond the steel of the door.

Leaning against the wall he fought to regain his breath and looked around. This was the lowest of the decks below the passenger levels. Store rooms and closets opened off the corridor that ran from here. There would be a long walk to reach the grand staircase lower levels, and from there around forty storeys of stairs – he did not trust the lifts – to reach the airlocks.

He heard a scream and the panicked chatter of an old woman pleading with somebody. Ducking out from the lobby at the top of the stairs he came across a group of passengers full of fear. Relief washed over them as they saw him.

"One of the crew! He'll know what to do!"

Before he could go they flocked to him like followers looking for their Messiah, expecting him to provide them with answers that he knew he did not know.

13

"The idiots," Ventura rumbled, "Abandoning the Starliner with barely two or three to a pod. Don't they know that they will leave thousands behind to their fate in their selfish drive to escape as quickly as they can?"

Dezza pressed his face to the cool curve of the screen on the promenade deck. On the deck above he could see the crush of bodies and the frightened fighting as a throng of passengers pushed and shoved for the lifepods. Further down the line he saw yet another pod fire away from its lock and flash away into space.

"Every one of those can carry a hundred people," said Ventura angrily, "And there must be barely more than half a dozen in each of those. The selfish fools!"

"By the time we get to them there will be no pods left," said Philipa.

Ventura glanced sideways at her. "It seems that we have to fight this thing whether any of us likes it or not."

Through the glass Dezza saw another dozen lifepods rock away from their moorings and fire away into space. The crush of passengers on the deck visible continued to fight; though the sounds of their turmoil did not reach them through the vacuum. Even as the very last of the lifepods jetted away, there was still a steady crush of bodies visible. He saw some pounding with their fists on the closed airlocks where the lifepods had launched as if somehow venting their frustration might bring them back. But it was a lost cause. Slowly the passengers left on the deck dissipated as some began to realise that there were other banks of lifepods on the opposite side of the Starliner. Dezza knew that there would be other fools there, and the chances were that the lifepods had already gone.

"How did you stop it on the *Cerberus*?" Ventura asked quietly, never taking his gaze away from the line of empty lifepod bays.

Dezza thought back and felt the pang of regrets and fear that always came when he remembered the old Starliner. He remembered Tracker, and his sacrifice by taking the Starliner into the meteorite swarm whilst Dezza and Toze retrieved the core. Then they had had a means of escape and it had not mattered that the *Cerberus* was destroyed. But looking at the banks of empty lifepod bays, he knew that whatever plan he could persuade them to follow would have to include freeing the *Persia* from the creature, or die in its destruction. He could not bring himself to tell Philipa that they might have to die to defeat it, so he plucked up his courage and resolved to find a way.

"We managed to stun the creature by shorting out portions of the *Cerberus*' power grid. The creature seems capable of existing between matter and energy, and a jolt held it at bay. There were other things that seemed to work too."

Ventura turned his back on the empty bays to look at him. "Like what?"

"It can travel through the ship in the electrics. Where there was no connection, it could not physically pass through bulkheads. It could however use security cameras and radio signals to bridge the gap."

Ventura nodded. "Kill the power and kill the creature."

"How exactly do we switch off a Starliner?" demanded Philipa unconvinced. She waved her hand at the Plexiglas. "Everything we could have used to escape is gone. I would have much rather got off this ship and let someone else with better equipment come back and clear up the mess."

He felt his ears run hot. Why did so many people assume there was an expert for every occasion? "Who exactly were you expecting to come?" he asked, "Once upon a time that person was me and a group of military boys who had enough firepower to level a small country. We got our arses handed to us gift-wrapped on a plate."

Undeterred, she folded her hands and stared intently at him. "So what do you propose that we do?"

Dezza was suddenly aware they were both looking to him. Were they expecting him to have the answers? The old Dezza would have backed away and made excuses, running to the nearest bottle for solace. But he knew there was no option. If he wanted to get out of this as much as these two did, he had to find a way – something that they missed on the *Cerberus*. There the creature had somehow managed to survive.

That first trip aboard now seemed so long ago, muted by time. Back then he had known little about what awaited him. How much ignorance was bliss. If only he could have warned off Zoë and sided with Tubs. He shook the thoughts away – somebody else would have blundered into the *Cerberus*. Besides, there had been no way of knowing.

The machine room of the vessel had revealed that the original crew had thought of a way. They had not succeeded in completing what they had started. Somehow they had put the Starliner and the creature with it into hibernation. They had almost managed what they had aimed to do, but not quite. With a shudder he remembered his blissful ignorance as he had restarted the ailing drive systems, and with it woken the creature from its enforced hibernation.

He realised the demons that he had carried with him all these years – he had been the one who had brought the creature out of its slumbers. If he had not dared to reactivate the Starliner and had instead pulled the plug and waited for Tubs to fix the core and tow the prize back as nothing more than a dead hulk, would the creature have never resurfaced.

No – these were dangerous thoughts that if left unchecked would lead to the slippery slope of depression that had ended his career and ruined his life from that moment on. He had to rise up and face those demons. The biggest demon of all that haunted his mind was the unsettled business with the entity.

Dezza drew himself up and turned to Ventura with a confidence that he had not felt in many years. "Captain Ventura," he said, "How would a person go about shutting down the *Persia*'s main drive cores?"

"Main engineering," replied Ventura quickly.

"How do we get there?"

"I know the way."

"What about this thing?" demanded Philipa, "It's chased us before, won't it figure out what you are doing?"

"A risk we have to take," shrugged Dezza.

"Will it chase us?"

He could not lie. "Probably. We can shake it off if we need to by shorting the power grid."

"Oh yes," she said sarcastically, "I carry shit to do that around with me all the time."

"If we have to, we shall find a way," said Ventura firmly.

He sounded so confident, but Dezza wondered how much he really believed what he said.

*   *   *   *   *

In the grand staircase they met a mob of passengers who seemed determined to take out their anger at any crewmember that they could find. In their dirty and damaged uniforms, Philipa and Ventura were still the figures of authority that they sought.

"I don't like the look of this," hissed Philipa, "Let's get out of here."

"Too late," said Dezza, and he was right. He was pushed to one side as the crowd swarmed up the staircase and surrounded them. To the mob, he was just another passenger. In an instant he found himself separated. He heard Philipa and Ventura trying to make themselves heard over the crowd, but they were fighting a losing battle. All the passengers wanted to do was shout each other down, as they demanded answers though they never paused to let Philipa or the captain speak.

He began to push his way back into the crowd, but several men batted him to the side and kicked him to the ground.

"Wait your turn, buddy," one snarled as he raised his fist to strike again.

Dezza feigned left then rolled last minute to the right catching the man off guard. Over balancing with his swing, Dezza took the opportunity and brought his legs up and kicked him under the ribs. The man collapsed into a wheezing mound, taking another man down too. But others were piling in fast, incensed at the fight. It had taken only a spark to ignite the powder keg that had been brewing.

They carried weapons that they had liberated - mostly pieces of wood, torn from furniture. Others brandished fire extinguishers and all now seemed bent on venting their anger on him as a convenient target.

The first man came at him, but Dezza had the advantage from being further up the stairs. As the man raised his extinguisher to strike, Dezza rolled back and jabbed him neatly in the stomach and he went down from the blow. Pushing the coughing man aside, he grabbed the extinguisher. Hitting the release he hosed the rest of the advancing crowd with a choking cloud of powder. He played it across the men until they were forced to retreat, coughing and spluttering and figures faded into shadows in the white haze. Just as the extinguisher spluttered and failed, two people appeared from the cloud and he braced for a fight. But it was Ventura and Philipa, shielding their eyes and noses from the dust.

"Let's get out of here," he shouted to them.

Already the mob was regrouping, realising that those they had thought that they had cornered were getting away. They charged back up the stairs, but Dezza, Philipa and Ventura had gone, darting into side corridors off the balcony and making sure that they had disappeared from sight.

They ran down one corridor after another. They heard the mob advancing, but somehow they managed to keep away from them. Finding a stair well, they used it, doubling back in the hope that the passengers would not have figured that they might go back to the grand staircase. At last they came back upon the staircase, listening a moment from the cover of the balcony before venturing out. The mob had gone now leaving only a slick of powder across the carpet.

Ventura tore off his tie and began plucking the badges of rank from his uniform.

"If we run into any other pissed passengers, we need to blend in." He looked at Philipa. "Get your epaulettes off."

Even before he had finished, she had flicked off the stewardess' badges and thrown them over the balcony's edge.

Above them, through the clear dome, Dezza scrutinised the shape of the lifepod that still lay tangled in the Starliner's antennas. It made him feel cold with fear – from the moment the engineers had brought in that body, the horrors had started.

"What did they do with the body they brought in?"

Ventura glanced up. "To the morgue. Why?"

He could not explain the feeling he felt. What if the dead man's body had harboured the creature? From the moment the airlock had been opened it would have been into the ship and able to infiltrate the electrical systems.

"Just a hunch," he said out loud.

On the *Cerberus* there had been no-one left, apart from the dead bodies in the lift. It had seemed less real them – just a few barricades and evidence of fighting that had grown old and the damage had been muted by the dust and decay. Now he was seeing here first hand how it might have been aboard the *Cerberus* when the creature had first struck. Was this how the crew and passengers had reacted then? Human base instincts never changed. Some of them back them had fought back though. someone had even done their best to shut down the drive cores.

*　　　*　　　*　　　*　　　*

Ventura never pressed his question, and Dezza was happy he hadn't. Instead they made their way down each staircase, wary of there being more angry passengers, though they met only the occasional lone survivors who seemed more interested in hurrying for the last of the lifepods – if there were any left by now. When the steps ran out and there was no way to get any lower, Ventura took the lead and led them on into the lowest cabin level.

"Through here – we can get into one of the engineering level access points easily enough."

Turning a corner they came face to face with a level of destruction that sullied the name of supposed civilised culture. Doors lay ripped from their hinges and the cabins beyond had been ransacked. Furniture was broken and strewn across the floors mixed with remnants of belongings. It looked like the mob had been through smashing up everything that they could lay their hands on. Small fires smouldered in places, not severe enough to trigger the ship's fire suppression system, but enough to add an acrid overtone to the air.

"So much for the blue rinse crowd on the outer rim cruise," Ventura spat. "Show them a disaster and they all throw their toys out of the pram and start acting like thugs and vandals."

"I thought people came on cruises to get away from the worst of human nature," said Philipa.

"I guess we were wrong." Ventura pointed through the haze of smoke. "We have to keep going. If we're lucky, the idiots who did this are those we got passed on the staircase."

They began picking their way over débris; then Philipa stopped unexpectedly in shock. Dezza followed where she was pointing, and saw the body lying face down in the destruction, a pool of blood lapping slowly across the tattered carpet.

He pushed her to one side and knelt at the body. It was still warm, but when he felt for a pulse there was none. Gently he rolled the head to one side. Eyes glazed in death stared up at him unblinking. Across the man's forehead a jagged gash showed that he had never stood a chance.

Dezza rolled the man's head back and wiped the blood from his fingers on the carpet and stood up. "Nothing we can do. Let's get on." He ushered Philipa past the body, trying to sound upbeat, but he felt far from it and he guessed the other two did too.

They moved on along the corridor, but the destruction got worse and worse until at last the pattern of damage could no longer be blamed on the fighting mob. Here the walls were smashed too, ripped apart and scored with jagged marks that no person could ever inflict, even with a variety of improvised weapons. The plating underneath the décor was buckled too, in ways that even heavy machinery would have struggled to do. The further they went, the worse it became.

"This isn't the mob," Dezza whispered, fingering some of the marks on the walls. The gashes felt smooth, despite their torn look. In places they were still warm and he could smell the burnt paint that had been scorched from the surface. The metal had been melted as if seared by an acetylene flame.

"What is it?" asked Philipa.

He was forced to concede that he did not know. The patterns of damage looked strangely familiar though and nagged at memories he had hoped that he would forget. Casting him mind back he thought of the *Cerberus*'s lower deck, and the fall through the ruptured plating into the machinery.

"Watch your step," he warned, "Some of this floor might not be stable."

Philipa followed him gingerly, but Ventura scoffed and strode on ahead. "Don't tell me that your creature could turn my ship into nothing more than paper!"

In a moment it was over. The metal creaked and sagged and Ventura fell to the floor. Grasping the lip of a cabin door he managed to get a good hold as the floor from underneath him slipped away with a roar.

Dust filled the air and for a moment Dezza could no longer see the captain. He felt Philipa's hand grasp his as the deck beneath them began to shudder. Together they stumbled through the dust; coughing and choking until their way was blocked by broken furniture piled up almost to the ceiling. They must have taken a wrong turning in the maze of corridors. He pulled Philipa close and tried to tell her to follow him, but the roar of collapsing steelwork was too great and the dust caught the back of his throat and threatened to make him vomit every time he drew a breath.

Dropping on all fours they crawled as the floor bucked beneath them. Through bleary eyes he saw the outline of a fire door and reached up to push it open letting Philipa dart through, then he followed. The stair well beyond resonated with the rumble of falling steelwork, but the structure here stayed firm and didn't give way. There was dust in the air, but at least it was thin and not much more than a light haze.

The rumbling reached a sudden crescendo and the vibration knocked them both to the floor. The lights flickered, and for a moment it seemed that they were going to die. Philipa pulled him closer and he ended up with her head tightly held to his shoulder. He knew she was scared as he felt her sobbing into his arm.

But the structure held and at last the rumbling began to die away. As quickly as it had started, the vibration was gone. Gingerly Dezza opened his eyes and looked over the stairwell. Everything looked normal, except for the light dusting of fine grey that had settled giving everything a matt sheen.

Philipa looked up at him, tears stained down her cheeks where the dust had stuck. Her clothes were a grey, and even her hair had turned the same colour. He wagered that he was unlikely to look any better. Rubbing a hand across his face it felt gritty.

"What just happened?" she cried in between sobs.

He looked back to the door that they had come through. It had closed behind them and showed no signs of damage, but he wondered what they would find when they looked back through. On the *Cerberus* there had been areas of floors that had disappeared. He remembered Tracker stopping him from stepping out into a massive abyss that had been on the other side of an innocent looking door, just like this one.

He gently eased it open a crack. A small amount of dust rolled through, but beyond it he could see the corridor and the piles of furniture that had blocked their way, all looking like they had been spray-painted in a uniform shade of light grey. It had muted even the walls and the ceiling. There was no sign of a collapse of the deck, and even the lights were still working, though dimmed by the layers of filth that encrusted the glass shades that remained.

"What do you see?" Philipa asked.

"One hell of a mess."

"What about Ventura?"

Dezza remembered the image of the man falling and reaching out last minute to grab what he could before the waves of dust obscured everything.

"I don't know," he replied.

She pushed past him to the door. "Then we go and find him. We don't just leave him behind."

*   *   *   *   *

Every corridor looked the same, yet unfamiliar. There was damage where the mob had been, but nothing looked like it had before the dust. Even the fires had been choked out and the air had cleared of any acrid smoke. It took a long time for them to find their way back to where they had been.

Most of the ceiling had collapsed and narrowed the corridor down to a slit of just a foot or so high. Ignoring the dirt, Dezza crawled in as far as he could go on his hands and knees. There was not a complete way through, but he could get far enough to see the huge void that had opened up.

No more than a couple of feet in front of him the metal was torn away and all that was left were a few tatters of carpet flitting in the air above a void. He strained to see how far it went down, but there was nothing to see but darkness. Above, what was left of the deck above slanted down and ended at the same point. There was no room to get through, even if he had wanted to. Scrabbling with his hands and feet he worked his way across to where the edge of the corridor had been.

"Can you see anything?" Philipa's voice drifted to him.

"No luck," he gasped. It was hard to move in the confined space.

Reaching the edge of the void he found what was left of the corridor wall. As the deck above had been pulled down it had buckled back into a cabin leaving a semi-circular shaped void that was just large enough to wriggle into on his elbows and get a better view out into the hole. He heard Philipa calling, but it was too cramped and too dusty to make any meaningful reply.

The corridor wall did continue bent almost double in places until it straightened out and joined the floor of the corridor at the other side. Twisting around, he saw that the other side of the corridor was gone, but that other fragments of the room beyond remained. As his eyes became used to the gloom he found he could make out the edges of decks below, ripped clean away by the force.

Where he had seen Ventura in the moments before the dust cloud had rolled over them all, the metal was frayed, but looked to have held. It was possible that the captain might have survived, if he had been able to keep his grip and haul himself up. Dezza strained to see any sign of tracks in the dust of the corridor over the gap, but it was impossible to see in the meagre light.

"Captain!" he called out. His voice echoed in the void before dying away without an answer. He repeated the cry again, trying not to choke on the dust he was kicking up. Still no reply came.

He heard Philipa calling to him again, but could not make out her words. Backing up on his elbows took a lot of effort. In the tight space it took far more time than getting in had. There was more than one moment when he felt the narrow hole narrow or pinch behind him that the fear of getting stuck washed over him. Then he felt the grasp of hands on his ankles, guiding his legs and body and he knew he was clear. Rolling out of the tight gap he collapsed in a heap, struggling to regain his breath. Philipa sat down beside him, her eyes pleading for information.

"Was there any sign of him?" she asked as soon as he had regained enough breath to talk.

"No." He saw her shoulders sag and the tears begin to well in her eyes. "That's not to say he did not make it," he added hurriedly, "There's a chance he made it out, but he would have to find another way through."

"I guess so," she said, but he figured that she did not share his optimism.

They retraced their footsteps back to the stairwell that they had hidden in. Nothing else looked the same amongst the cabins under the blanket of dust. At least the stairs might find them a way to another level that hadn't collapsed.

14

The passengers came in their ones and twos until David found himself with more than a dozen walking behind him. He had not wanted to be anyone's saviour, but they saw his uniform of sorts, and looked to him as a leader who could get them to safety. He did not dare tell them that he had no idea where that 'safety' they spoke of was. So they followed him as he tried to find his way back up through the ship. All the time he could not help but ask himself why there were no other crewmembers.

When the floor beneath them began to shake most of the motley group of overweight tourists and old aged pensioners scattered in all directions, screaming as they went. David dropped to the floor, his vision blurring as the vibrations got worse. Dust began to flutter in the air and the lights flickered off then came back on at reduced brightness.

The sound of metal ripping grew, louder than the rumble and he felt the floor beneath him jump and writhe as if something had taken hold of the steel plate and was flexing it like it was nothing more than a sheet of card. The wall down the side of the corridor splintered as wall fittings and plaster pulled away and fell in a shower of fragments. A line of paint ricocheted in flakes that shot out like they were being fired from a machine gun, and a jagged line followed them across the wall as the steel twisted and buckled. More dirt fell; it rolled over him in thicker waves and all he could do was press his face to the carpet and try to shield every breath he took with the fingers of his hand. It was hard not to choke.

It seemed like forever, but at last the rumbling subsided and the rending stopped and the floor beneath him stopped bucking up and down. He waited a while longer, bracing himself in case something else happened; but nothing did. Carefully he lifted his head and wiped the dust from his face. The whole corridor had turned to grey and a haze hung in the air. He looked around, but the passengers who had followed him had all gone.

Dust rolled off him as he stood up and he had to pause for a moment trying not to breathe until it had settled again. Where had all this come from? He did not know how so much filth could appear from nowhere in a supposedly clean ship.

The wall in front of him was a uniform grey now, but it seemed to dip at crazy angles over a length of over twenty metres. The ceiling had buckled in places too. When he rubbed a hand over the grey it fluttered away revealing patterns of cracks in the paint. At one point he found that the wall had split entirely from the floor and there was a gap under which a determined person might be able to crawl. Taking out his torch he shone it into the gap in case there might be someone in there, but the beam picked out only the wrecked insides of a cabin. The wall on the other side had been shoved in at an acute angle and most of the fitted furniture had splintered into matchsticks that were now heaped on the floor. There was no-one in there; he turned off the beam to save the battery.

It took him a moment to work out which way he had come before the dust had descended. Every step he took left marks in the dust, but there was no evidence of anyone else. He imagined it to be like being in the aftermath of nuclear fallout. He paused mid stride and his heart jumped at the thought - could a drive core have ruptured? He weighed over the idea for a moment. The atmosphere was still intact and no warning sirens blared. Putting the thoughts aside he cautiously followed the corridor, testing each step carefully before applying any weight.

Reaching the edge of the distortion he walked with more confidence. Looking back down the corridor his footsteps lead out in an unbroken line and was taken aback by the distortion that was more evident than ever in the structure. The dust helped to mute some of the damage, but it could not disguise the twist to one side that the whole corridor had taken on over a twenty-metre stretch.

At the end of the corridor he came upon more destruction. A whole section of the ceiling had collapsed, getting progressively lower until it met the floor ten metres further on. Testing the débris with a firm push it was clear that the entire structure above had shifted and there would be no way for him on his own to break a way through. Even then, what else might there be on the other side?

He retraced his steps and tried another turn off. This one seemed untouched at first, but eventually he came to a section where all the lights had failed and the corridor ahead faded to darkness. It was impossible to see anything more than a few metres. He felt his way on a few metres until he remembered the torch and flicked it on.

He stopped in surprise, as the beam of light illuminated only a few metres of floor before the corridor ended at a black abyss. Silently he cursed himself for not being more careful. Blundering into the darkness might have got him killed. Testing the strength of the remainder of the floor, he edged as close as he dared and shone the torch around. A couple of decks above the beam faintly picked out the outline of structure still remaining. There were the lines in the steel where walls and floors had been, looking incongruous and strange with the mix of different décor colours now shoved side by side by the collapse. Shining the torch further he saw a haze of dust through which intermittent jagged edges of broken girders reached up like a Petrified Forest of twisted steel several decks below. It would have been an instant end to fall into all that.

Retracing his steps again he tried another corridor. This time it came simply to a dead end, forcing him to return back to where he had started. That covered all the different ways that the corridors could go, and every one of them was a dead end or blocked. Of the passengers who had been following him, there was not a trace. Maybe they were the lucky ones? What if he was now trapped in a small section of the Starliner? Who would rescue him?

The dust in the air had cleared quite quickly. That meant that the air conditioning systems had to be working, and that in turn meant that there would be ways though the ducting if he was determined enough.

There were large ventilation grills set in the walls the length of every corridor. Raising himself up on tiptoe at the nearest one he was rewarded by the feeling of movement in the air on his face has he pulled himself up so his face rested level with the grill. It was too far up to be able to climb in unaided, so he looked around for something that could be used as a step. There was nothing in the corridor, but here there were plenty of cabins he could search. The doors to them were locked, but it did not take much effort to break down the flimsy wood and gain entry.

A part of him expected that there might be passengers cowering inside, but the cabin proved empty like the rest of the corridors. Some of the furniture had been thrown to the floor by the quake, but there was enough undamaged for him to pick out a chair and liberate a length of slender wood from a small table. He dragged them back to the grill and rested the chair against the wall before testing it with his weight – it would be more than strong enough.

It was easier to see how the grill was fastened from the tabletop. Four screws quickly yielded to his screwdriver set, and he lifted the panel away and let it fall to the deck. Dust fluttered from behind the panel catching him off guard and he nearly fell from the chair in a coughing fit. But the ventilation soon cleared the air as he peered inside.

The opening led into a square passage that itself dropped into a larger ventilation trunking. Once he got in, it would be big enough to walk crouched down. The breeze was strong and fresh meaning that there ought to be a clear way through. Hoisting himself up, he used the slender piece of wood from the table to hook onto a join in the passage and pull himself in.

It was hard work for a man who was more out of shape than he would care to admit, but he made it at last and rolled over into the main ventilation trunking, pausing to catch his breath. There was not much to see; just a long metal tunnel that led off in either direction fading out towards nothing. But the torch beam showed no obstructions, and that meant he could get far enough to be clear of the collapse and kick out another panel to drop into another corridor.

It was harder to move in the ventilation trunking that he had thought. Forced to stoop by the low roof, the panelling had too many sharp edges where it was joined to be able to crawl. Every step made the metal flex and bounce threatening to trip him as the panels dipped and exposed the flanges that connected them. It did not help either that the light from the torch was failing.

He struggled on as fast as he dared, but it was difficult to see in the near darkness that was quickly obscuring what he could see. The torch's light was now next to useless. Waving his hand across the beam there was barely enough light now to illuminate the tips of his fingers.

A hasty look around located the next connecting passage out to an adjacent corridor. A feeble wash of light came through the distant grill and he could just about see his way by it as he climbed the passage. If this did not lead out into a corridor beyond the collapse then he had no means to see his way any further down the ventilation ducts and he did not trust scrabbling in the dark with risk of further voids that he could fall into.

There was definitely a breeze blowing this way, and he could feel it on his back as he neared the grate. The panel was firmly mounted, and feeling around its edge he could not feel any means of release. Like the others, he knew it would be fastened from the outside with screws that he could not reach from inside. He beat it a few times with his fists and the metal louvers bent under the rain of blows but would not release their grip on the frame. Working in the tight confines was hard and there was not enough room to get his full weight behind any of the blows.

I didn't come all this way just to be stopped by a thin bit of cheap metal, he thought.

He caught his hand on a flange in the vent in the process and wincing from the pain.

"Damn!" he exclaimed and rubbed the bruised knuckles.

It was hard to work crouched as he was and he had to concede a temporary defeat and settled down as comfortably as possible to catch his breath and plan what to do. It was difficult to gauge the passage of time in the dark. Lulled by the passing breeze it was easy to let his mind wander and lose track. Even if he held his watch up close to the louvers, there was no way of reading the dial in the meagre light.

The voices were there in the distance for a while before he registered them, and then he was left wondering how long he could have missed them for. He listened with an ear to the grill, trying to see who might be there. It was hard at first to make anything out and it occurred to him

170

that maybe his mind, hungry for human contact again, might be warping any sounds into those he wanted to hear. Once or twice the voices seemed to stop altogether and there was just the gentle hum of far off fans. Then the sounds would return, faint but definitely human.

He was suddenly afraid that the people out there might make a turn in the maze of passenger cabins and not pass this vent by. Filled with a fear of being trapped here, he beat at the panel and shouted at the top of his lungs. His voice echoed loudly around inside the trunking, almost deafening him. But he kept it up until he had no more breath. Then he stopped and listened.

As much as he strained to hear anything, there was nothing. He began pounding on the grill. Just as he was about to give up and curl into a ball of despair, a shadow passed across the grill and he heard the sound of someone testing the metalwork from outside.

"Hey!" he called, "Can you hear me?"

"Yeah. Relax – we'll get you out of there."

The voice was muffled and he could barely make out the words, but it was good to hear another human voice and the feeling of elation ran through him like electricity.

The shadow flitted and disappeared then for a long time did not return. He began to fear that the person was not coming back and hit the grill again with his fist.

"Are you still there?" he called, "What's going on?"

To his relief the shadow passed across the grill again and he heard the muffled man's voice.

"Take it easy. I just had to find something to stand on. You haven't made it easy hiding in there."

"I'm not hiding."

"Whatever."

The grating rocked to the sound of screws being undone, then it rocked and finally dropped. After so long in near darkness, the light that flooded in was bright and it was painful to look without shielding his eyes. Edging forward he peered out and as his eyes grew used to the light he saw the rough looking man who had been his saviour.

"Cheers bud," he said thankfully. "David's the handle."

The stranger extended a hand to help him out of the panel. "Dezza. But don't expect that you're going to get my number too."

David laughed and eased himself down with Dezza's help over the pile of furniture that had been used to get at the grill. "I wasn't in there for my health. I got trapped after several decks collapsed and that was the only way out."

"Anyone else in there?"

"They disappeared when the shit hit the fan. I couldn't find them and like to assume they got out before the collapse."

David noticed for the first time a woman standing a few steps behind Dezza in the remains of a stewardess' uniform who regarded him with a hint of a smile. "Friend?" he asked.

She cast him an indignant look. "I only work here, pal. They'll never catch me asleep on the job yet."

Her face looked a little familiar and he struggled to recall where from. On a ship this big usually he could go an entire tour without running into any of the hotel services staff. Actually, they were both familiar when he put his mind to it. "You were at the airlock," he said at last, "I went out with one of the apprentices to check over that lifepod. When we finally found a way back in this whole place had gone to shit. Maybe one of you could fill me in on what happened?"

"Wish I knew," she replied. She glanced to Dezza. "Ask him; he seems to have calamity follow him wherever he goes."

"That true?" he asked.

Dezza nodded. "Yeah. Looks like the same shit is happening to the same guy for the third time. And I'm that guy."

David whistled between his teeth. "Unlucky you."

"It's a creature that can move seamlessly between energy and matter. I first encountered it on the *Cerberus* and it's been haunting me like a bad penny ever since."

"*Cerberus*?" David rolled the word around in his mouth as he thought, before shaking his head. "Never heard of her."

"Don't you read the news?" Philipa demanded sharply.

He shrugged. "Never had to yet. I'm an engineer, and call me old fashioned, but I've always found that the engines head in the same direction as the rest of the ship whether I know what's going on or not."

She rolled her eyes.

"Well the engines might be going, but we won't be unless we can stop that thing," Dezza interrupted, "News flash pal. If we don't stop that thing then this nice big floating palace of fun will become a nice little tomb for everyone on her."

"Might not be much left. The cooling system has been damaged and gone into overload. How long will the cores continue before they overheat? Who knows what will happen then."

"You've been in the machine rooms?"

"Yeah. The boy and I had to get in through an emergency tube. Bastards on the airlock level locked us out." His voice trailed off. Judging by the destruction and panic inside the Starliner, he began to realise that they had probably not left him and the boy outside on purpose."

"Have you seen any others of the crew?" he asked, changing the subject.

Philipa shook her head. "No. Just the captain."

David brightened up. "Is he still here?"

"We got parted in the collapse. Hopefully he got through okay."

He grunted in acknowledgement. "What about the cores?" he asked again, "Shouldn't we be looking to get off this crate before they go?"

"They should shut down," said Dezza, "There will be safeties."

David saw the wide-eyed look of shock in Philipa's face, though she said nothing. Maybe Dezza hadn't told her everything. "Depends on whether the systems are damaged that control them. The computer was going ape-shit down there when I went through." He remembered the hologram – that cold, evil look it had had on its digital face and the way it had just consumed the boy without trace.

"Whatever this thing is, it sucked the boy in with no effort. It made a hologram eat a man without even leaving a smudge on the floor, for Christ's sakes. If I were you two I'd be getting out of here on a lifepod."

"That might be a little hard," said Philipa quietly.

"Why?"

"Lifepods are gone," she finished flatly.

"Gone? All of them?" he demanded. There were enough lifepods for the entire compliment of passengers and crew one and a half times over.

She nodded slowly. "Passengers panicked and took off in them. Some of them were being fired off with just half a dozen people in. There were practically riots on the upper decks."

He shook his head in disbelief. "Shit. Tourist-class Muppets So they've left us behind to die? But there are people still aboard. There's us for a start, and I've seen others."

"They didn't care."

"Bastards," he spat, "Save their selfish skins without a care for anyone else."

"The world is full of them. I've spent a lifetime trying to beat them all. Trust me – it's a losing battle."

"So how do we get out of here?"

"The only way to survive now is to get in there and turn off the power. Everything. Until the Starliner is completely offline, that creature will find a way of surviving somewhere in the electrics," Dezza explained.

"Give the bastard no live circuit to hide in," added Philipa, smiling at him.

"You said it could move between energy and mass," David said slowly, "What's to stop it just sitting around as a thing?"

Dezza waved his hand. "No. Doesn't seem to work like that. On the *Cerberus* they nearly managed to shut everything down. It was forced to hibernate, but there was enough power to keep it alive. Without power it doesn't seem to be able to do anything."

"Sucking on the grid then," he said thoughtfully. "Only problem is that without power we're going to be out of luck too. No gravity, no air circulation or anything. The long range aerials were torn to hell when that lifepod crashed into us, so there's no way of calling for a rescue."

"We turn it all back on," said Dezza firmly.

David was taken aback. "Just turn it off and on again like an errant computer on your desk? I really don't think so."

"You have a better idea?" said Philipa harshly.

Without lifepods there was no way of getting off the Starliner. If they stayed, the creature would attack. If they managed to get the ship shut down – and nobody had *ever* tried that to the best of his knowledge anywhere other than in the safety of space dock – they would die unless they could turn it all back on. He did not even know if it was possible to turn half the systems back on without outside assistance. He saw the resigned look in Philipa's face, then looked to the expectant Dezza.

That man really thought they had a chance, and she was going to follow him to try and make it work whether they got help from him or not, he knew. She was that kind of woman – he had seen them all come and go, but she was stubborn enough to still be working the tourist cruises as a stewardess way past her prime.

"Okay," he said at last, "If you reckon it's the only shot we've got then I'm with you."

Dezza smiled. "So how do we get down into engineering?"

David looked at the removed grill and the darkness of the air conditioning trunking beyond. He did not fancy another crawl through those ducts.

"The ventilation is still running but there's no light in there. In that labyrinth we could end up anywhere. There are emergency access points that would get past the computers."

"Why do we need to do that?" demanded Philipa.

"That thing seems to have taken control of all the systems down there. It was closing hatches left, right and centre. If we want to get in, we have to do it unnoticed." He looked at Dezza. "I hope you know what you're doing."

*   *   *   *   *

At the lowest point of the stairwell the hatches were locked down. Dezza felt around the edges, looking for some way they could get a lever in and pry the seals apart. But there was no use; these hatches were made to withhold a vacuum in case of hull breach.

"We won't get through that," he sighed. He saw David looking over the control panel and added, "Any attempt to trip it will only attract its attention."

He stopped, and blinked. Of course! Why had he not thought of it before? He pushed David aside and pored over the panel.

"I thought you weren't interested in tripping it open?" said David.

Dezza waved him quiet. "I've got an idea. Instead of blundering in, why don't we flush the creature out?"

Philipa began to back away. "Hey, hold on now!" she protested, "That wasn't part of the deal. You really want to invite that damn thing out here? What will it do if it gets ahead of us?"

David looked over. "I already saw it kill the boy," he said calmly, "Maybe the lady is right."

"It feeds off the power," Dezza explained, "If we can disrupt that, we can get a breathing space and get into engineering before it knows what's hit it."

"We can't turn the ship's core grid off except in there," David warned again.

Dezza sighed – he wanted them to understand, but of course they had not been on the *Cerberus*. "We shorted the power on the *Cerberus* and it bought us time. If we use the same tactic here it should work."

He saw the idea register with the engineer.

"I get it." He snickered. "You know, the damnedest thing just crossed my mind. There's something I always wanted to do. There's the mother of all pools further down this deck if we can get to it."

"You're not going for a swim!"

"Nah, not my scene. But I've always fancied chucking a television into it. Real rock and roll shit."

"You're serious?" Philipa asked, not seeming to quite believe what he had said.

Dezza could not help but laugh. "Be my guest buddy. Lead the way."

It was like following a kid ready to do the biggest of schoolboy pranks. They had to backtrack once from a collapsed deck, but they found a way through and took it. The pool was in a gym level, like the one that Dezza had weight trained himself into the ground on. Even now looking over the silent empty gym equipment filled him with memories that he would rather have forgotten.

The gym led through to a changing room complex that could have easily housed nearly a hundred people at once with ease. Tiled in white with decorative scrollwork, its designers intended it to look vaguely Roman in its style. The lights burned brightly but their footsteps echoed alone, and any other people here had long departed.

There was a diagonal crack through one of the walls that had shed chunks of tiles to the floor. Other than that though the area seemed to have escaped unscathed, and had not even become tainted by the flows of dust.

Occasional piles of clothes neatly laid out on the benches hinted that there had been people here when hell had broken loose. What could spook people enough to make them run away without their clothes? Dezza could not help but wonder. He half expected to find tourists cowering in the cubicles, but the doors they passed were ajar and the changing areas beyond were empty.

The exits led through a foot pool and opened out onto a sandy beach. It took Dezza aback – he had not expected to see a Caribbean coast line accurately presented in a glass topped atrium so huge that it was difficult to tell where the coral reefs and palm trees ended and the walls began.

"Pretty impressive," he said, whistling in awe at the sight.

Even the waves were still lapping at the shore as if nothing had gone wrong elsewhere in the Starliner.

"No time to admire the view," urged David, "We need to find a way of giving the electrics a good dunking. Just make sure none of us is anywhere near the water when it all goes off."

"Remind me why we can't just jam a fork in a wall socket," Philipa asked, unconvinced.

"Because we need real juice that's at a high voltage." David pointed up to the roof of the atrium. "Up there will be a central feed piggybacking onto the main grid. No circuit breakers except on the high voltage – it's a direct line to the core."

Dezza found himself looking up at the vast roof of the atrium. He could see the stars outside faintly, but there was a warm blue glow that was somehow being projected across the curve of the dome, making it friendlier and like a pleasant day on Earth. They were lighting gantries up there, and that meant that there would be plenty of power sources. He squinted, trying to see, but it was deliberately set up so as to disguise any of the meant that made this whole place look like nothing more than an island paradise.

He pointed up to the lights. "Is there a way up onto the rig?"

David stroked his chin. "Should be. I've never been up there myself, but there will be a way out for maintenance. We'll need some heavy duty cabling – enough to go down into the water. Whoever throws it in had better hold on tight though, because when it blows it will fry anything in the water or nearby."

*   *   *   *   *

In the changing rooms they found storage and clearing lockers and ransacked them all. Mostly they contained nothing but an assortment of mops and buckets and the cleaning chemicals to go with them and the occasional spare uniform.

"This stuff's just junk," David moaned. He aimed a kick at a pile of mops and buckets and sent them flying across the changing rooms.

Philipa recoiled at the noise. "This isn't a game," she scolded.

He ignored her jibe and kept looking, but the lockers really did hold very little.

"There must be maintenance stuff already up there," Dezza surmised. He looked at David. "How do we get up to those lights?"

"Stairs around the other side – I'll show you."

He led them back out onto the sandy beach. It seemed surreal to see it all laid out without a soul in sight though he tried to ignore the fact that it would be unlikely to remain that way for long. The waves lapping at the beach began to roll in covered in foam; they seemed to be getting stronger. At first he thought it to be the wave machine going through a cycle, then he stopped as the sand began to shimmer and flatten under their feet.

"Tide's coming in," said Dezza.

The water was climbing up the beach with every wave and began to swamp some of the abandoned sun loungers along the shore.

"It shouldn't – there's only a fixed amount of water," said Philipa. She looked around, concern clear in her expression, "The whole beach is moving."

She was right. It was not the tide that was coming in, but the beach that was slipping out into the water. Already a gap had appeared along the top edge of the sand where it had dropped against the wall and faux rock escapement. Metal supports came into sight as the beach continued to slide.

Underfoot the sand seemed to swirl and flow like a liquid. He lifted his feet but each time he planted them down they sank in up to the ankles. The others too were struggling to avoid sinking in.

"Quicksand! Get back!" he shouted.

Dezza jumped and Philipa tried to. Where she stood gave way and she fell flat on her face. Before she could cry out the sand seemed to flow over her back and legs and suck her down. Around her sun loungers and umbrellas dipped and fell as the sand and sea consumed them all.

"Help!" she screamed.

Dezza reached out and grabbed her outstretched hands. From the safety of an exposed metal beam he leant across too. He felt her fingers on his and for a moment he thought he would not be able to get a grip. Dezza was slipping and could not hold her for long. Leaning as far as he dared he tried again and was rewarded by the feel of a handful of her jacket in his grip.

"Pull!" he shouted, and he and Dezza pulled together. The structure beneath them was vibrating now, and the water out in the vast pool had become oily and flat. The beach began to hiss as the sand moved faster. The sound became overpowering. Sand trickled from Philipa's back as she struggled to break free from the downward pull. Her legs reappeared, and as the two men strained she floundered to the edge of the exposed steel and pulled clear.

"That was too close for comfort," she gasped, looking back at the slithering sand.

The last of the sun loungers sank from view and only a handful of umbrellas remained, drifting about buried all the way to their garish coloured canopies.

A crack zinged across the faux rock escarpment behind them, and a shower of cement fragments rained down. David scrambled to one side, grabbing Philipa as he went. Dezza followed as fragments of the rock began to rain down and be consumed by the sand. With a rumble a palm tree descended, dislodged from above and the rocks peeled away drunkenly revealing the twisting structure behind.

David led them from one platform to the next as rocks began pinging all around them. The structure was shifting, under stress from the shaking; the décor of the Starliner had never been designed for this. He looked up to the arched dome high above and hoped that it might be better able to deal with the stresses. One crack in that and the whole Caribbean paradise could be sucked explosively into the vacuum of space.

But the rumbling began to subside and the sound of shattering rocks faded away. As they climbed the last of the mound that lined the beach end of the curved bay the ground had all but stopped vibrating and the water had lost its oily sheen as the light waves returned, though the sand of the beach remained strangely smooth.

There was a path that led across the top of a cliff and they followed it. Lined with palm trees and bushes it should have been a beautiful place to sit and watch the world go by below. But the soil that held the trees had cracked and moved, and several of the once fine plants now lay in tatters across the path leaving them to scramble carefully over.

In one place the path had slipped away, taken by the crumbling of the cliff's structure. Bare steel now poked out, covered only by a few fragments of cement and twisted reinforcing rods. They picked their way carefully over these. Finally they reached the end of the path. It opened out into a wide area that was flanked by a balcony rail. Halfway to the top of the dome, it afforded a view out over the entire beach world. Backed by a bar, it had many tables for tourists to sit and enjoy a quiet drink.

The quake had dislodged everything from behind the bar. The sweet smell of spilled liquor hung thick in the air and a slick of browns and yellows ebbed across the concrete flecked with fragments of broken glass. Tables had been upset, and the once pretty area looked like it had played host to a riot.

Dezza looked over bar. "No-one here. I guess they all made it out."

"What a waste of the finest scotch," David said quietly, shaking his head as he looked over the mess. More than two dozen bottles lay smashed amongst mounds of fractured glass. Every single bottle was a dead loss.

"No time to cry over spilt alcohol."

He saw that Philipa had climbed around and was going through the cupboards behind, gingerly trying to avoid the broken glass. She waved her hand at the other cupboards that lined the length of the bar.

"Get looking and see what you can find."

He had to admire the girl; she certainly could keep herself focussed when she needed to. Their searches turned up several lengths of electrical cable of the heavy-duty sort with large industrial plugs at both ends. Spooling them out one by one he measured their lengths – they were all standard ten metre reels designed for working maintenance equipment. Glaring at the lighting rigs that were still a good deal higher than the bar level, he gauged the distance down from them into the water. Must be around two hundred feet that they would need, he reckoned. That ought to give a bit of slack to get to any power sockets.

The lengths joined together end to end on their plugs. He discarded any that felt loose and pulled easily apart. If they came away whilst being lowered it would leave them too short to reach the pool. Some of the cables weren't as strong as he would have liked; as much as they searched the bar there were no more available; they would have to make these do.

The cleaning equipment designed to use the leads was too bulky for one man to carry. Instead David suggested that they find something else that could be botched into the plugs. A lamp from above the bar did the job with its lead hurriedly taped into the final open power socket on the makeshift reel.

Then he was ready. Hoisting the reel over a shoulder and tucking the light under the other.

"As soon as it goes in this place will light up like Chinese new year," said Dezza.

David nodded. "Once the power grid is shocked out, we make a move straight to engineering."

*   *   *   *   *

From the bar the first stage of the climb was pretty easy. A secluded metal grill ran further around the top of the cliff that surrounded the beach area from here. At several points it followed the contours up on stairs that were easy to climb. Once he reached the end of the walkway, however, the climb became much harder.

A ladder went up vertically, making up the last seventy or so feet to the overhead gantries. Sure, there probably was another easier way up there, but there was not the time to find it. At any rate, it would probably require access codes that David did not have.

A steel mesh surrounded the ladder in a gentle curve. Shielding his eyes from the glare of the lighting under the dome he squinted at the climb that lay before him. He would need at least one hand free to make that climb, and the cable and light he was carrying currently left him neither. Slinging the coil to the ground he rigged the light into the cable bundle then hoisted it back onto his shoulder. That left an arm free for climbing, as long as the bundle was not so big as to jam in the safety mesh around the ladder.

Thankfully it fit – just. He had to be careful not to let it snag, and it made the climb a slow and tiring one. On the flip side, whatever happened he would not have to bring the bundle back down with him.

It made for slow and difficult progress. Time and again the bundle would catch on the mesh and he would have to carefully wriggle around to free the cables, trying to not let go of them. If they fell they would unravel all the way down the ladder and he would have no hope of retrieving it. Each time he worked them free and heaved the coil back with aching hands onto shoulders that cried out in pain at the weight and awkward angles. Forcing his legs and arms to work together he pushed himself on; giving up was not an option he was prepared to entertain. He had no concept of how long had passed; it did not matter as long as he made it to the top. Then the steel safety cage opened out and at last he sprang up the last few steps onto the gantry.

It took a moment for him to regain his breath. His arms and legs felt shaky and he had no strength to his grip. Whilst he rested he took stock of the new surroundings. The gantry was wide enough for one man with equipment

184

to comfortably walk along it whilst on either side banks of powerful lights lay on projecting beams that were topped with the narrowest of walkways, protected by a single handrail designed only for clipping a safety cable to. He did not have one of those, and the thought that he might have to crawl out on one of those beams was not one he relished.

It was darker up here, despite the powerful glow of the lights that picked out the miniature world far below in the brightness of day. All the light was angled down and to the side, leaving the gantry tight against the curve of the dome and the starscape of space spread out across overhead. He expected it to be cold; usually pressed up tight against the Plexiglas screens it would be. Here though the heat given off from the lighting rigs was powerful and he was quickly drenched in sweat despite the leaching cold that tried to reach down from the dome a few feet above.

Leaving the bundle, he began to search the gantry for power sockets. But the power leads that led from the topside of the lights were fitted into sealed connectors and he had no tools that would loosen them. Tracing back along the gantry to the edge of the dome the walkway ended at a recess that contained a huge bank of consoles decorated in an array of small lights and switches. Beyond, settled into the darkness at the end of a short tunnel was the closed entrance to a freight lift.

Searching on his hands and knees under the console revealed no power sockets there. Angrily he banged his fist on the wall. How easy this plan had seemed far below in the bar with the others. Now he realised that without the right tools he was going to have a great difficulty in hooking the heavy coil of cabling that he had brought into anything. Even if he could find adapters and tools, he would still be faced with where to plug in. Back on the gantry he leant over the edge, trying to ignore the dizzying drop beneath to reach the back of one of the lights. The heat radiating off was stifling and when he touched the cable with his hand he recoiled from the surface heat.

He took off his top and wrapped it around his hands. Leaning back out he was able to get a grip around the cable and try and work it loose. The angle was awkward, but to his relief he felt the cable shift a little. The heat must have made the fitting expand, but with brute force it was working loose. Maybe there was no need for any special tools after all.

As the fitting worked loose there was a buzzing and the stench of ionised particles, then singed cloth. The light flickered beneath him then died, and he felt the heat suddenly drop as he let go of the cable in a reflex action. It dropped and swung just out of reach in the glare of the adjacent light. He looked at the material wrapped around his hands – it had singed in a crescent where it had got close to the edge of the connector. Better that than his hand, he decided. Cursing himself for not thinking about it sooner, he returned to the console and looked over it for the controls to switch out the bank of lights he had been working on.

He found the right one and the first twenty metres of lights faded together. Retrieving the swinging cable he tested the pins gingerly with a screwdriver wrapped in his top for insulation. As the blade crossed the pins there was no flash, confirming that the power was dead. Now he could work to jury-rig a connection between the cable and the coil that he had slaved to bring up the ladder.

*   *   *   *   *

Dezza felt the pang of jealousy to see Philipa so easily getting on with searching the bar area, looking for anything they could use. He would have offered to help her, but he was not sure what exactly he could do. Best to leave her to her own devices, he decided. At any rate, the smell of spilt liquor was not one he particularly enjoyed being around. It was a temptation he would rather not have had, even if it looked as if all the bottles had been well and truly broken. There was always the chance of finding one undamaged and it was a temptation not worth exposing himself to. The fear had made a big enough impact on him for him to realise that even without thinking about it, he had sat himself at the furthest table from the bar. If only he could have found some resolve in the last few years to have always been like this. Maybe then he would not have pissed his life away into the gutter.

He tried to turn his thoughts away from the slippery slope that they were leading to. He had been down that path many times before, and it scared him to think what was at the bottom of that pit of depression. It was not somewhere he wanted to be. It made him feel bad to feel the envy inside him as he watched Philipa ducking behind the bar and bringing out odds and ends. As he watched she heaved onto the counter a first aid box and flicked it open to check its contents.

    *   *   *   *   *

The sound of the explosion caught them both off guard. One minute he was watching her carefully laying rolls of bandages out across the bar top, and the next he was sprawling on the floor amongst shards of broken glass with the table rolling beside him. His heart raced wildly as he scanned around for Philipa. The bandages were scattered across the floor and she was nowhere to be seen.

"Philipa!" he called out.

He heard a whimper from behind the woodwork and scrabbled across the floor on all fours ignoring the glass and the stench of whiskey. At the end of the bar he saw her huddled on the floor, grasping her head with a roll of bandage, stemming a trickle of blood.

"Are you all right?"

She nodded, distracted by the bleeding. He went to take a look, to see that she really was all right when a second explosion rocked the floor. An uprooted palm tree branch whipped across the bar above them, showering them with more glass.

Dezza raised himself up carefully to peer across the bar top. His first thoughts had been that maybe the dome had given way. If that had happened they would need to get out of here fast. But the air pressure had not dropped and he could feel no difference to the pressure. To his surprise he saw a wall of mist rolling across the water from the far side of the pool. Several of the lighting gantries above were no longer on, giving the whole atrium an air of a brewing storm.

"Stay under cover," he hissed to Philipa. Without waiting for her reply he darted around the end of the bar to the edge of the balcony.

The view was clearer from here. Looking down he could see the mist had nearly reached the beach. It looked as if it was spreading from a point on the far side, but it was hard to pinpoint the exact spot it came from. As it hit the beach it rolled up in a fine haze, then headed upwards over the cliff until it began to come through the gaps in the balcony.

It had a curious smell that reminded him of dust and rotting garbage and it felt humid too. As he watched, the centre of the mist cloud seemed to reach up and swirl and for a moment he thought he saw a figure with arms and a head forming. Then the mist moved around and the shape melted away.

A scream echoed across the water. He cringed at the sound – had David fallen from the gantry? A part of him wanted to rush down to the beach and help, but the more wary and suspicious part of him held him back and made him crouch unseen a little longer.

Lightning arced across the cloud in a jagged finger of brightness and he realised that this was not the result of David's work on the gantry. The cry came again, this time from a little further around the edge of the pool. Something flickered in between two columns and he was certain there was a figure of a man. Then the stutter of gunshots rang out, and he knew it most certainly was not David.

The mist cloud rolled and bunched and he felt the humidity in the air change direction as the haze sucked back to the centre of the cloud with an eerie precision. A shiver ran down his spine as he watched and his blood ran cold. The mist was forming into a form that rippled and crackled with blue arcs of static. It was not a mist cloud anymore; it was the creature.

An arm of white reached out in a ghostly shape through the columns. Gunfire stuttered again and he saw the figure of a man darting past the edge of the beach where the sand had settled in the quake leaving exposed steel showing. With a feeling of shock, Dezza recognised him – Ventura. He wanted to stand up and shout to him, but he knew the creature would turn its wrath to him too. Dezza looked desperately to the gantries above. Where was David?

A splash echoed from the water and he looked back to see Ventura floundering in the shadows. Any icy feeling clawed Dezza's mind – if the cable dropped now then Ventura would be a dead man whether the creature got to him or not.

He dashed back to the bar. Philipa peered white faced from the edge, clutching the bandage to her forehead.

"What's going on?"

"Stay here. It's Ventura."

"Ventura!" she cried, trying to stand up.

Dezza held her down. "The creature too. I've got to do something. Ventura's in the water."

The realisation flickered across Philipa's face, and she held a hand to her open mouth in shock. "But the power cable? " Her words faltered.

Dezza nodded. "I know. I'm going to try and get him out before it's too late."

"The creature?" she squealed.

He waved her back. "I'll take my chances," he hissed.

The stairs hurdled by three at a time underneath him as he ran. He heard Philipa shout, but did not look back. Something crashed behind him and immediately the creature was around him too. Everything went white, then something buzzed in his ears, and the cloud was gone.

A deathly quiet consumed him. He could hear the far off sound of an explosion, but it was like someone had muted it into the distance. There was a flicker in front of him, and a figure poured itself from the air and coalesced.

He fell backwards onto the steps in his haste not to run into it. It lunged forward, the arms turning to tentacles that thrashed around wildly. A palm tree got in the way and split in two as if nothing more than a matchstick.

He braced himself, feeling the air move as the creature took on a firm physical form and lashed out. With his eyes scrunched tightly shut he tensed for the pain that he knew would come. But it did not. Cautiously easing an eye open he looked up to where the creature had been, wondering for a moment if he might have imagined it.

The creature was still there and the tentacles thrashed around wildly, but they seemed to be caught in a paralysis that had stopped them inches from Dezza's face. As he watched, the tentacles turned to tendrils of mist and receded in on themselves. In their place a figure of a man formed bent over and glaring at the ground. A flash of recognition shot through Dezza's mind and he leant forward, almost not believing what he was seeing.

"Tubs?" he asked, uncertain.

The figure looked up with sudden move that sent a wave of fear cursing again through Dezza's body. But the creature did not morph anymore, and the eyes that regarded him were filled with a sad emotion that he knew could not be the creature that he had met before.

"Tubs?" he asked again.

The body pulsated, not quite fully formed, but the face remained stable as if in a deep concentration. Finally the lips moved, and a voice that sounded strange floated from the apparition in a voice that Dezza had not heard in many years.

"Dezza?"

"You recognise me?"

"Yes." The voice was strained and sounded somehow distant.

Dezza realised that whilst the head remained stable, the body was morphing wildly and thrashing as if trying to escape some unseen force that was holding it at bay.

"I cannot hold it back for long," the voice of Tubs hissed hesitantly. "The creature's mind is strong and it works to fight me." Tubs' head looked up, and the expression flickered for a moment. It was only a split second, but the eyes in Tubs' face changed and for that moment he saw the evil eyes of the unadulterated creature looking back at him.

"Go. Quickly," Tubs said, his voice ever more hesitant, "I cannot distract the creature for long. When it turns its full strength against me I cannot fight it."

"What happened on the *Cerberus*?" Dezza demanded.

"It can take my body, but it will never have my soul," Tubs said defiantly.

In an instant Tubs' head began to ripple and change. The mouth opened, as if to scream, but the only sound was the banshee wail that Dezza had heard so many times before. Heeding Tubs' words he rolled over and launched himself down the last of the stairs. Behind him, the creature became tendrils of mist again, that thrashed around trying to regain their form. He did not wait to see what form that might be.

On the sand of the beach he saw the footsteps leading across the otherwise smooth surface and knew that only Ventura could have made them. The sand was hard to run on and sucked at his feet with every step. But he made it across to the water's edge and glanced again up to the dark patch on the gantry above, hoping that David had seen him and would not drop the cable just yet.

The water was warm, but he still shivered at the thought of how close to death he might be. Around an outcrop of rocks that shielded off an islet he saw the ghostly shape of the creature scything through the water and somewhere beyond it was Ventura. Hearing the crackle of another gunshot, Dezza knew he was still alive. Wading into the deeper water he forged to the edge of the rocks as fast as he could, sending waves racing across the millpond smooth water.

Beyond the rocky outcrop Ventura was there, but he was fighting a losing battle. The creature had formed into a bulbous mass with limbs that thrashed at great many odd angles. At its extremities it did not have a clear defined form, but faded out into the mist as if it and the vapour was one and the same thing.

It had the captain and was rolling him over and dragging him into the water that had been whipped up into white foam. The gunshots had made no mark and even as Dezza watched he saw Ventura's finger tug desperately at the trigger. He ducked, in case the shot came close, but there was no sound; the chamber was empty.

Perhaps feeling victory, the creature threw the captain back and forth until the gun flew uselessly from arms that waved under the onslaught like a ragdoll's. A blue flicker of static discharge crackled across the surface of the creature and over the water until Dezza could feel every hair on his head standing on end. Ventura hung limp in its grasp, but it seemed to stop until Dezza realised with a leaping heart that it had seen him watching it. In a moment the creature was around him too, but it seemed to have stretched itself too far. He felt the electric touch of its presence coursing through him as the blue charge enveloped, but he had enough strength to break free and dive under the water. When he came to the surface the creature was thrashing around, maybe looking for him.

Dezza looked desperately around and saw Ventura floating dazed, in the water. He grabbed hold of an arm and with all his strength managed to pull him to the rocky edge of the islet and roll him onto its flat top.

He felt the touch of the creature from behind, but did not dare to look around. Any second he expected to feel the tug and the deadening blow as the creature found its strength and struck him down. Instead there was a far off shout from the cliff top above. Philipa!

In a flurry of activity the creature was torn between Dezza and the captain, and this new human who had stood up at the top of the cliff. As he rolled onto the rocky ledge clear of the water, his heart sank. Why had Philipa done that? She had brought danger upon herself.

From the corner of his eye he saw something fine drop from the top of the dome. It took a second to realise what it was; then he remembered David and the plan they had had all along.

Scrunching his eyes shut he waited for the moment. Then that moment came, and he saw the world light up through the inside of his eyelids. The scream the creature made seemed to go on forever, but it could not have been for more than a split second. There was a smell of ionised particles in the air, then the scream faded and so did the blinding light.

*   *   *   *   *

It had come along the walkway as he had finished the connection. Far below the fighting had raged; too far away to see clearly, but with sounds earnest enough to tell him that the creature had arrived. As the last connection had been made he had retreated to the console. To his shock the hologram he had seen in the engineering spaces was there, looking at him with that piercing stare. It had seemed to consider him for a moment before glancing over the walkway. He had not remembered the figure changing, but it did. In the blink of an eye it was the figure of Tom, the boy, standing there before him. Perfect in every detail except one; the eyes were still the darkened holes into the psyche of an alien creature.

The console had been easy to reactivate. The creature had not seemed to realise what he was doing, and watched impassively from Tom's form as David had made the circuits live again. It had seemed to David that the creature was distracted, perhaps by what was going on far below. There came from below a splash and a cry and the stutter of gunfire. David cursed – if they were in the water then they would be dead.

The creature had taken hesitant steps along the gantry, as if too late realising David's plan and was trying to find a way to walk in a form unfamiliar to it. But he had reached the coil again and in a second had heaved the bundle onto the guard rails and looked the creature in the eye.

"Give my regards to the other side," he had hissed, and leapt clear as the coil had unravelled into the drop.

The creature lunged, but the blinding flash had erased it in an instant. As the echoes faded, the creature was gone and David had found himself alone on the walkway with the cold leaching through from the dome above.

*   *   *   *   *

Water dripped from the rocks, but it was too dark after the suddenness of the flash for Dezza to see where the noise came from. He remembered the creature and the fight they had had, and groaned. Every inch of his body ached and protested, but he was still alive and despite the cold of the water, he felt good.

He heard Ventura groan alongside him – the man was still alive, though Dezza knew it had been close. Another few seconds and the shock of the power spike would have fried them both.

It took a few minutes for his eyes to get used to the gloom. To his surprise he saw Ventura was sitting up, looking intently at the mangled remains of the photograph he kept of his brother.

"You okay?" Dezza asked, hesitantly.

Ventura looked up. "Yes." He seemed to consider the picture a moment longer, then tucked the remnants back into a pocket. His eyes harboured a faraway look.

"You look like you have seen a ghost," Dezza said slowly.

Ventura nodded. "I guess I did," he said at last.

He looked across, and Dezza saw that the burning hatred that the captain had always had before for him was gone.

"I saw my brother, in the corridors after the collapse. It looked like him, but I knew in an instant that it was nothing more than a facsimile. It taunted me with his voice, but it was not alive."

"You saw the creature. On the *Cerberus* it defeated us one by one. It feeds off our minds and our emotions."

Ventura snapped out of his daze and looked to Dezza as if seeing him for the first time.

"I guess I owe you thanks for saving me. I really thought I was gone."

Ventura looked up at the stars that were visible through the dome. A narrow thread dangling from the gantry glowed with the last gasp of flames where the power had arced into the water.

"What happened?"

"We shorted the power grid. You were damn lucky I got you out of the water in time."

Dezza heard a scrabbling on the rocks behind them and turned to see Philipa approaching.

"Did you see that?" she gasped.

"Hard to miss," Ventura replied. He stood up and shook water from his hair. "We ought to get going."

"It's good to see you back, captain," she beamed, "I was scared we lost you in the collapse."

"It takes more than that to keep me from kicking some butt."

"So I saw." She looked to Dezza. "You were close – too close."

Dezza waved her comment away. It sent a cold shiver through him to think about how close they had come. "Let's get David and get out of here before that thing recovers."

She looked at him, shocked. "Recovers? I thought we killed it?"

He could not help but shake his head. He wished that it could have been destroyed so easily, but bitter memories told him that it would just provide a lull. "Sure we've sent it off to lick its wounds, but it will be back. Quicker too if it works out what we're up to."

15

Whole sections of the Starliner were coming back into life as the power grids cycled back online. Through the vast Plexiglas dome of the pool atrium, visible now the lighting gantries were dead, a thousand porthole lights had winked back looking like stars being switched on in the sky. But they carried a more sinister undertone. For every section that the computer reactivated, it was a sign that the creature would not be that far behind.

The group had left the pool atrium quickly. If the creature were to search them out then surely it would be the first place it would try, returning to haunt them. So they had headed through the deserted changing rooms by the light of flashlights they had scavenged. After a brief discussion they split into two groups to go their separate ways. The creature would come looking; Dezza was certain of that. Ventura and David would head for the engineering levels whilst Dezza and Philipa had the unenviable task of attracting the creature away. That was Dezza's theory anyway. He had made it sound so simple, but David had seen the look of terror etched on Philipa, though she had kept quiet and gone along reluctantly.

*　　　*　　　*　　　*　　　*

At the bottom of the stairwell David and Ventura came upon the locked down airtight door rolled into place and sealed. The control panel was dead, just like the last they had checked.

"Every one locked down tight," Ventura muttered.

"Try another?"

Ventura shook his head. "No. They'll all be like this if that crazy son-of-a-bitch Dezza is right." He looked over the hatch's seal and tested the rubber seal with a finger, though David knew as well as he did that it was designed to hold back the vacuum of space. Nothing short of a small explosive charge would open it without power assistance.

"Tool locker."

Ventura led him back to an alcove on the mezzanine hidden away behind the bottom flight of stairs. The door wasn't locked and inside was an assortment of pry bars and other basic equipment.

"How do you know all this is here?" asked David, his eyes glittering over the haul of new-looking tools that still had their factory-fresh cellophane wrappers.

"I'm the captain – it's my job to know what every compartment holds."

David whistled through his teeth in awe. "I'm the engineer and even I don't know every compartment. You must have spent every night in your cabin poring over schematics."

Ventura ducked behind the locker and felt for the edges of a hidden panel. Under pressure from his fingertips the covering slid back and David watched with amazement as a hidden chamber opened up on the other side.

"More or less," Ventura said, "Hey, it's coming in handy."

David shrugged and ducked through into the open hatch after the captain. "Sure, but you can't pick up chicks with a detailed knowledge of blueprints."

"Depends on the chicks. Most chicks just dig the uniform of a captain. Apparently the shipping line loses more captains to being married off to rich eligible spinsters than you would imagine."

"No kidding? So where's your rich trophy wife?"

"Haven't found her."

The small compartment looked more like an emergency store. There were dim emergency lights, but they did little after the glare of the outside mezzanine had dazzled his vision.

"Shit, I can't see in here," he exclaimed.

Ventura grunted. Somewhere in the darkness a locker door rattled before he felt torches being thrust into his hands.

"Take this and use it."

It had fresh power packs and worked first time. In the small space the light was pretty effective.

"Shine it over here."

In the light Ventura slung tools from the locker into two belts and slid one across. David fastened it quickly about his waist as the captain did the same with his.

"When we get down into the machine rooms there's no telling what we'll need, and we may not find it to hand. This ought to be enough."

David flashed the beam over the small low-roofed compartment. Along one side the mesh-fronted lockers contained a utilitarian mix of safety equipment and rudimentary tools. At the other side of the room fire suits hung like lifeless dummies waiting for a disaster that their designers hoped would never come. At the end of the small chamber, sat squarely in the middle of the floor was a circular hatch bolted shut.

Ventura saw him trying to read the warning plaque set into its lid. "Back door into the engineering spaces," he said.

"How do you know about these places?"

Ventura shuffled to the back of the chamber and began to prise the dog clips off a hatch set out in the floor. "Blueprints make good bedtime reading?"

"You don't get out much."

Ventura grunted and started springing the clips that held the hatch tight in its frame. They were old and probably had never been used in all the time the *Persia* had been in service. How long was that? David thought back; she had been considered old when he had first joined her crew.

"Give me a hand here." Ventura waved him to the hatch.

Putting the torch carefully on the floor he strained to free them off. He was tempted to use a hammer from the tool belt, but as soon as he slid it out the captain waved him to a stop.

"No. That will vibrate through miles of steel structure. No point in advertising where we are."

So he slid the hammer back and struggled on with the clips. Just as he thought they would not go, the last flicked open and he cursed as the metal caught his fingers. As he rolled back, a central piece in the hatch popped up unexpectedly and he recoiled to the edge of the chamber.

"What was that?"

Ventura eased himself in for a closer look. Picking up the torch he played its light across the new raised piece.

"Just a safety device," he said at last, "Tells us the pressure differential before we pop this thing open. Better than stepping into the backdraft of a fire, or worse still the vacuum of a hull breach."

"Cool toy."

"No toy. You wouldn't want to pop a hatch onto a hole into space."

"I guess that's true enough."

Ventura checked the raised piece. "All clear. Pressure normal – there's an atmosphere in there and it isn't on fire. Let's get this thing open."

David shuffled forward and eased his fingers under the lip. With a bit of gentle persuasion the hatch moved upwards and clicked neatly to one side leaving a hole down into another chamber below. Light flooded up bright enough that they could both turn off their torches.

"Engineering is still live," whispered David.

"Yeah. Lights are on – let's see who's home."

Without waiting for a reply Ventura swung his legs over the lip and eased down to drop onto the deck below. David waited for him to give the all clear than soundlessly dropped through to join him.

*   *   *   *   *

After so long in the dark finding their way by torchlight the sudden brightness came as a shock. One minute the *Persia*'s corridors were dead and the next section after section of the corridor lights flicked on. He saw Philipa's unease.

"It hasn't found us yet," he tried to reassure her.

"It's cold."

She was right. It was possible that without the air circulation systems running, the decks with a power outage would have quickly lost their heat, but a vessel would be better insulated than this. In the new light his breath curled in front of him in the air, as did Philipa's.

This corridor was completely untouched by the destruction and the dust that they had seen elsewhere. It was strange to see it stretching out with its plush fittings looking as if the cleaners had only just left.

He pulled a chair from an alcove where it might have been intended for weary passengers on the walk to their cabins to rest and pushed it beneath an air conditioning vent. Climbing up on it he pulled his head level with the vent checking for a draft.

There was nothing coming through. Licking a finger he checked again to be certain, but there was no movement at all. Pressing his ear to the panel there was no sounds in the ducting behind.

"Air circulation is off line," he said at last.

"Meaning?"

He jumped down off the chair. "I don't know. Maybe the power spike caused damage to the systems. Without an engineer to physically reset the breakers maybe some things won't come back on."

She shivered and hugged her arms to her sides, glancing up and down the corridor. "Something feels wrong. I think I liked it better when the lights were off."

He shivered too, but not just from the chill in the air. It had felt cold like this on the *Cerberus*. Of course that ship had been a derelict, cast adrift without crew or passengers for nearly a century. But the same feeling was here aboard the *Persia* where it did not belong.

"Keep moving. Walking will keep us warm," he said, trying to keep her spirits up, but it was difficult when his own mind was filled with doubts.

"You really want to attract this thing's attention?" she said hesitantly after they had gone no more than a few steps.

He tried to sound confident. "If we are going to give the others a clear run, then that's what we have to do."

Her face flushed with anger. "You never stopped to ask me. You never bothered to ask whether I wanted in on this. What makes you think I want to die?" Her voice was raised now and tears welled in her eyes.

He tried to comfort her, but she pulled away from him.

"Leave me alone. Bastard! I should have known you were trouble from the moment I set eyes on you. Why I got involved I don't know. Emma warned me, and I didn't listen. Now she's gone. Everybody's gone."

"There might be others still alive. We can help them," he tried to reason.

"Help them my goddamn backside! We can't even help ourselves half the time. I've been chased, dropped in a lift shaft, nearly crushed and damn near electrocuted. And that's just for starters. Is this how you planned to show me a good time? Is that the usual night's entertainment that a girl can expect from Mr. Desmond Booth?"

He thought of the moment their eyes had first met on the shuttle. "I don't know what I planned," he muttered, avoiding eye contact with her. "Certainly not this. I wanted it to be normal – I didn't want Tubs' message to be true." A part of him wished he had never come – but then, it would have still happened with or without him. At least it gave him the chance to face his demons. Not that he really thought he wanted to.

She sobbed, louder than before. A part of him wanted to comfort her and make her happy again; he had preferred it when she was happy. But it would do no good, he knew.

She sat on the chair at the side of the corridor and refused to talk to him or follow him.

"The others need our help," he said softly.

"Do they?" she snapped.

He did not answer. Instead he began to move away down the corridor.

"Where are you going?" she called out after him. He could hear the waver in her voice. She might have argued with him, but she did not want to be left on her own.

"Getting on with what I have to do," he called back, never breaking stride.

The patter of her footsteps came quickly down the corridor and he smiled as she drew level with his side.

She still would not walk too close but she was going to come with him. He had not wanted to leave her behind; at least now he did not have to. He would have gone back if she had refused to move. Just so long as she didn't know that he would.

*   *   *   *   *

The corridor ended at a huge open lobby. Comfortable leather suites and small drinks tables were arranged here in a semi circle facing the bank of elevator shafts that lined one wall, for passengers to wait on the arrival of their lift. There was no-one here now, but a neatly folded newspaper and a half empty glass of water showed that someone had been. Dezza took a closer look at both and sniffed the glass – soda water; it was flat now. Whoever had been here had been gone a while and would be unlikely to return. It was a strange reminder of how normal things had been right up until the creature had come aboard. Where was the passenger who had sat sipping their water and reading their paper? He did not like to think – if they were lucky they had made it to one of the lifepods.

"We missed the crowd," he said out loud.

Philipa didn't answer. She was so quiet that a warning feeling told Dezza that something was wrong. He looked around the lobby for her, and did not see her.

"Philipa?" he called out. Had he left her behind in the corridor?

"Over here," came a voice from behind the furthest leather sofa.

He breathed easier. "Shit. Don't do that to me."

"You'll have to try harder than that." Her head bobbed up above the top of the sofa. "Come look at this."

Her urgency set off warning bells. At the end of the sofa he saw the feet sprawled out at awkward angles and knew that the calm normality of the corridor and lobby were hiding much more than met the eye.

"Dead?" he asked slowly, kneeling at her side.

"Yes. But look at the way he died."

She traced along the outline of the man's clothes, and Dezza realised that the body was bent in the wrong direction. Not once, but several times. "No man's spine curves like that."

She looked concerned. "You remember when they brought the engineer back in through the airlock? It looked like he had been crushed. This man is exactly the same. It's like something squeezed him. Hard."

She stood up and looked around the lobby nervously. "There's nothing here that could have done that, and he didn't get here afterwards on his own."

"What are you saying?"

"Look, I don't know how your creature works, but no human did this to him. The monster's here!" she hissed.

A shiver ran through him. How long had the man been lying behind the sofa? He checked the neck and pulled back in surprise. "Skins still slightly warm. This can't have happened more than thirty minutes ago maybe. But I'm still not totally convinced."

"What do you want to convince you," she stormed, "A bear hug from this thing until your ribs explode? Smell the coffee, Dezza!"

He was about to scold her; to tell her to shut up and stop getting carried away. Hell, it had seemed like the natural response. But the words never made it out as the lights in the lobby flickered once, then died away to nothing. A rumble echoed from far away down the corridor to the lobby.

"Dezza?" Philipa's voice whispered, subdued. "What was that?"

He felt around in the darkness, trying to remember where exactly she had been before the lights had failed.

He tripped on something and fell heavily to the floor and swore.

"What happened?" Her voice sounded stressed, and he heard her fumbling around in the darkness trying to reach him.

"Relax," he reassured her as he picked himself up, "I just tripped, that's all."

Delicately he swept his foot out until it brushed against the object he had tripped on. It was just the corner of one of the low tables. He felt around with his hands and his fingers touched glass for a moment.

"Shit."

The glass bumped unseen to the floor, not breaking but spreading the flat soda water across the carpet with barely a sound. So much for the dead man's drink.

A hand fumbled in his own and he heard Philipa squeal in shock and knew that he had found her. Pulling her tight he shushed in her ear "It's just me."

Her hand nestled in his and squeezed tightly.

"I don't like this," he heard her say, "What if the lights don't come back on? What do we do?"

It was a barrage of questions that he did not have answers to. But he tried to reassure her anyway.

"Forget the stiff. Feel around until we reach the walls and see if we can find our way around to the lift cars. There should be emergency kits inside them in a locker; there always is. There will be torches."

Feeling her steady grip, he took her with him slowly, feeling out with his free hand waving it like a blind man in front of him. They stumbled on the edges of sofas once before he found the cool, hard feel of the wall. He tried to strain his eyes, to see something. The darkness was so complete that it played tricks with his mind. It was almost like there were walls and doorways there, but when he moved towards them they dissolved away; tricks of his mind.

Inching along the wall he tried to remember which way the lifts had been. They had been opposite the passageway in. But they had moved around a lot since then, and there was nothing to hint which way they were now.

There was a rumble in the darkness, far away but closer than the last time. He felt the adrenaline spike in his body in time to the bass growl.

"It's getting closer," Philipa squeaked.

"I know. Just keep moving."

The rumble did not die away, but instead grew in volume and intensity until Dezza could feel the floor begin to shake under his feet. The lights flickered again, and in that instant he saw in photographic relief the horror in Philipa's face as she stood beside him. Behind her he saw the doors of three sets of lifts. Then the light faded to shadows again.

"Over here."

He dragged Philipa in the direction he could remember, trying his best to think and concentrate. The air began to move in a breeze and he could almost feel the sensation that something was coming up behind them.

The lights flickered and flashed again, this time remaining on but dimmed for a few seconds. It was all he needed to get Philipa to the lifts and jab at the buttons on the central control panel before the lights in the lobby died again.

To his surprise the fascia around the button lit up and he saw his hand and the ghostly outline of Philipa illuminated in the feeble glow. From somewhere behind the wall the came the sound of machinery kicking into motion.

He could smell the dust now that had been stirred up in the air. It made his eyes smart and he had to rub at them with the back of a hand and it caught the back of his throat setting off a choking splutter as he fought against the acrid taste. It made Philipa cough and retch too.

The motor whine slowed and came to an end. For an agonising few seconds there was no sound, and Dezza started to think that maybe it had been too good to be true and that the lift had failed just like the rest of the electrics in the lobby. Mimicking his thoughts the light in the fascia flickered and died, leaving darkness around them. A bell chimed sounding so out of place against the background rumble. Then the doors in front of them slid back revealing the light inside a lift car.

He stepped forward, but Philipa hesitated and held back.

"The lift is safe," he said quickly, "It isn't going to fall."

She looked him squarely in the eye, her eyes pleading with him. "Are you sure? I've had the optimism to take promises at face value ground out of me today."

In the reflection of the light from the lift car he pointed in the direction of the approaching rumble. Already the bass tones were becoming edged with something more sinister, which wailed and screamed just as they had heard at the pool under the dome.

"You saw the body on the floor; we have to get out of here."

"Damn you!" she cried, but he felt her resistance slacken and she let him pull her into the lift car.

The dust was swirling strongly in the air now. It hung like smoke in the lights within the lift and left a fine white film on the glass of the car's mirrored walls. Dezza scanned down the control panel.

"Push a button, any button!" Philipa screamed behind him.

He felt the air moving from the lobby, suddenly changing direction and taking on a sentient humidity that made the skin crawl up his back. Looking to the door he saw the shadowy forms of furniture in the lobby and the shape of the walls. Beyond them, from the black opening that led to the corridor, he saw the dust start to twirl and coalesce into shapes that dust could never naturally fall into and he knew the creature had found them.

He jabbed at the buttons – any level to take them as far as they could get from this creature. The doors began to respond, but they slid with an excruciating slowness as the shape in the lobby folded inwards and ghostly limbs and tentacles began to flop around the furniture. One bulbous limb that seemed to be covered in green sucker cups slid across the carpet towards them. The creature let off a banshee wail, so loud in the gloom that Dezza had to reach up and cover his ears with his hands. The limb found its mark and caressed the edges of the closing doors triggering them to open again. Still it continued forward as it probed for them both.

"Do something!" Philipa screamed, moving as far as she could into the back of the car.

Dezza dodged the limb as it felt in his direction, stepping neatly over it then jumping to the side as it came back. The searching limb threatened to stop the doors a second time, but at the last moment Dezza aimed a kick and managed to push it clear before it could react. The creature hidden somewhere in the lobby, let out a squeal the sound of a stuck pig. Then the doors shut, and Dezza heard the thump on the outside of the door.

"Jesus. That was close."

"Too close," gasped Philipa.

He looked at her; she cowered in a corner hugging her knees with her arms. Tears were welling in her eyes. He went to comfort her, but she thrashed out at him making him keep his distance.

"Stay back. I don't want to be touched by anyone or anything today. I am not having a good day."

He listened to the fading sounds of the creature somewhere several decks above them.

"We have to get out from the lift as soon as it reaches the top floor," he said matter-of-factly, "Now it knows, it's going to follow."

"That's what you wanted," she spat.

He ignored the intended insult. "If it keeps it away from the others until they can shut the Starliner down, then we'll have done all we need."

She did not reply.

The lift came to a halt as the last button on the panel illuminated. He felt the car rock, and waited the agonising seconds before the doors rocked open. He had expected more darkness, but the corridor that the doors opened onto were bright and well lit making him hesitate a second before he darted out. Untouched by any hint of dereliction, even Muzak still played softly in the background, and he could feel the steady healthy breeze from the air conditioning system.

Its normality was unnerving. It was just like everything else on the Starliner had never happened. It was a large lobby, set out with furniture just like the last and it looked like there ought to be people here, sipping their gin and tonics and going about their relaxation. But the lobby was deserted and the corridors that led off it were empty too.

Philipa followed him from the lift car cautiously. As she cleared the door he reached back inside and pulled open a locker hidden discretely by the control panel. Inside there were torches and a harness all neatly clipped in place. Ignoring the harness he levered out the torches and tossed one to Philipa.

"Take this. We might need them."

Then reaching back inside he hammered a dozen of the floor buttons at random and dodged neatly back out as the doors slid shut. That would ensure that the lift went to several different decks before it finally came to a halt. If the creature had any true sentience and logic, that would at least leave it guessing as to where exactly they had got out. He hoped that it would be enough.

*   *   *   *   *

The upper machinery levels were strangely clean and tidy with every computer terminal sat cycling through pre-programmed routines. But there were signs that something was not quite right. Here and there the personal effects of crewmen who had been forced to depart their stations became clear the deeper Ventura looked. On that console a mug of tea, half-empty and stone cold, sat next to the crumbs of a half eaten biscuit. Over there a jacket lay draped on the back of a swivel chair. There were no bodies to be found. Maybe that was a good thing; he did not know that he could stomach the deaths of more of those he was responsible.

They travelled through several corridors and down a level before seeing any crewmen. Legs protruded from a side room, lying at an angle that no living person would tolerate and the smell of death lingered in the air, musty and sweet. Air conditioning had purged it from creeping into the corridor, but in the side room it overpowered the usual smells of machine oil and paint. There were more bodies in here too. Stepping carefully into the gloom he looked over a dozen consoles that lay bent and burnt. Of the bodies, none were properly recognisable. An occasional bloodied limb here and there and scraps of uniform were all that remained.

His feet splashed on something sticky on the floor and he fought the urge to throw up, knowing that it was human. Every time he breathed in his nostrils filled with the stink of charred flesh. The smell could have easily been mistaken for the smell of hot pork scratchings. But there was no hiding its true origin. The dead bodies made it real, and added a greater sense of urgency to what they were trying to do.

"There's nothing gained in lingering."

He looked around and saw David's silhouette at the doorway, watching him impassively.

"I just wanted to see if there were any survivors," he replied blankly. The engineer shuffled nervously on his feet and they moved on, more sombre than before.

The closer they got to the main drive room, the more tense the atmosphere felt. It seemed strange to think. Then it struck him that there was a hum, almost but not quite out of hearing range, that was definitely getting louder. He hadn't really noticed it before, but now he thought about it, maybe it had been there in the background all the time. It gave him a sense of foreboding.

"Can you hear that?" he whispered.

David stopped and listened. "Yeah, sure. That's the main drive cores," he said with a nod.

"Do they always sound like that?"

"They're pulling quite a load," said David, "That's why we've got to shut them down."

They moved on, treading with caution. The corridors in this section seemed darker than before, unless it was a trick of the light. Ventura looked up at the light fittings and saw that the bulbs looked somehow more yellow. Or was it just his imagination?

At the next bulkhead David waved him to a halt. Then the engineer crept to the edge of an open hatch and looked through. The seconds went by until Ventura grew impatient. Just what was the engineer doing?

"What's up?" he hissed.

"Just looking for the hologram."

"Are you expecting one?"

The engineer added an explanation. "It killed the apprentice I came in here with. It isn't just the ship's hologram anymore; it's like it's been possessed. Watch out for it."

"You think it will really be in there waiting for us?" Ventura demanded, finding it hard to believe that a hologram could kill.

"It just sucked him in and there was nothing left. I'm not going to risk that happening for me; not for any man." In his eyes Ventura saw the look of a man who had faced up to death and felt that he had only just escaped. The engineer was deadly serious.

"Okay," he conceded.

*   *   *   *   *

The little voice that sang was so out of place that at first Dezza thought that it could have been part of the annoying Muzak. Only when the tracks changed, was it clear that the singing was something else as it just carried on following its own tune.

His first thought was that his ears were playing tricks on him. Stress had a curious effect, and it might not have been the first time that his mind had led him into believing something that was not. He remembered the nightmares and shuddered at the thought of them.

Philipa could hear it too so it wasn't his imagination. He wished that he could turn off the background Muzak and listen more clearly. The voice was somewhat faint and it was difficult to tell the direction that it came from. They looked for it as cautiously as they dared, but the first turn into a side corridor led them further away and the singing grew so faint. When they retraced their steps the singing became louder once more.

At last they came upon the source of the singing. A child sat in a large airy meeting place alongside a bar that had escaped the ravages of both rioting passengers and the quakes that had struck other parts of the ship. She was a young girl, about ten years old. Dressed in a party frock and with ribbons in her hair, she looked more like she was waiting to be picked up to go to a birthday party. She did not see them come in; her back was to them both as she sat swinging her legs over the edge of a sofa that was too tall for her. Even as they approached the singing carried on as if nothing was wrong.

Dezza held back a little. Children weren't his thing and if he were to admit the truth to anyone he would have said that the age difference made it impossible for him to know how to deal with them. Philipa, however, seemed unencumbered by similar feelings. Ignoring Dezza, she marched across the room to the sofa and cleared her throat to attract the child's attention.

The singing stopped and the child looked around. She did not seem surprised in the least to see either of the pair and her feet continued to swing at the edge of her seat.

"Hello," began Philipa slowly in a friendly voice, "What's your name?"

The girl looked to her fingers and grasped her hands in a ball on her lap.

"Mummy says I shouldn't talk to strangers," she replied in a matter-of-fact voice.

Dezza laughed – it was the last thing he had expected to hear from the child. It was possible that the child had not seen anything of what had been going on across the ship. In a way he envied the child's naïveté. Perhaps it really was better to be completely unaware, and let the world pass on by.

Philipa persevered in that way that only women could. "Then where is your mummy? Perhaps you wouldn't mind if I spoke to her?" she said.

The child's feet swung more vigorously, and she looked to the floor with a hint of sadness. "Mummy won't speak to anyone."

"Why not?"

"Because mummy is scared."

She glanced across to Dezza and he saw the look in her eyes. Perhaps the creature had been here? Did the child really understand what might have happened, he thought.

Philipa leant closer to the child. "Do you know why your mummy is scared?"

The question hung in the air as the legs kicked back and forth furiously. The little girl was getting nervous, though Dezza was not sure whether it was because she was uncomfortable talking to them or because of something else that she did not want to let on to.

"Mummy says I should not talk to strangers," she said with more urgency.

"Well, my name is Philipa." She held out a hand to the child. "If we know each other's names then we aren't strangers anymore. What's your name?"

The child seemed to consider the logic.

"Lily," she said at last. "Mummy says it's short for Tiger Lily, but I don't believe her," she continued matter-of-factly and more confident now. Her face scrunched up as she looked at Philipa's hands. "You're all messy. Why are you so dirty?"

Trust a small and naïve child to take the edge off the tension. He could have thanked the little girl; suddenly the corridors of the Starliner did not seem quite so frightening.

"I know where you can clean up," Lily said suddenly. She slipped forward off the sofa and took Philipa by the hand. "There's a washroom in our cabin."

Dezza hesitated. "Is that where your mother is?" he asked.

Philipa stopped and a look of uncertainty returned to her face.

Lily was unfazed and did not seem to notice the sudden unease of the two adults. "No. The monsters took her. I've got the key though."

As if to prove it in case Dezza and Philipa had any doubts, she fished in a pocket of the party frock and pulled out a keycard that looked unnaturally big in her little hands. "I'm a big girl," she proudly said, "Mummy gave me this."

As they walked slowly along the corridor, Dezza wondered what they might find. He had no idea how to explain to the child about what was going on. He would most likely struggle to find words the child even understood.

Lily brought them to a stop in front of one of the nearby cabin doors in a corridor that led off from the lobby and bar. The girl produced the keycard from the pocket and, because she was not a tall child, she had to stand on tiptoe to fit it into the lock. The electronics clicked, and the door swung open on the darkened cabin behind and the girl marched in.

Philipa entered slowly and felt along the wall for the light switch. Over her shoulder Dezza saw the lights flicker on and he craned his neck to see in. There was nothing out of the ordinary to the cabin and it looked rather like the one that he had had. Except that this one had clothes strewn all across the floor. Drawers hung open and underwear hung limply over the edges. It looked to Dezza like someone had tried to pack in a hurry, failing to get a single thing in their suitcase. Of any bags or suitcases there was no sign.

Lily seemed undeterred by the mess. "The washroom is through here," she said, looking up critically at Philipa's torn and dirty uniform. "Mummy says I should always look my best, and you should too."

Dezza exchanged glances with Philipa, but she followed the girl's direction into the washroom.

"Is she your wife?"

Dezza found himself looking down into the expectant eyes of a ten year old who seemed to be regarding him with a strange fascination.

"No," he said hurriedly, slightly panicked.

She screwed up her eyes and looked at him intently. He felt a little nervous under the watchful gaze; it was strange to be looked at so unashamedly by another person. He was not used to the scrutiny.

"You've grown through your hair," she said at last after thinking for a moment. "Daddy grew through his hair too."

He tried to avoid her gaze, but subconsciously found himself stroking a hand through his hair. Perhaps he was going a little bald and he had not shaved for a couple of days. He knew that, but it seemed odd to be told that by a child. He stepped nervously over the discarded clothes and sat down on the edge of one of the bunks.

Lily sat down on the bunk opposite him, and stared back at him in the manner of a child who has not yet learnt social graces. He tried to look anywhere but her direction but he felt at a loss over how he should react. Children weren't like adults. An adult would never stare this intently, and even if they did he knew how to deal with that sort.

He turned his attention elsewhere, listening to the tinkle of water from the washroom. It occurred to him that he must be filthy too, though Lily had not mentioned it. Perhaps she expected boys to be dirty, but not girls.

The running water came to an end and he heard a towel rail squeak. He heard Philipa moving around – and stop. Her sudden silence made the hairs stand up on the back of his neck.

"Philipa?" he called out, "Are you okay?"

He was relieved to see her emerge from the bathroom, walking slowly. But her face was ashen and white and it made him nervous. What had she seen? He began to stand, not wanting to rush and surprise or scare the little girl.

"What's wrong?" he asked.

"Have a look in there; in the bath."

The blood drained from him and he felt light-headed all of a sudden. But he fought it back, for Lily's sake. The girl stood up too, but Philipa hurried to her side and sat down next to her.

"Don't worry, Lily. Let's talk about dolls. Have you got any dolls?"

216

She shot a glance to Dezza, and he knew that she did not want to alarm the girl. That meant there was something Lily was not supposed to see in there.

He went into the washroom and closed the door behind him.

"Is he going to get a wash too?" Lily asked Philipa. As the door clicked shut he heard Philipa steering the conversation back to dolls once more. Lily was a child with normal curiosity. But also like most children she was easily distracted, and Dezza was thankful for that.

Water dripped from the taps in the sink, and he could see where Philipa had splashed water on the fascia. The hand towel had slipped from its holder and lay in a crumpled heap on the floor. Stooping down he picked it up and felt its dampness in the palm of his hands.

The shower curtain was pulled all the way across the bath alcove. The *Persia* had generous sized bathrooms to cater for the larger of the American tourists who were valued custom, and outnumbered other nationalities two to one. This cabin was no exception and he wagered the tub could probably hold enough water to make an ecologist wince. A steady drip of a tap in the alcove sounded like it already had some water already in it.

In a former life he might have been shocked, but the years had been harsh and whittled down any sense of optimism of what Fate might bring. One end of the curtain was untucked from the tub and he suspected that Philipa had brushed against it when she had gone for the towel. Otherwise she may never have thought of looking. He grasped hold of the edge of the light material and gently drew it to one side. Then he pulled back, thought a while, and turned away.

He vomited as quietly as he could into the sink, hoping that the noise would not arouse Lily's interest. Running the taps he flushed the vomit down the plug and washed his face clean. For a moment he stood staring at his own haggard expression and hang-dog eyes in the mirror, wondering if what he had seen had really been as bad as his body's reaction had suggested. Summoning up the courage, he cautiously turned and pulled the curtain back aside for a second look.

He had not expected to be shocked, but a part of him still reeled. A woman lay in the tub – or at least all that was left of her. She was in her mid thirties and he suspected that she was probably Lily's mother. Not that he was going to put that kid through hell to identify the body. The head was still perfectly recognisable, down to her neat hair and applied makeup. She could have just stepped out of any of the salons aboard the Starliner, except that from the neck down the body was a mangled mess.

The body looked to have been pulped, with tattered remains of flesh almost liquefied. Here and there he could make out the shape of bones and organs. The ribcage was still present, poking through the gore, but the bones were shattered in several places. The right arm was there too, complete and untouched except for a light splattering of blood. A watch was fastened to the wrist and he could see its second hand still ticking round the dial as if nothing had happened. Of the left arm there was little trace except a stump of bone that jutted out with tatters of flesh and muscle hanging from them. A slick of red ooze stretched from the torso to the plug and lumps of human flesh, almost unrecognisable in their texture, blocked it enough for a pool of blood to have formed along the bottom of the tub.

He did not know how long he must have stood staring at the mess. Somehow he could not quite bring himself to believing that it could be real, though his empty stomach churned and filled him with waves of nausea that he fought down with willpower.

He realised that the talking in the main cabin had stopped. A knock on the door made him jump.

"Are you all right?" said Philipa's shaky voice.

He rubbed a hand over his face and felt the dampness that had come from washing it.

"Yeah. I guess," he said with some degree of uncertainty. It was hard to find an emotion faced with the mess of human remains.

He was about to leave and rejoin the others in the cabin. He figured there was nothing in the remotest that could be done for the woman; she had been dead a while. How she had died he did not wish to think.

A bubbling noise stopped him in his tracks, his hand poised on the handle of the bathroom door. He first thought was that he had imagined it, but in the eerie quiet it came again. This time he was certain that it came from the bath. *Was the woman still alive?* Incredible as the mess had been, he was almost willing to believe that she could have survived – just. He could not leave her there to suffer in what would be agony.

Pulling back the curtain he was just in time to see a geyser of filth splatter up from the plug. That was not normal. The woman's face remained motionless and the eyes stared, glazed in death, did not blink and the face remained fixed. The body seemed to spasm and he took a step back in surprise. The intact arm flopped down off the edge of the tub and slapped against the bloodied torso.

He knew they had to get out; instinct told him this was more than the plumbing backing up. As the body jerked, he saw the residue and filth in the bottom of the tub start to pulsate and take on a kind of form. Without looking back he rushed out of the bathroom and hustled Philipa and Lily off the bed.

"We have to go."

"Why?" asked Philipa.

"It's coming through the plumbing; it's found us."

Philipa's mouth opened to question him, but the words never came as she turned to the bathroom door at the sound of air bubbling rapidly through liquid. Turning to Lily she seemed to smile as best she could and scooped the little girl from the edge of her bed onto her feet.

"We have to get on dear," she said calmly, belittling the fear in her expression.

"But what about waiting for mummy?" the little girl protested.

"She isn't here," Dezza blurted. It was the only thing he could think of saying. Behind him the noises from the bathroom were getting louder and more intense. He could see Lily looking around him, wanting to know in child like curiosity. He could not let her - they had to go.

Once in the corridor he shooed Philipa on with the girl and stopped only to make sure the cabin door was shut and latched. Not that such a flimsy piece of meaningless décor would do much to stop the creature when it finally came.

"My key! I left it on the bed!" Lily wailed.

"You don't need it anymore," Philipa assured her.

The sounds from the bathroom were louder now and though muffled, could be heard in the corridor. They quickened their pace, as the child complained again about the lost key. Damn that thing!

"We have to hurry," he said as Philipa scooped up the little girl and they began to run.

16

The machine room was empty, like it had been before. The consoles with their detritus of human habitation were still there, unchanged. Coffee mugs and discarded jumpers on the backs of chairs made it look like the crew would return at any moment and the computer screens still scrolled through their programming locked into cycles that no codes could penetrate. Ventura tried entering his own personal codes. These should have overridden everything but just as they had with David before, the screens flashed up error messages and refused to recognise them.

David looked up at the glowing masses of the toroidal drive cores. "We're going to have to manually shut this thing down," he said with a grim determination.

Ventura turned from the console. "Tell me what we have to do."

"All the power for the ship's systems is coming from the cores. We can shut them down either by closing the fuel valves or simply unhooking their power grids. Either way carries its risks."

"Risks? You didn't tell me anything about risks."

"You didn't ask."

"Let's consider that I'm asking now," Ventura snapped. "Tell me the risks."

David considered the options. It wasn't that he was absolutely certain; he wasn't. No-one that he knew of had ever tried shutting down a Starliner completely out in deep space away from docking facilities. Certainly not with a load applied to the cores. The Starliner's entire grid was technically live, and that meant that there was a lot to go wrong. If it did, there could be no dock crew and no call for help to get them out of a fix. It had never been done. He wasn't even sure that it could be done; theoretically it could – just pull the plug and everything would go offline. Of course the practical side was that they would have to reboot it all to bring the life support systems back online. Without them, there would be no happy conclusion for either of them.

"If the fuel flow goes into flux, it could cause the drive core to blow. If the power shutdown spikes the main computer, nothing will come back online without replacing a good number of the circuit boards in the main computer's brain hub."

"Can we deal with either?"

"No."

"Then let's not make any mistakes then," Ventura finished grimly.

"It's a big job and what scares me is the room for mistake."

"Where do we pull the plug from?" asked Ventura, giving up on the computer terminals that refused to even acknowledge his personal codes. "Down here?"

David shook his head and pointed to the gloom at the top of the enormous drive room above the cores. "Not entirely. Up there's the core control boxes. It's the only way to be certain of bypassing the computer control. I'll be down here re-routing the panel feeds to stop the grid cycling over to emergency power sources."

The captain squinted into the gloom. It was a long way up. "And it'll work?"

"Sure as hell. There's nothing the computer can do to re-route power – we're pulling the only plug it knows."

"Show me what I'm looking for."

David held his arm up and pointed under the gantry. "There's a bundle of cables all along the edge. The walkway is for maintenance access and there's a ladder at either end – take the climb steady. You'll see a junction box over the core with heavy armoured cables feeding in to it. Pop the top and pull the plug."

Ventura looked at him. "Simple as that."

David smiled back. "In theory. That's what the manual says, but you'll be pioneering a world first."

"Great. Just great," muttered Ventura. "Save me a drink at the bar."

As the captain headed for the access ladders and swung himself onto the slender chromed steel for the long climb up, David returned to the computer terminals.

"Okay baby; let's see what you've got."

At the first set of computer consoles he ducked down and began removing the panels underneath. Behind lay the maze of cabling and circuit boards that were the Starliner's means of control. Sure he could have smashed them out, and that would have been quicker by far. But it was permanent too, and in the back of his mind he knew that they had to take a shot at powering the whole damn thing back up again afterwards, or they were all as good as floating in their own airless tomb. He had no doubts that the computer in its present state would interpret anything they did to take it offline as something it would do its utmost to override. It had to therefore be stopped before Ventura made the final connection.

He undid the screws on the next panel and a couple of tugs brought it free from the frame. Behind it came a rat's nest of cables. Swearing, he pulled himself up to trace the bundles to the upper side of the console. It was a maze that he would have to figure out, and quickly. Glancing up at the gantry he saw Ventura hard at work. At least for now there had been no signs of the creature. The longer it stayed that way, the better.

Feeling his way into the bundles of wires with a hand, he grabbed hold of the connectors that made the link between the computer and the console. With a silent prayer he hoped that he had the right one, he shut his eyes and tugged. The connector came away cleanly on the second pull and the ribbon of cable dropped down loose into a coil on the floor.

He had not known what to expect, but the actual result was an anti-climax. No warning sirens blared and no appearance from the hologram came. Instead when he levered himself upright all he could see was a flashing cursor on the flat screen, waiting for input.

He had no idea how to check whether it had worked or not. Should he pull other wires loose to be sure? He glanced feverishly across the console, looking for any indication that he had succeeded. Flashing red lights flickered across the console, and that meant that the computer was registering that it no longer had any control over the backup systems that would have kicked in once the core was shut down.

"It's all up to you now captain," he whispered under his breath and turned skywards to see how close the captain was to the gantry above.

The gantry was hidden by shadows and he couldn't see exactly where Ventura had gone to. Had he reached the top and already got along to the cable junctions? He scanned across the structure, trying to find any sign of him.

"I've been watching you for some time now."

The voice was calm and matter-of-fact and came from right next to him. It was not a voice he had been expecting so close to his ear, but it was a voice that he still recognised even if it did send an icy chill racing through his body. He turned on the voice, and his skin went cold and numb. In front of him, not more than a few feet away and with piercing black eyes that regarded him with an intense curiosity, stood the figure he recognised as Tom.

"Tom?" he asked, as a part of him wanted to think that the boy could really be there. But his sanity screamed at him that the piercing eyes told their own story and this was nothing more than a manifestation of whatever had been in the hologram that had swallowed Tom whole.

Tom's figure smiled, but for the first time David realised that there was a translucent edge to the figure, and that he could see the consoles behind him dimly through the rendition of the body. Now Tom was the ship's hologram, of sorts.

David looked around, as if the soulless figure of the hologram that had taken Tom might be stood there too. But there was no-one else; they were alone together. He felt the sweat begin to bead on his forehead and he knew the figure in front of him was not the Tom he had known.

"You aren't Tom."

The figure feigned being taken aback, but it was a poor facsimile.

"What makes you think I am not?"

224

The voice made David waver; only for a moment. It sounded just as he had remembered; the same edge of youthful curiosity and enthusiasm. Yet, it was tinged with a more sinister edge that rang alarm bells in his mind.

"You're not Tom," he repeated, involuntarily taking a step backwards, "I saw you die. The hologram took you."

The figure seemed to shrug and look around itself. "I don't see any hologram. Just you're old friend Tom standing here asking you what you are doing." The figure shot a look to the open panel and the maze of wires on the floor.

David felt a cold shiver run down his spine. This was not Tom; somehow the creature had found a way of mimicking the boy. It was a good copy, but the small details that were not quite right set him on edge.

"What did you do with Tom?" he demanded, more sure of himself this time.

The hologram threw its head back and laughed, but the sound was a baying alien cackle that grew sounded more like a wild animal.

He took another step back, wanting to put more distance between himself and the aberration, but the thing seemed to anticipate what he was doing, and at once the cackle stopped and those sharp eyes were scrutinising him with piercing precision.

"What's the matter, David? Don't you want to stay and play with your friend?"

His eyes narrowed. "You are not my friend."

Tom's face creased into a smile that oozed contempt. "Is that how you treat a friend?"

I know you aren't Tom," said David, holding his ground. He hoped that outwardly he did not show signs of feeling intimidated. All the time the hologram continued to stare with a gaze that felt like it was boring a hole right through him.

The eyes darted before David could stop himself.

"Are you cold?" the hologram said with mock concern.

"No."

"Then why do you shiver? Is it because you are afraid?" It's voice dripped more and more with menace.

It wasn't Tom anymore, but some evil thing hidden behind a façade that it wore like a pantomime costume. There was nothing left in its act that even pretended to be the boy now; the mannerisms and movements were changing and evolving like an actor slipping from one part into the next. David took another step back and felt a swivel chair behind him. He grabbed it and flung it forward to where Tom's image had been.

But the chair rolled through nothing; the image was gone. He watched with disbelief as it bounced unhindered off the consoles on the opposite wall. Tom's laugh, contorted by the creature into sinister tones, echoed across the machine room.

"Aren't you going to play with me?" a voice hissed at his ear. He could feel the hairs on the back of his neck move as if something was there. Terrified, he swung around, but there was nothing but empty air. He thought he saw a wisp of white drifting in the shadows, but he could not be certain and as quickly as he thought he saw it, it was gone.

On the gantry above, he saw too that there was no sign of Ventura. He could see it from end to end, and there was no-one up there at all. Fear gripped him even tighter as he realised that the creature could have despatched the captain all the time that it had been here as the hologram.

The machine room suddenly seemed a huge and foreboding place. The thirty metres across the grey steel floor looked to him now more like a gaping void. The creature was in here, somewhere. At any moment he expected it to strike again.

Plucking up the courage, he ran the thirty metres. Skidding to a halt at the foot of the access ladder alongside the first of the toroidal drive structures, he

226

turned to make sure nothing had followed. But the machine room was still empty and the hologram was nowhere to be seen. Without a pause he launched himself up the first few steps of the ladder, climbing at a record speed. Reaching the top he rolled off and looked down, but the ladder was empty; nothing had followed

Where Ventura had been he found tools strewn across the metal grill of the gantry. Some of the necessary plugs had been disconnected, but others remained untouched. In frustration that he had let the creature trick him, he knelt to finish the work.

"I hope you aren't planning on doing anything that you will regret," said the facsimile of Tom's voice.

The tools from his hand clattering over the walkway and plunging over the edge to fall with to the floor far below. The sound of their impact seemed faint and far away. In front of him, knelt cross-legged on the steel mesh was the hologram of Tom, sitting patiently as if he had been there watching all along.

Tom's facsimile glanced to the cables. A dark look flickered across his face, and he turned slowly to look at David. The hologram never actually stood up, but one minute it was sat cross-legged, and the next minute it stood towering high over the engineer. The morphing in between happened smoothly and almost instantly.

It was not Tom anymore, but an archaic looking man in a fancy uniform that looked as though it belonged to a different age in the past. He opened his mouth in surprise, to say something, but the creature moved too fast. A limb thumped out of the darkness, wrapping itself around the gantry. Metal sheered with a scream of rending bolts and he felt the jolt as the walkway lurched several inches and stopped.

The strange man seemed unfazed by the movement and took a step forward. David scrabbled on the floor, trying to get a purchase to get up and get away. He wanted to run, but the walkway vibrated again and dropped more. It was leaning at a perilous angle now, threatening to tip him down and off the buckling edge.

Another limb flopped over the walkway, and a chunk of the handrail snapped off and cartwheeled down to the floor of the machine room below. As the walkway dropped with a final lurch, David swung around and managed to grab onto the stump of metal. The weight of his body jarred against his shoulder joints. Every bit of his body felt like it was being pulled apart, but he hung on with grim determination. In a superhuman effort he managed to pull himself up on his arms and find purchase with his dangling feet. Easing himself up the nearly vertical walkway, he grasped at the bent handrail at the top and rolled over clear of the collapsed gantry.

"Nice to see a man of your age keeping himself in shape."

The shock of the voice so close by nearly made him roll back over the edge, but he caught himself just in time and held on. Almost next to him on the walkway, stood nonchalantly like nothing was wrong was the figure of Tom. It shimmered slightly and a crackle of static ran through the image. For a moment the hologram seemed perplexed. The static rolled through it again, this time more severe. David could hear the buzzing in the air as the image began to break up. As it dissolved, the image of Tom changed, and for a split second a ghostly figure stood like a demon from another world without anything other than a vaguely humanoid form, then it too was gone and he was left breathing heavily on his back on the gantry.

"Hey! Are you all right?"

His ears pricked up at the sound of Ventura's voice. Spinning himself around he peered out between the bars of the walkway's grab-rails and looked down.

"The hologram's offline," Ventura shouted up. He held above his head a bundle of cables that ended at a neatly severed connector. "I've pulled the plug on it. I don't think it's going to bother us any more."

Forcing aching limbs to react, David swung himself up and hammered along the walkway to the far end where an intact access ladder led back down.

Ventura met him at the bottom. "Did you get the safety's deactivated," he demanded.

David nodded. "Yeah, I think so." Suddenly he remembered the cables he had seen on the gantry. "The cables up there. You didn't get them all?"

The captain opened his hand and showed David the tool he held within it. "I didn't get a chance. The creature attacked me." He glanced back up at the walkway. "I'll go. Just get ready to fend that thing off."

"I thought you pulled the plug on it?" protested David

"The hologram, yes. As for the rest of it..." his voice tailed off.

Even as he spoke, a banshee wail echoed through the engineering spaces from somewhere close by.

*   *   *   *   *

Dezza heard the thing break out of the cabin long before they were far enough away that he would have felt safe. Lily and Philipa heard it too. Lily did not understand, and he envied her for that.

The groan echoed down the corridor behind them; the thing was coming. He felt the air begin to move around them, caressing them with a humid touch. He could smell the scent in the air that the entity brought with it. It smelt like ozone mixed with dust.

"In here!" he called, ducking into a branching passage that led off the main corridor at right angles. Just inside there was a concealed case that held a fire hose, extinguishers and an axe and he pulled it open. Philipa and Lily stopped beside him, breathing hard from the run.

"Keep going!" he urged.

Another wail echoed from the corridor, louder this time, and Lily began to cry as the pair ran on.

Rifling in the cabinet, the fire axe though felt good to his touch. Pulling it from its retaining clips, he tested its weight.

Like all ceilings across the Starliner, this one was punctuated with discrete sprinkler nozzles. He did not know how many would go off if he activated it, but it was worth a try. Heaving the axe up and over his head, it caught the glass vial beneath the spray head and shattered it in one. Immediately a jet of water hammered out, followed by more jets up and down the corridor. The carpet was quickly sodden through and he smiled at the thought of the cleaning job that he did not have to do. Clutching the axe close to his chest he turned and ran after the others as fast as he could. Hopefully the water sprays would confuse the creature long enough for them to get away.

The passage ended at a large opening out onto a promenade deck along the edge of the Starliner. The lights were dim and the spray from the sprinklers played over the Plexiglas and ran in rivulets to the pools that were growing on the floor. Wary of having been followed he was surprised to find Lily and Philipa stood in the centre of the promenade The spray of water had saturated their hair and clothes and Philipa's hair clung limply to her head and shoulders. Her once white blouse had become almost transparent, tracing the outline of her bra beneath.

"Hey?"

They did not answer, or even look to him. What the hell were they playing at? Then he saw the aberration that sat quietly in the middle of the promenade, regarding all three of them with beady little eyes that sat on top of stalk-like protrusions.

It was hard to know what shape it was. Whilst it was physical and solid, it kept changing at its extremities as if it could not quite decide what shape it really wanted to be. Portions of it appeared at various moments to be of human origin. An arm here or a head there would appear in silent poses, in a macabre display of body parts.

Philipa finally acknowledged him, and he realised that she was almost frozen in fear.

"It was there when we came; like it was just waiting for us."

The creature pulsated again, and in a moment Dezza realised that he was looking at the head of the woman who had been in the cabin's bath and a shudder ran through him.

"Don't look, sweetie," Philipa said to Lily, and tucked the little girl's head into her chest so that she could not see.

"What do we do?" she hissed to Dezza.

He took hold of her and began to pull her back. "We go. Slowly," he urged.

She took a step with him, but the thing turned and took a sudden renewed interest in their movement. A limb unfolded from its torso, then another and another. In a moment there were nearly a dozen long slender tentacles that felt their way out along the water-streaked floor towards them all.

He felt the weight of the axe in his hand, and bounced it tentatively from one hand to the other. All Starliners had a failsafe system for dealing with hull breaches. They figured it wasn't going to ever happen, but they prepared for it anyway. Board of trade regulations could be a real pain in the butt, he thought. His face sneered into a lopsided grin – out here on an exposed Plexiglas promenade there was nothing but a thin bit of synthesised plastic keeping the vacuum at bay. It wouldn't take an awful lot to see just how well the designers had calculated for a hull breach. He glanced behind them; they were pretty close to the way back into the *Persia* proper. He could get out quick if he timed it right. Looking over the

Plexiglas he reckoned all it would take was a couple of good hits in the right place.

"Get back into the passage," he hissed.

She took a step, but the thing began to slither again towards them, as if it knew they were planning something and she stopped. Dezza got the impression that the damn thing was playing with them. His grin widened – how little it knew about the new all-improved Desmond Booth!

"Ignore it. Keep going," he ordered. They started moving again, back to the steel hatch rim that was descretely contained within an outcrop of fake décor at the edge of the Plexiglas.

Dezza turned to face the creature. It tilted what could be loosely described as its head – at least, where its eyes were. Then a lopsided mouth sneered into a grin, and the limbs slapped greedily towards his feet.

"Run!" he called out. Philipa and the girl turned on their heels and splashed to safety. Now it was just him and the creature. Just like old times, he thought, as he shifted his grip on the axe.

The creature's head reformed, morphing into a form that Dezza shuddered as he realised he knew. Within a second, the grinning face of Exbo with that leering lopsided smile was there in front of him and the rest of the creature folded in on itself and was suddenly no more than the cocky arrogant marine from Dezza's past.

"I've waited a long time for this," the voice of Exbo hissed. "You really think you can take me down with that little tiny axe?" Exbo taunted. He took a few steps forward, moving dangerously close now to Dezza.

Dezza tested the axe in his hands and glanced to the exposed Plexiglas along side him.

"No," he said with honesty, "But I can take you piece by piece."

Exbo threw his head back and laughed. It was a laugh that Dezza remembered all too well from the *Cerberus*. Some things just have a habit of sticking in memory.

"You don't have the balls," Exbo taunted.

"Neither do you. You just got pissed on vintage liquor."

"You left me to die," accused Exbo.

He felt a mix of emotions. Inside the anger seethed and boiled. All this time he had had to face the gauntlet of people's accusatory stares and the stigma of being suspected of being a crew killer. Now here was the slimy little tosser accusing him too, after Exbo had sat there at the bar and taunted him with that priceless booze drinking himself into oblivion.

The anger boiled up, to the delight of Exbo. He clearly enjoyed the turmoil he was causing, just as he had done before. Then Dezza realised; it was just an imitation. That was how the creature worked – it fed off the fears. Work you up and make you so scared you were on the edge of a heart attack, then take you and consume you.

So he relaxed instead. A feeling of safety washed over him, and saw the worried look flicker across Exbo's face as the creature seemed confused. The figure of Exbo dissolved and morphed with a sickening grinding noise. Dezza fought the urge to look away, and brought the axe crashing down on the Plexiglas with a blow that resonated like an explosion. The Plexiglas was tough, but there was a white splinter star was left where the blade had bitten into it. Another good hit, he reckoned.

A mouth formed on the pulsating mass of the creature. "You are going to die!" it hissed in an alien voice that hissed and wheezed.

His second blow landed straight on top of that white star – a perfect shot! Dezza saw the white cracks appearing, snaking out across the screen with silent precision, and grinned. "Not before you," he sneered at the creature.

It could not react quickly enough as Dezza launched himself backwards and rolled through the hatchway. Before it could morph into a fixed form, the Plexiglas turned white and cracks snaked wildly in all directions. Then the wall began to bulge and with an explosion louder than thunder, it folded out into the vacuum and disappeared. Air and water followed, sucked from the promenade with a force that tossed Dezza's body with more power than he had felt before. Letting go of the axe he lunged for something to hold onto. In the gale the axe disappeared towards the breach as if nothing more than a flimsy toy.

As the hatch neared the bottom of its track, the roar turned to a whistle. A flailing tentacle fought to follow him, but it was too late as the hatch thumped closed on the rim and the whistle squeaked to nothing.

"Pleasant journey Exbo. Consider yourself expendable," he hissed.

17

When it came, it came with the speed of a hurricane. The lights in the machine room began to flicker and David looked around nervously, trying to see where it was coming from as the roar of its approach echoed louder and louder drawing out into a low moan. Somewhere close, electrics shorted and buzzed and he felt the air move. A rumble echoed from the corridor that connected the machine room on to the rest of the engineering level and he dashed to the side of the room and tore open the tool cabinet there. There was not much to make use of inside it; an assortment of meters and laser pen supplies. He picked up one of these in his hands and searched for a power pack for it.

It arrived in a rolling cloud of dust with static bristling in the air. In the flickering glow of the lights David saw a nebulous cloud of white gas, flowing and undulating in ways that his mind could not quite fully keep up with. Faces appeared to come and go within the cloud; tilting back open mouthed locked in a perpetual scream from which no sound ever came. He saw the face of Tom, and gasped. Then the faces morphed and it was someone else. Then it changed yet again. He saw some faces that he recognised; some of them were crew from the Starliner who he had come to know though several years of working with. With a pang he realised that every face that the creature was pulsating through was the face of one of its victims, locked in their death screams. His fingers grasp tightly around the laser pen and vowed he would not be taken without a fight.

The creature seemed to detect the presence of the engineer and the cloud flowed and twisted, turning across the open grey deck until he felt the humid breath of the cloud getting closer to him. It carried with it a curious smell of ozone and ionised particles. Mixed in was the tainted odour of must, mould and ozone.

Unable to take it any longer, he held the laser pen out in front of him and energised its controls. Shielding his eyes from the glare, he heard the arc lance out and felt the heat of the unprotected beam. The creature screamed and he felt the pull of the air moving as it retreated from him with lightning speed. Opening his eyes again he lowered the laser pen; in a flash the creature seemed to roll and swarm back at him. A fist flew out of nowhere and hit him across the chest. The blow was unexpected and knocked him sliding across the floor.

The laser was jolted from his grasp and slid across the floor coming to rest several metres away. Dazed by the blow, he looked around for the creature, expecting it to be moving in for another attack. But the white pulsating cloud had gone. The air was still tinged with the stench of ozone and he could feel the residual humidity that the creature had brought.

"Shit!" he exclaimed. His voice echoed empty in the cavernous void of the machine room and for a moment his heart sank as the adrenaline rush subsided. He looked at the laser pen; could something so simple have despatched the monster? He shuffled upright, feeling the pain from the blow running through his body. It had been quite a punch, though nothing was broken. He reached for the pen to have something again to protect himself. In an explosion of static the air seethed around him and the pen was knocked from his grasp, to skid across the machine room and be lost in the tiny gap beneath a console.

He shuffled backwards as fast as he could, retreating from the burning air. He felt the cold harsh steel of a supporting girder graze past his arm and the lightning shock of pain lanced across the exposed skin.

Then at once the air subsided and David was left hiding beneath a pipe run wondering if he had imagined it all. He tried to see where the creature had gone, but there was still no sign of it.

"I can see you!" hissed the voice of Tom, taunting in its tones.

"Show yourself," he called out.

The sound of Tom laughing drifted through the pipes though it was impossible to tell where it came from. Shuffling backwards, he managed to find a way back into the darkness, hoping that perhaps the creature would not be able to find him.

"Hide and seek!" a voice hissed by his ear.

He jumped at how close the voice was; he saw the outline of a figure crouching with him in the darkness, the eyes piercing red in what otherwise looked like a normal human form. His heart leapt in horror – how could the creature end up beside him without making a sound at all?

"I'll count to fifty," said the voice of Tom from a leering mouth, "And you have to go and hide."

The voice oozed menace, and filled David with thoughts of what fate the creature planned if it caught up with him.

The head tilted to one side, and for a moment the red eyes flickered at the creature blinked. "What's they matter? Don't want to play? Here – I'll help you."

He felt the creature lift him up and toss him aside as easily as if he had weighed nothing at all. Flailing in the air, he landed heavily into a bank of consoles. The steel frames buckled beneath him and pain lanced through his whole body as he crashed to the ground.

"One. Two. Three…" the voice counted, still coming from under the pipes. The creature actually seemed to be enjoying its taunting.

"Come now my little engineer friend," the voice said, breaking from the counting, "It isn't very sporting if you won't play. I can be all of your nightmare's if you like? Run away and hide, or I'll make it slow and lingering for you." Then the voice started counting again, and he heard the click of what sounded like talons drumming on the pipes.

A shiver ran through him, and the memories of all the childhood nightmares came flooding back.

The creature cackled in its hiding place. "So you remember me now? All those years you thought I was under your bed every night?"

His heart jumped – how did that thing know? He felt a buzzing feeling in his mind and the creature's cackle grew louder.

"I know everything that makes you tick. I know all your fears, and I know what you fear the most. If I were you, David, I'd be running and hiding." It resumed counting its numbers.

Without hesitation, driven by the welling fear of memories of the childhood nightmares, he scraped himself up off the floor and ran for the laser pen. He had nearly reached it when he felt the buzz in his ears and the console in front of him seemed to spring into a renewed life. Peering at the flat screen, he saw a fuzz of static that seemed to be forming into a face. A noise stuttered from the speakers, and he realised that it was a voice.

"Oh no you don't," it buzzed.

For a moment he could not think, then he realised too late that he had been duped. The static on the screen poured itself forward. One minute it was just an image, and the next it was reaching out to him. A stump of a hand grasped out, draped with tatters of clothing and blood. It really was there, reaching out of the screen at him. He felt its claw-like fingers brush across his arm, the sharp nails clawing at his clothes. He tried to reach the laser pen, but the claw got there first and yanked it away from his grasp.

"Poor sport," a voice hissed, "No weapons allowed."

He tried to jump clear as the laser pen was activated with a hiss. Its beam played across the metal of the console, striking bright sparks into the gloom and sending up plumes of acrid smoke. He rolled away just as the beam sliced neatly into the floor at his feet. Picking himself up he tore off across the machine room to the connecting corridor, and dived into the seclusion of its darkness.

From the safety of a hatch rim he looked back, panting and out of breath. Sweat trickled into his eyes and he wiped it away feverishly with the back of a hand.

"Fifty!" The voice of Tom floated to him, ghostly and far away from somewhere back amongst the gloom of the pipework. "Coming, whether you are ready to die or not."

David turned and ran.

18

The man had appeared in front coming from nowhere. He looked haggard and down at heel and his clothes were torn and beneath the shreds of a shirtsleeve, congealed blood glistened on long scratch marks.

He looked to Dezza with eyes that had seen too many strange things in too short a time to find anything a surprise; then he looked to Lily and Philipa too. His expression lightened as he saw what was left of Philipa's uniform.

"Finally. someone from the crew," he said.

Philipa glanced to Dezza with a worried look. He remembered only too vividly the results of the baying mob they had met on the grand staircase, looking for somebody to blame and vent their frustration on. He braced for something similar, but the man's face showed none of the hostility.

"There's about thirty of us," the man continued, "Waiting down by the shuttle."

"Shuttle?" The word filled Dezza with surprise. When the last of the lifepods had left the *Persia* he had not thought that there would be any other way off.

The man nodded. "Yeah. Down in the docking bay. It's the orbital shuttle and it's still there, but nobody knows how to get the damn thing working." The smile faded a little and he glanced across at Philipa with hope and desperation in his face. "You do know how it works, don't you?"

She looked panicked and backed away under the scrutiny of his hopeful gaze. "Hey now, hold on. I'm just a stewardess. I don't pilot anything; just serve the drinks, look pretty and smile."

Dezza cast his mind back to coming aboard. Of course! The orbital shuttle; why did he not think of it sooner? He could have kicked himself given it was where he had first met Philipa and fallen for the spell of her brusque exterior. He pulled his thoughts up from where they were leading him – had he really fallen for her? In that moment he realised that perhaps he had.

"I can pilot it as long as someone else has the codes," he said quietly.

Locked in their conversation, they did not hear him at first, so he said it again. "I can fly it if you can get it online."

239

The words stopped mid sentence and both looked to him. "What did you say?" Philipa asked slowly.

"The shuttle," he repeated, "I can fly it if you can activate its systems."

A pang of fear ran though his heart – what if she did not have access to the codes? Without computer control, the shuttle was marooned in the docking bay and would be useless to them. His eyes darted to the man, hoping that if she could not help that he would not turn like the crowd on the grand staircase had.

"I can get the computer active," she said at last, much to his relief, "But from then on you are completely on your own."

He looked back into the expectant face of the man. Dezza knew that he was taking a huge leap of faith – it had been a long time since he had sat in the pilot's chair of anything, and back then technology had been more simplistic. Hell, the salvage tugs had been cheap and cheerful old-hat technology. What might a modern shuttle from a shipping line where money was no object be like?

"You can fly it?" the man asked.

Fighting back the feelings of doubt, he nodded his head. "I guess so." He did not add that it had been a long time since he piloted anything. Ever since the *Solitude* had returned from the *Cerberus* he had not flown a single flight. Forcing down the doubts he told himself to think positively – how hard could it be?

"Just like riding a bike," he murmured, but no-one heard him except Lily. She looked up to him with the sweet naïve innocence of a ten-year-old child. Not for the first time he envied her and the stresses she did not have to think about.

The man introduced himself as Grant, a survivor from the economy class lounges, he told them that he was one of a group who had realised that something was wrong the moment they started seeing the crew in a panic. He told them about how a radio call had drawn every person in uniform away. Told to sit tight, they had until nobody had come back to them. When the floors began to shake, they knew it was time to get out.

*   *   *   *   *

The walk to the shuttle's docking bay was eerily familiar to Dezza. He had not paid much attention at the time, but looking around he remembered walking up this way with Philipa and the abrasive tone she had had when they had met for the very first time. Looking to her he saw that she seemed unencumbered by such memories. He guessed that by now she probably wanted to get off the Starliner; didn't they all?

The lights glowed much dimmer than he remembered, but the corridors were the same. It was strange how a change in lighting could make a place that had been so airy and open become oppressive and dark. It led out into an open area at the top of the shuttle's connecting ramp. He stopped in surprise as the glimmer of lights picked out a mass of frightened faces cowering in the shadows. He looked to each of them in turn, and saw in their faces the fears of people who have came to realise that their fate hangs so close in the balance. They were desperate, looking for a way out and they were looking to Philipa and Dezza for that way. He shivered under the scrutiny.

"I've found one of the crew," Grant announced to the downbeat crowd, "She says that she can activate the shuttle. This man says he can fly it."

Before Dezza had a chance to gauge the reaction, a second man stepped forward and in him he recognised the same look that he had seen on the faces of the mob in the grand staircase.

"She's just a stewardess," the man spat, "What does she know about the shuttle?"

There was a power struggle within the group. Dezza had seen this man's type before – the perpetual pessimist who works hardest to bring those around them down. He had seen too many like him in officialdom and hated every ounce of them. They were the people whose can't-do attitude left a bitter taste in his mouth.

"She can turn it on and he can fly it," Grant pleaded.

But the other man was having none of it. As he talked, his voice raised higher on his soapbox, preaching to the crowd behind him. He was a powerful speaker, and Dezza could see that the crowd was wavering; they were looking for someone that could lead them, and this man was showing the most leadership, even if his words were of defeat.

Anger welled up inside Dezza. He did not tolerate fools gladly, and right now he saw in front of everybody a fool who would happily talk the others into death.

"I didn't catch your name?" Dezza asked carefully, stepping forward next to Grant.

The man looked at him with a look that screamed venom, and Dezza realised that he was a person who hated his authority being challenged. "Stanton – the man whose going to stop fools from firing us all into space and getting everyone killed. Just who the fuck are you?"

It was as much as Dezza could do to keep his anger in check. He wanted to plant his right fist square in this man's jaw and wanted to lay him out cold and take out on him all the anger he felt for the frustration of a lifetime of being held down by others. But the sea of faces looking at him made him realise that to do that would make Stanton the martyr. Make him so, and this ship of fools would follow him into their own graves. There was a risk that the lives of them all hung in the balance of how he dealt with Stanton here and now.

"I'm the guy who's going to be piloting us all out of here. I think therefore," he said slowly, picking his words with care, "The bigger question is: who the fuck are you?"

He saw Stanton's face turn red and he watched the anger seethe and boil beneath his cold exterior. But

Stanton was no fool either; at least with how he dealt with people. He too must have known that authority was only as good as the people who followed you. He crossed his arms and stared at Dezza with defiance.

"So you think you can pilot it. What experience do you have?"

The words were cold and icy - a deliberate challenge for Dezza to fall into a trap. He knew he could not rise to the man's bait, nor could he show any weakness. The crowd of expectant faces filled him with fear that they might choose to ignore him and instead follow a fool just as much as they inspired him to try and save them all. He could do that, couldn't he? His thoughts turned treacherous and nearly too late he realised that Stanton was a powerful man and could sow seeds of doubt through his pessimism. He had nearly turned Dezza's own mind against him. Could he really fly this thing?

He looked past Stanton and the crowd, to the umbilical connector that led to the shuttle's airlock. Offline and dead in its docking clamps, it would not have been infected by the creature – he knew that much from experience. But try as he might he could not remember what the shuttle looked like. Only the memories of his daydreams of looking through the viewing port came to mind; he could remember the white hull of the *Persia* and nothing else.

He fought back the feelings; he had to at least put on the façade that these people wanted to see. Only then would Stanton lose his power over them all.

"Can you get the shuttle hatch open?" he whispered sideways to Philipa.

She nodded.

"Good. Then do it."

The crowd was hesitant as she walked forward to the control panel on the wall, but they parted for her and Stanton looked on, arms still crossed and staring daggers at her back. Dezza could see Philipa trembling; she was scared of the man too, just as most of the passengers here were. Curious about the man's past, Dezza wondered what sort of figure Stanton had been before he had joined the cruise. A man like that went through life always a bully.

The lights flickered on the length of the umbilical corridor. In the glow he saw more faces, clearer now. There was real hope amongst them, but he saw the flicker of dissent sown amongst them by Stanton's words still ready to come to the surface. They would just need one excuse to turn the tables to Stanton's favour, and they would follow him. It was a delicate balancing act. No doubt he had sat with them waiting for Grant's return, poisoning their minds. How could such a person truly exist? Surely he had to know that the shuttle was the last chance?

Philipa walked to the shuttle's hatch and hesitated. Stanton seemed to draw renewed strength from her worried look and the glance she made back at Dezza without even realising she was doing it.

"See!" Stanton poured out with vial, regaining his confidence quickly, "She doesn't have a clue – she's only a stewardess. All she does is serve the drinks and keeps the peanuts flowing."

Dezza fought the urge to punch him out. Instead he called out to Philipa. "Go ahead. Pop the hatch."

With nervous hands she typed in her code. Dezza closed his eyes and prayed that it worked. If there were a problem now it would only hand the power back to the power monger and he feared that the mob mentality brought on by stress would let Stanton whip the crowd into lynching them.

Hearing the hiss of the seals he breathed a sigh of relief. Stanton was annoyed but silent as the crowd's attention turned to the dark interior of the shuttle. Some of them started to shuffle towards the opening, desperate now in their chance of escape. The crowd was wavering, and

Stanton was losing his grip. But the fight wouldn't be over yet.

Stanton held his arms up and called out to them, but with a smile Dezza realised that his spell over them was being broken. A few stragglers hung back, but they no longer seemed to hang on every word that was said. They just wanted to be free of the Starliner and the nightmares they had witnessed.

Dezza was one of the last few to head for the hatch. Stanton side-stepped and blocked his way. "You know you're just building their hopes up," he sneered, "How do you think they're all going to feel when nothing comes of this? They'll tear you apart, and I won't be able to help you."

Dezza felt taken aback. How dare this man try and belittle him under some flimsy sham of extending an olive branch. "I suppose you had a better idea?" he said, standing his ground.

Stanton faltered. In the shadows behind him he saw Grant watching, the look of relief that someone was finally standing up to the bully. He could not let him down.

"If you want to stay here, be my guest," Dezza snapped. He looked to the dimly lit corridor that led out of the docking bay and back into the rest of the ship. "I'm sure you'll get on just famously with the alien." He side-stepped the man before he had a chance to retort.

The lights in the shuttle were on when he got to the hatch and ducked through. Most of the passengers had found their way into seats in the cabin and the stragglers shuffled through, more upbeat than he had seen them when they had waited outside. Philipa was knelt by the front row, strapping Lily in and speaking to her in reassuring tones. She looked up at Dezza. "I hope you really can do what you said."

Behind, several of the passengers regarded him with suspicious looks and he realised that Stanton might still hold some grip over some of them yet unless Dezza could prove himself.

"Show me the cockpit," he hissed, ignoring the sharp looks he was getting. It was as much as he could do to project an image of confidence; inside he was anything but.

"Let's see if you really do know what you're doing and weren't just yanking our collective chains."

He turned in surprise at the venomous voice so close. Stanton was standing behind him, looking like he was about to reach down and grab him by the scruff of his neck. But he didn't. His eyes glittered angrily as he spoke, and Dezza caught the impression that if he failed, Stanton would be the first to lead the lynch mob. He could imagine the guy waving a pitchfork and flaming torch in the air.

"I'll show you," whispered Philipa.

He followed her to the front of the cabin. From the corner of his eye he saw Stanton coming too.

"Make sure giggles here doesn't come in and get in the way," he told Grant. He almost expected Stanton to punch him, but he didn't. As he passed through the door into the cockpit, he almost wished he had. Then the passengers might have seen him for his true colours.

19

With the voice of Tom still echoing in his mind, David blundered on through room after room, desperate to get away from the threats of the creature. Every turn he made seemed to lead him into dark ways and ducts that threatened to engulf him in a maze. Out of breath, he leant against the wall, fighting to breathe as his heart hammered in his chest.

"You aren't any sport at all!"

His heart leapt at the hissing whisper of the voice, so near though as rapidly as his head darted from side to side he could not place where it came from. It had sounded so condescending and patronising, yet the malice had been clear.

"Where are you!" he screamed in anger, "Can you only hide and speak to me from the shadows?"

His voice echoed hollow as he listened against the faint hum of air conditioning panels. For a moment he thought that maybe he had dreamt the voice, but then with gut-wrenching precision, the hovered close to him and he spun on his feet towards it.

"Would you prefer if I showed myself?" it said, as if the hidden creature was smiling at the invitation.

David felt his skin creep. He had not bargained for this. How could he fight something that seemed to prey on the fears in his mind? He stuttered, trying to form the words but none came.

The voice of the creature laughed. "I can see your mind, David. I can see your fears and everything that makes you afraid."

"Liar!" he snarled, finding words at last.

"What makes you think I lie?" the voice questioned, a new tone to its words.

"You think you can scare me? I've found scarier things in my laundry."

Another laugh echoed about the gloom. "You don't believe me? You soon will."

It sounded so sure of itself; it made David shiver, despite the fact that he was sweating. The air around him buzzed and crackled, and he felt his hair stand on end and static leap across his body. In the shadows he saw the blue-tinged glow reflect on the walls and ceiling. Maybe the creature was trying to electrocute him? But there was no pain. Then the buzzing was gone and the glow faded.

He looked around, but there was nothing in the corridor but himself. Had the creature gone? No – he doubted it. The minutes ticked on by, but still nothing happened. Finally he took a step forward.

"Going somewhere?"

He stopped dead in his tracks, frozen to the spot by the voice that had sounded somehow different from before. It was nasal and whiny, but still possessed a sinister edge that warned him this was the creature. He expected it to step out of the darkness in some hideous form, but instead he merely saw the suggestion of a shape moving in the darkness.

His heart leapt as some deeply buried childhood memory fought to be remembered. He wanted to turn and run away, but his legs would not respond and he found himself rooted to the spot with a gathering sense of fear.

The figure moved forward in the gloom and David's heart felt as if it was exploding with the stab of adrenaline mixed with fear. The figure that stepped into the pool of light was the clown that he had learnt to fear as a child. His eyes opened wide like saucers and he felt the icy grip of fear across his skin.

"You're not real!" he stuttered, "You died with my childhood!"

The clown's painted grin contorted revealing dark yellowed stumps of teeth. "Are you really so sure?"

"I knew you weren't real when I reached my teens. You weren't really in the closet every night."

"So why were you still so frightened? Tell me why you still cannot sleep in a room with an open closet?"

In David's mind the childhood memories flooded back. At the age of three his parents had taken him to a circus, and he had recalled in shock at the garish painted faces of the clowns and their strange antics. His parents had told him not to be frightened, but he had been. Every night afterwards he had had nightmares of the clowns living in his bedroom closet and only coming out at night. It had turned into an obsession that had stayed with him into adulthood, even though he eventually convinced himself they weren't really there. It didn't dispel the subconscious feelings he felt at that open closet door in the darkness. It was the one fear that he had never had the strength to admit to anyone. Only his parents knew, and they had been dead for many years.

"You can't possibly know that," he cried, shaking his head in disbelief.

Nothing he did dispelled the creature from its taunting. "Of course I know that – I've read your mind. All your fears are there for me to see. Come and play with me David."

Finally he found the courage to turn and run. In the gloom behind him the clown figure through its head back and laughed before stepping out of the light and dissolving away into the shadows.

"I'll be back to get you David. You can't hide forever! Can you really make sure that all the closet doors are shut tight enough to stop me coming out?" the voice taunted as he ran.

*   *   *   *   *

Lights blinked on across the control consoles of the shuttle as Dezza slid himself into the pilot's chair. It was not like any vessel he had flown before. The bridge of the *Solitude* and the *Magellan* had been simpler and more robust affairs. This craft looked like it had taken a crash course in electronic toys and gadgets and was light years ahead of the commercial craft he had seen. He ran a finger over the console, and hesitated with his hand poised just above the buttons.

"This isn't what I expected," he said.

Philipa glared at him. "You said you could!" she snapped, angry with him.

He looked up at her, pleading with his eyes. "I said I had flown before. What is this thing? It looks like someone sprung for the full optional extras package and then some." He looked back over the console with frustration. "I'm expected to drive an intergalactic amusement arcade?"

She leant forward and snapped on a series of switches on the panels. More lights came on, and the flickering glow of the computer's holographic display reflected off the underside of the canopy.

"The amusement arcade's upstairs," she snapped, pointing through the canopy at the dull utilitarian metalwork of the *Persia*'s underbelly, "Think of this as the family run-around if you have to. But please just drive it or Stanton is going to make a pilgrimage from whatever banjo country he came from and string you up."

Dezza knew that much only too well. The controls weren't too bad once he leant forward and read off the panels and their functions. Most of them he reckoned he could do without; as long as they cleared the *Persia*'s hull, he could get to grips with the rest of the controls at leisure. A knock on the door made him jump and he looked to see Grant poking his face around the door.

"I've shut the docking hatches. We're ready to go."

Dezza nodded. "Sure." Then a pang of recollection hit him, and he felt his face go hot and red. "The captain and the engineer!" he gasped.

Philipa looked at him; she had forgotten too.

Grant did not understand. "Who?" he asked, "Are there others alive still on board?"

"Two," Philipa said hurriedly, "They were going back into engineering." She looked at Dezza.

"What do you mean?" said Grant. He was confused.

"They were supposed to be going into engineering to shut the Starliner down – kill the power and kill the creature at the same time."

"When the systems come back online the creature is gone – it can't live outside of the power," Dezza finished, "That's the theory anyway.

Grant was about to say something when he was pushed aside from behind. With a sinking feeling Dezza saw Stanton push into the cockpit.

"So there *is* another way," he exploded, "You bullshitted us just to take the easy way out." He stared at Grant and the poor man lowered his gaze to the floor, not wanting to make eye contact. "Why are we fleeing in a shuttle that we don't even know for certain that you can fly?" he said, pointing an accusing finger to Dezza, "We could just stay and wait for the power to come back on. Only fools would abandon ship so soon on a whim."

"It's not a whim," snapped Dezza, "It might not work. There's still a chance that the systems might not reboot. They may not even shut down locally."

But Stanton was no longer prepared to listen. He had heard the excuses that he needed to go back into the passenger cabin of the shuttle and proclaim to the group that there was another way. He ignored Dezza and pushed past Grant roughly. Even before the door had drifted shut, Dezza heard Stanton's voice, urging the crowd to follow his idea and to stay, not go.

Grant looked embarrassed. "I'm sorry. I shouldn't have let him in here."

Dezza burned again with the anger inside, but it was directed at Stanton and not Grant. "Don't sweat it," he said, as calmly as he could. It was not his fault – Stanton was a bully and a thug.

"What now?" asked Philipa. Already the sounds from the other passengers in the cabin suggested they were more keen to wait here than to leave.

Dezza looked back across the cockpit controls. It no longer mattered that they looked so unfamiliar to him; if Stanton had his way, they would not need to be used. Gritting his teeth, Dezza made up his mind – they could not just abandon the men to their fate. If Stanton was going to take the opportunity to sow seeds of doubt in the minds of the others, then that was a risk he would have to take. He pushed himself out of the pilot's chair.

"Stay here. Let no-one in or out unless they can identify themselves to you. Don't plug the shuttle's systems into any of the *Persia*'s in case the creature gets across through the computer hook-up. Keep it sealed down – the air units on board should be good for a long time. Try and keep everyone occupied so that Stanton doesn't get too much of his hooks in them."

"How?" Grant demanded.

Dezza smiled. "What am I - the party King? Show them an in-flight movie or something. I'll be back as quick as I can."

Outside the cockpit the air in the main passenger cabin was hushed. Stanton regarded the trio with suspicious eyes, and some of the other passengers did too, but no-one else seemed determined enough to stand up and confront Dezza.

"The man reckons that we don't need to leave after all," Stanton said with quiet venom, directing the words to the people behind him.

"That's not what I said, and you know it," Dezza hissed.

Stanton ignored the rebuke. "I say we stay and wait," he snapped.

Some of the other passengers behind him were taking an interest. Looking from face to face, Dezza saw that they were looking for reasons to stay in what they saw as the relative safety of the Starliner. They did not want to believe that they had to leave and Stanton was playing on those feelings.

"I don't have time for this shit," Dezza snapped, turning away and laying his hands on the locks for the hatch to open them.

Stanton's sudden move surprised him; he had not thought that the man could rise above his weasel words and actually do anything physical, but he did. The punch did not particularly have much strength or skill to it – maybe he was not the kind of man who often felt he had to live up to his own bullshit and deliver. But it caught Dezza off guard and that was enough to knock his head into the metal of the hatch. He saw stars as the metal bar of the handle glanced across his forehead. In an instant the man was upon him, raining down blows as fast as he could. Dezza rolled as fast as his frayed reflexes let him, but he was caught on the back foot and spots of light swam in his vision.

*   *   *   *   *

Ventura cursed as the lights on the gantry flickered and failed. It took nearly a minute for his eyes to grow used to the feeble glow from the drive cores as he fumbled around trying to feel his way over the joins in the cables. Which of these cables had been which? He tried to remember but it was no use. Feeling in the darkness, he tried to find the edges of the walkway and the handrails that would be there. He knew there would be torches in the emergency lockers on the main floor that he could use to see his way, but it was a long walk – especially in the gloom.

Halfway across the walkway the lights came back and he froze in mid step, uncertain of what to expect. The floor far below was still empty. Had David managed to trip the circuits back on? A feeling of edginess bristled in his mind and he felt the as if he was being scrutinised, like a specimen in a jar on a laboratory bench. For a moment he felt as if there was something behind him, and he spun around to face it. But there was nothing there except for the empty walkway and his tools left scattered across it. If he hurried, he could get the job done here and now without a need to go down. He hurried back to the cable junction and his tools and knelt down to continue.

"Hey bro!"

The voice came from nowhere and filled him with a shock that made him drop the wire clippers he was holding. They cartwheeled down disappearing out of sight.

The voice had not sounded like it had come from anywhere in particular and he was not sure where to look. But when he turned, a figure stood less than ten metres away on the metal walkway.

It looked strange, as if formed from white marble. Smooth and vaguely humanoid, there was no detail whatsoever. Its movements were exaggerated and slow. Where there should have been eyes, nose and a mouth, there was nothing but a smooth ovoid sphere that seemed to reflect the lights of the gantry.

"What the hell are you?" he stammered, looking feverishly behind for a way out. But the walkway ended not far away in a twisted edge of torn steel from the earlier collapse. There was no other way down.

The faceless figure tipped its head to one side. Without ears or any other features, it seemed a strange gesture to make. "Don't you recognise me?" the voice said.

There was a memory in Ventura's mind; the voice was familiar. He had not expected to hear it ever again, but his face wrinkled into that of shock mixed with surprise.

"Bobby?"

The figure's head tilted upright again, and it crossed its featureless arms in front of its torso.

"So you do recognise me, bro."

It was Bobby Ventura's voice all right, but it did not match with the figure before him. Before he could stop himself, he found he had reached into his jacket and could feel the creased edge of the photo that he carried.

The figure took a step forward, and Ventura instinctively scrabbled backwards. "You're not him," he spat, "I knew my own brother well. You're nothing but an alien!"

His brother's laugh filled the air, though the figure did not move. Where was the voice actually coming from?

The figure moved with a motion so fast that it was impossible to detect. One minute it was stood ten metres away, the next it was next to him with its hands around his throat. He felt the choking grip, and the tingle of a touch that felt not quite physical, but as if electricity was moving between the fingers. He tried to twist away, but found that the grip was too tight. Trying to prise the fingers loose they felt like icy cold stone beneath his touch and would not yield. Looking straight into the face of the figure all he saw was the ghostly image of his own contorted face being strangled reflected in the mirror finish back at him.

"Remember how we used to play together, bro?" The voice continued, never changing its tone as Ventura felt the grip tighten.

*   *   *   *   *

It was Grant who threw the deciding punch. As Philipa helped Dezza to his feet he was only dimly aware of the moment that he had stepped up and dealt Stanton a blow to the side of his jaw. Bullies never saw it coming – they only took on people they thought were weaker than them, or who they had an advantage over. Dezza had been taken by surprise, but Grant had had enough and the blow was enough to floor the man. The passengers that had hovered close behind Stanton looking to him as a sort of leader melted back into the crowd.

Dezza nodded in Grant's direction. "Cheer's buddy."

"Any time. Now get on out there and do what you have to. We'll wait for you here."

He pulled open the hatch with Philipa's help and felt the cold air from outside play across the sweat that glistened on his face; he had not even realised he was perspiring. Philipa tried to follow him as he stepped on through, but he held her back.

"No. You stay here with the others."

She protested, but he stood firm. "Lily needs you," he said, "So do the others." She turned back reluctantly.

Grant took hold of the edge of the hatch. "I only pop the seal for you," he said, "If it looks like you aren't coming then we'll detach the shuttle without you and take our chances without a pilot." He put a hand on Dezza's shoulders. "Don't let us down."

*   *   *   *   *

As fast as it had started, the choking hands around his throat were gone, and Ventura was left slumped on the gantry's walkway, fighting to regain his breath. Feeling his neck gingerly there were a string of bruises and breathing still hurt. But the featureless figure had disappeared without trace.

"Hey bro!"

Back where the figure had been some ten metres away now stood his brother, in military fatigues just as he had seen him last before he had shipped out from home for a tour of the planets with his mercenary division. It had been the last time he had ever seen him alive.

"You know," Exbo said, "I never thought I would run into you. It's strange how small the galaxy can really be."

Exbo's face leered into a lopsided grin, just as Ventura had always remembered. They hadn't got on that well when they had lived together at home, but that did not change the fact that he was family. He stopped himself – Exbo was dead. He told himself that what was stood in front of him was nothing more than a fraud.

"Get lost, freak," he hissed with measured words, leaning down to scoop the last of the tools up off the walkway. "I'm not interested in a ghost. My brother is dead, and nothing's going to change that."

He felt the air move, and from the corner of his eye he saw the figure of Exbo seem to pour its way across the ten metres then recombine back into shape next to him. The movement was almost nauseating in the way that a human form could melt and twist like that, all the time retaining that same impassive grin on its face.

"You blame Dezza for my death." It wasn't a question, but a statement.

Ventura felt the pain burn again inside. "I blame you."

Exbo seemed taken aback. "Me?" he said in a high pitched squeak, "It was Dezza who left me to die."

Ventura's eyes narrowed. "I don't listen to the poison tongue of an alien. You're not Bobby, so why don't you stop pretending and show me who you really are?"

Exbo laughed as the figure dissolved into a flowing mass. The laugh continued even after the face had disappeared, and the mass slowly oozed its way through the metal grill then poured itself into an electrical junction box. It silently kept flowing until there was nothing left and the laugh finally disappeared.

The length of cable caught him unawares; it moved like it had a mind of its own, coiling in the air with a whipping sound and thrashing about wildly. The end crackled with electricity and he felt the sharp pain and smelt the tinge of scorched flesh as it whipped across his arm.

He cried in surprise, but the coil swung back and thrashed across exposed skin again, cutting his cries short. An end of the coil looped around his arm, and the tool he had been holding was flung out at high speed, disappearing over the tops of the drive cores and into the shadows on the other side.

He had only a split second to register before the coil pulled and with it he was launched over the safety rail to plunge towards the floor below. He braced his arms in front of his face, expecting the pain of the impact, but it never came. With a stomach-churning fling of acceleration, the recoiling cable tossed him into the air.

A bundle of pipework seemed to come towards him, and he reached out blindly and grabbed it. The force of the impact jolted the breath from him, and it took him a moment to regain his senses and work out where he was. From the corner of his eye he saw the glowing mass of a drive core; he had been flung to the very top of the room.

The explosive sound of steel cable under tension brought him rapidly to his senses, and he managed to roll around the pipework just in time for it to barely miss him. Sparks leapt from the tortured metal; a split second sooner and that metal would have been his head.

The cable whipped around, glancing off light fittings sending glass showering with sparks as the lights winked out one by one. Below him he could just about make out a tangle of cable runs and a further walkway. With a silent prayer he let go of the pipework and let himself drop, just as the coil of cable whipped through the air again. He heard it hit the pipework above and whip round and round, crushing the exposed metal.

He hit the edge of the walkway at an awkward angle, and the impact sent him sprawling. There was a twinge of pain from an ankle that might be twisted, but in the narrow area between the cores the whipping cable could not find him.

*   *   *   *   *

David heard the clown. There was no mistaking the steady sound of the large shoes flapping along the floor of the corridor. He did not know why it filled him with fear, but it did. Clowns were his Achilles heel, and no amount of reasoning with his subconscious could change that fact.

At the next intersection, the clown was there; there was no way though past it. The creature took a step forward and extended an arm that seemed to telescope on and on down the corridor. It grabbed hold of David and began to draw him in. He struggled hard, but the grip was unrelenting.

The closer he got the more detail of the ghostly white and red makeup he could see. It was ragged and the eyes were cruel and cold.

258

"Time to face up to your fears," it barked. The voice was harsh and loud, and resonated in his head.

The clown's head enlarged until it dominated David's view. Every direction he looked in, it was there. Wriggling free of the grasp, he ran back the way he had come. The haunting echo of the clown followed him all the way. "You can run, but you cannot hide!" it called.

In a blind panic he ran on, turning corners and dodging through hatches. The walls passed by in just a blur now; he could not think of anything but the face of that clown.

"Poor sport, running from a childhood nightmare." The voice seemed to follow, spurring him on.

Looking around, he did not recognise the corridors he was in. The voice too had changed, and had morphed from the clown to something else with an accent that sounded unfamiliar.

"Who are you now?" he called angrily.

Hearing a buzz of static, he looked around to find a man standing a few feet away, bent over and looking like he was injured and his movements were slow and sluggish. Ripples of static flowed through the image.

"Hologram?"

The figure looked up, its face twisted into a grim expression. "No; not a hologram. Dezza knows who I am; I was on the *Cerberus* with him. I've been watching you all, when I can. But the mind of the entity is strong, and I'm trapped within it."

"You're one of the victims?"

A smile flickered on the man's face. "Yes. It took me as I died, but I've been fighting it ever since. It had my body, but it can never fully take my mind."

It seemed to guess his next question before David could speak. "I can't explain it all. Maybe the others it took were the lucky ones – I am trapped in a living hell as part of an alien hive mind." The man looked wistfully to the ceiling as if recalling some faded memory. A flicker of static buzzed angrily through the image and he winced.

"The creature, it renews its grip." He looked David in the eye. "The only way to defeat it is to send the Starliner on a journey to the edge of the stars and beyond. It cannot escape the ship in the Rösenbridge. If the drive is locked, the ship will go until the cores are exhausted. Then the creature truly will be no more, and I and the others within it will finally be set free."

His final words twisted and contorted. A ripple spread through the image, growing and spreading until before his eyes it morphed and grew. The image that remained was stronger and clearer and was of a completely different man. Dressed in an archaic uniform, he regarded David with piercing eyes that were black, cold and unforgiving.

David did not wait to hear the figure speak. He turned and ran as fast as he could, knowing he had to carry out the suggestion of the first man who had spoken to him.

*   *   *   *   *

The whipping coil of cable stopped as quickly as it had started. As the slender strip of black dropped away, Ventura expected to hear it slap across the floor and fall still as the creature perhaps grew tired of taunting him in this way. But instead there was a sound like wet leather rubbing on steel, and the shadow cast by the cable expanded. A heavy rasping of breathing filled the air and Ventura heard the steady tapping of what his mind decided were nails dragging on the floor.

He heard the creature dragging its body across the floor. Darting around the back of the glowing drive core, he followed the walkway all the way round. Behind him he heard the creek and groan of metal as the creature attempted to follow, then the grunt and the sound of bending metal as it got stuck. *How could the alien be so stupid*, he thought. Its blunder had given him the time that he needed to get clear.

Dodging out onto the floor of the room he saw the shadow of the creature cast from between the drive cores, but refused to look. His heart was pounding with the expectation of what form it had taken, and he did not want to know. Already he could hear the wet liquid sounds of mucus dripping as the creature tried to turn. Going back up to the overhead gantry he stumbled forward along it until he reached the cables. Most of the work was done, and he knew that there would be only one more connection to break to trip out the cores.

The creature seemed to realise its mistake and he heard the banshee whine that sent a shiver down his spine just like it had done before when he had heard it echo through the ship. Now it was here beneath him, and the sound was so strong that he could barely think as his ears began to hurt.

He climbed the remaining ladder hand over hand and rolled out back onto the gantry. The part-finished work was there, just as he had left it. The cable connection was tight, just like the others had been. Leaning out as far as he dared, he used his body weight on the cable to try and sever the joint. Quickly he realised that he would have to swing his whole body out onto the other side of the protective handrail and jump up and down. Trying to put aside the thoughts that that would leave him in a perilous position if the creature attacked again or the cable gave way suddenly, he clambered out and rested all his weight on the connector.

It slipped loose and the banshee scream came again in unison, startling him so much that he nearly slipped. Only a timely grip on the metal of the handrail stopped his fall.

"You will die!" the twisted demonic voice of the creature boomed out. A tentacle swung up and reverberated off the edge of the handrail narrowly missing him. He felt the metal jump under the blow and was nearly knocked free. In determination he hung on, kicking again. The tentacle swung back, wrapping itself around the walkway. He thought it was going to flop along and find him to constrict him like a snake. But instead it morphed into a white polymer like liquid that flowed silently up until the walkway was covered several inches deep with the pulsating pool. Heads formed up out of the goo, followed by arms, limbs and other appendages that did not fit with anything recognisably human. They all lunged at one straight at him. Realising it was his last chance; he jumped and put all of his weight on the cable.

It parted with a crackle and he felt the glowing plasma it released burn up the side of his leg. The appendages of the creature lunged into the air, but missed and he watched it fade away as he fell. Jagged forks of lightning stretching between the cable and the collapsing mass of the creature.

As he hit the floor he felt the momentary jolt of pain and smelt blood before he slipped into unconsciousness, rewarded by the staccato of warning klaxons that told him that the drive cores were shutting down. As unconsciousness welled up to take him, he could only smile.

*　　　*　　　*　　　*　　　*

As the lights began to flicker he heard the banshee wail from a distance away. David hesitated at the final hatch back to the machine room as the sound grew from within. Fighting for breath, he leant against its edge keeping himself as much out of view as he could before leaning forward to get what view he dared around the edge.

He withdrew in horror – a tower of plasma stretched up from a pulsating lump on the floor to the gantry high above. He had seen something else too; the figure of the captain balanced precariously on the cabling.

He watched as the creature struck out at Ventura. David looked around desperately for a weapon to attack it, but there were none and it would have been a futile gesture.

There was a blinding flash of light and a cry from the gantry. Ventura fell amidst the forks of lightning that jetted along the metal work and over the creature.

Ventura landed heavily and David winced at the sharp, dry sound of bones cracking. A light spread over the plasma before it began to dissolve. The background hum of the drive cores had changed too and klaxons were sounding as the consoles lit up like Christmas trees and he realised that Ventura had succeeded – paying an ultimate price for success. Finally the hazy traces of the creature faded, and the lights in the machine room dipped as the glow of the drive cores winked out one by one.

The creature had gone. He dashed to where Ventura lay and knelt at his side but saw the blood spreading beneath the man's clothes. When he reached forward the man stirred and his eyes flickered open and he looked up into the engineer's face.

"Did I do it?" he gasped, his voice feeble and weak.

Consoles stuttered and closed down one by one. Screens rolled with data before shutting off, and he knew it was only a matter of time before the chain reaction would end with the Starliner dormant.

"Looks like you did," he replied, though the victory was sour.

The captain's face contorted into a grin and he coughed hard, blood trickling at the corner of his mouth. "I avenged my brother's death," he said; then he died.

There wasn't anything that David could do, even if he had any medical knowledge. He left the body where it lay and checked the banks of consoles in the withering light that remained from the Starliner's battery emergency lighting.

Had the shutting down of the *Persia* worked? Another console died, and the background hum of the air conditioning wound down followed by the sound of the klaxons weakening then stuttering to silence. Then the emergency lighting dimmed to almost nothing too.

For a minute he was certain that it had worked and let out a whoop of joy. Then it dawned on him that he still had to get the systems back up and running if he was going to live. What was it they had said? Wait for everything to shut down, wait some more for good measure then flick the switch back on.

He gazed across the consoles with one question on his mind – which switch?

"There aren't any bloody switches," he cursed, "They're all damn computer terminals."

It took him a while to work his way across the controls, looking at one blank panel after another. One panel, however, was different to the others. The screen looked different and looking closer it was because it was glowing. A line of text appeared in the top left corner, faint but legible enough to make his heart miss a beat.

Programme saved. Rebooting system from files.

Even as he watched he saw the flicker of lights across other consoles appearing and behind him one of the dark drive cores began to hum as the whole system began to reactivate.

"No!" he screamed, banging a fist on the console.

The computer had overridden the shutdown and was bringing the Starliner back online. Like a Judas it had faithfully saved everything – did that include the creature? Dezza had said that it could exist between energy and matter – did that include saving itself to the computer's hard disk arrays?

The lights in the machine room flickered back on and he knew there wasn't much time. Wrenching a metal back of an adjacent chair he rained blows down upon the consoles as hard as he could in a fit of frustration and anger. Fittings cracked open under the heavy rain of blows and several of the screens fizzled as they smashed. Out of breath, he flung the chair back to the floor and frantically searched the consoles until he found the one he was looking for.

The words of the faded figure that had fought its way out of the creature's consciousness in the corridor rang in his head as he keyed in his codes and hoped that the computer had not yet had the chance to lock him out – it hadn't. With a sneer on his face he typed quickly. Finally he typed in the command to execute the programme and reams of text scrolled on the screen.

"Put that in your rocket booster and flame it," he hissed. Then he turned and ran from the machine room as one by one the dead consoles flickered back into life.

*   *   *   *   *

The air conditioning rumble disappeared and the lights quickly followed to darkness; Dezza's heart spiked – so they had managed it? He blundered around banging into walls and tripping over objects in the dark, and realised that he was completely blind. What if the power did not come back on? He felt his panic rising as the minutes went by and he struggled to surpress the feeling that the Starliner had become his tomb. What would happen to him? There was a lot of atmosphere on the stranded vessel. Without an atmosphere breach would he starve to death before the air turned bad? There were too many questions that he wasn't sure that he really wanted to know the answer to.

He swore out loud before tripping over an unseen piece of décor in the darkness. Sprawling to the floor he began to fear that there was no way out. How long would it take them to turn the Starliner's systems back on if they could? Minutes, hours or never?

Then the glimmer of light appeared in the distance and headed towards him. *It's the creature,* were his first thoughts, but as it drew closer he realised it was the emergency lighting flickering back on up the corridor. It illuminated in sections, and quickly he found himself bathed in the sickly yellow glow.

At the side of the corridor a staircase led down to the lower decks and he took it three steps at a time. At the bottom though an airtight hatch had shut tight, blocking off further access downward into the crew areas.

He tried the controls set into the wall at the hatch's edge, but they were dead. The computer had not yet reactivated these systems and with a sinking feeling he realised that there was no telling whether it would. He could not hang around here indefinitely. Instead he scouted around. In the mezzanine of the stairwell he discovered a large panel that had been opened. It made him curious instantly; it had to have been opened recently by one of the crew, and a gut instinct told him that Ventura and the engineer were the most likely. Inside the panel was a small open area. The lights had failed in this compartment, but he could see the glimmer of light through an open hatch in the floor. It had to be an emergency access point to bypass the hatches, and it had been used recently.

There were open cabinets along one wall and he saw that tools and some torches had been removed. There were other torches left and he grabbed one and hooked its safety cord to his waist – no point in getting caught out a second time. He felt a little more confident now and tested the beam. It shone with a brilliant whiteness, picking out every detail of the small compartment.

In the edge of the beam he saw motionless figures and his heart raced. In his panic he banged his head and saw stars before he realised that they were just fire protection suits lined up along the other wall. In the semi darkness they had looked like ghostly figures ready to pounce. Cursing himself for being so stupid, he crawled gingerly to the rim of the open hatch and peered through into the engineering levels beneath.

A figure appeared and scrabbled up over the edge. The creature? But the beam from the torch picked out a face that he recognised. Streaked in blood and covered in dirt and sweat, it was the engineer.

David hesitated too, and in that moment of surprise Dezza saw in his expression a man who could not be a facsimile made by the creature. The engineer sprawled at his feet, panting hard from exertion.

"You did it?" Dezza asked.

A worried look crossed David's face and Dezza felt the twisting in his gut as he knew the news was not good.

"No. The computer stepped in and stopped a full shutdown. The damn turncoat computer saved everything faithfully to disk and began rebooting the system."

"The creature saved itself to disk?"

"Yeah."

Dezza looked past him at the hatch. "Ventura?" he asked.

"Dead." David grabbed him and pushed him back out of the small compartment.

He blinked in the sudden brightness of the lights in the stairwell. The main lights had come back on replacing the sickly yellow of the emergency lighting.

David ushered him onto the stairs. "Creature, computer; they're pretty much the same thing now. Quick – we have to look for a way off this thing. There has to be a lifepod somewhere; something that the passengers missed. We have to get off this thing." He hesitated a moment. "Where's Philipa?"

"She's in the shuttle with the other passengers we found – we got a way to get out; I came back for you and Ventura."

"Get us back to the shuttle," David commanded.

Dezza hesitated and held back as his mind raced through his thoughts. The creature was not defeated – he thought to the *Cerberus* and the way it had kept coming back like a bad penny. "If the creature survives, we can't run. There will be nowhere to hide."

"I put the Rösenbridge actuator into a loop. It's counting down now, and there's no way to override it. When it triggers the main drive, this Starliner is out of here."

"But it will just keep coming back," Dezza wailed.

David shook his head. "Oh no. I got the idea from a guy called Tubs – he's in the creature, fighting from the inside. This baby will drop into the Rösenbridge and keep going until the drive cores are sucking fumes. There'll be no power to keep it going anywhere else, or to support the creature. It dies with the power then and there's nothing it can do to stop it."

Dezza's heart jumped at the mention of Tubs' name. "You saw Tubs," he asked slowly, remembering the moment at the pool that Tubs had appeared to him. He had survived – of sorts – in the mind of the creature. That tough old son of a bitch never had been a one to lie down and take it.

"How long have we got?"

"Thirty minutes as best."

They were already scrambling back up the stairwell with Dezza leading the way before the significance sank in for him. they did not have much time at all.

20

The hatch vibrated with the dull thud of knocking making the passengers jump. Philipa looked to the inside of the hatch, then looked back to Grant. "What do we do?"

He turned to the hatch hammered his fist three times in succession on the inside. "See what the answer is, of course."

Through the tiny Plexiglas viewing port he could see very little past his own reflection. The glass was thick and domed and made seeing anything of any detail a hopeless task. But it showed enough that the lights were on again in the umbilical corridor and that a figure stood before the hatch. It was impossible to see if there was anyone else. "There's someone there," he whispered.

The knocking came again. "No use seeing who it is," he said, straining to see through the curved Plexiglas, "it's worse than the hall of mirrors looking through this thing."

"Do we open it?" Philipa asked. Behind her other passengers mumbled similar sentiments.

"Hey! You out there!" Grant shouted at the top of his lungs, "Can you hear me?"

He ignored the way Philipa and the others jumped. Maybe he should have warned them he was going to shout first.

A muffled reply came through the thick steel, but it was enough for Philipa to jump forward to the hatch. "That's Ventura!" she blurted.

Grant's forehead creased into a frown. "Ventura? The captain?" he asked.

"He was one of the two Dezza went to find." She turned to the hatch and shouted as loudly as she could. "Hey! Are Dezza and David with you?"

The figure mumbled something, but the hatch was too thick to hear. She shook her head. "It's no use."

"Do we open it?" asked a passenger.

Grant looked around to see more than a dozen hopeful faces looking at him. Even Stanton regarded him with narrowed beady eyes as if waiting for him to make the wrong call so he could pounce again. He decided he had to be strong and not give the man his chance.

"Open it," he said firmly to Philipa. He looked to the passengers and pointed out a trio of big men. "You three, get over here and get ready if there's trouble."

They obliged, and stood ready with him as Philipa unlatched the lock.

Air hissed around the seals, and the hatch revolved slowly inwards and around out of the way. In the umbilical corridor silhouetted in the lights behind stood the figure of a single man, his chest heaving as he fought to get his breath.

"Ventura!" Philipa said, helping him into the shuttle. The captain collapsed in, exhausted by running. There were wounds on his face and hands and he was nursing an arm that was broken.

"What about the others?" Grant asked.

Ventura slid into a seat, helped by Philipa and the other men. The umbilical corridor outside was empty.

"Gone," Ventura panted, fighting for his breath, "Dead. I only just made it out alive. The ship is set to drop into the Rösenbridge; we have to leave or we'll be sucked into it."

Grant cast a glance to Philipa and saw her worried face. "What does that mean?"

She hurried to the hatch and pushed her weight against it to get it moving. "It means," she said, "That we are leaving now."

"But Dezza, and the other he went after?"

He saw Stanton rise from his chair and glare over. "You heard him, or are you deaf?"

He looked dumbly to the man, not expecting him to pounce like this.

"If the Starliner is a goner, then I say we leave now," said Stanton, turning to face the rest of the passengers as if he was on top of his soap box making a political speech. Grant realised only too late that he was making his bid to take control of the group once again.

Stanton marched over and took hold of the hatch, pulling it shut. No-one challenged him; the rest of the passengers wanted a route to safety too. Stanton looked down at the injured figure of the captain, slouched in the chair and breathing heavily. "Do you think you can get us clear of the Starliner?"

The captain nodded slowly, the motion causing him to wince in pain. "I can. Just help me up."

Stanton sneered at Grant, then put his arm around the captain, helping him to stand.

A knocking on the hatch made them all stop as the echo shot through the hull of the shuttle. someone else was in the umbilical corridor

"There's someone else out there!" she exclaimed.

Stanton hesitated but the captain did not reply or look back.

"We ought to see who's there" Stanton began, but the captain reached across and flung him to the ground.

"We go!" Ventura hissed, but it was no longer Ventura talking. As he turned Grant looked into alien eyes that were cold and inhuman sitting within a waxy face that was not real. In a flicker of an eye he knew the truth.

"Open the hatch!" he screamed at Philipa.

She twisted the handle before the creature could reach her and the heavy door hissed and opened. Grant was not sure what happened next exactly. One minute the captain stood in front of him and the next there was a scream that rocked the whole interior of the shuttle. He put his hands over his ears, but the pain persisted. Then, it was gone and the pain, the scream and the figure of the captain had all gone too. There was a flicker of static in the air that poured itself into the electrical fittings and disappeared.

From around the edge of the hatch two figures half fell and half ran into the shuttle in time to see the last of the static cloud dissipate and disappear.

"Shut the hatch!" Dezza shouted, already fumbling with the controls.

"It's already in!"

"Where is it?" Dezza demanded breathlessly.

Grant pointed to the ceiling. "It went into the electrics."

"Shit. That's all we need," said Dezza and dived for the cockpit.

*　　　*　　　*　　　*　　　*

Across the consoles of the cockpit, lights blinked and wavered and the holographic display was already spluttering back into life. Dezza slammed down into the pilot's seat and flicked banks of switches, but nothing happened. David hauled himself into the cockpit behind him.

He looked over the holographic images that were flickering in the air, trying to decipher the unfamiliar controls. "It's trying to get a connection to the *Persia* over the docking links."

Then he stopped, realising the significance. The creature was not whole – it wanted the rest of the entity that was probably still on the *Persia* struggling to get itself free from the hard disks that had saved it from the core shutdowns. The damn thing was trying to dial in for reinforcement!

"It isn't all here," he hissed, "It's trying to upload the rest of itself before the *Persia* drops into the Rösenbridge."

"Kill the power," shouted David.

"How?"

The engineer propelled himself out of the seat and ran back into the passenger cabin and Dezza followed.

They did not stop until he reached the back of the cabin. Bending down he ran his fingers over several almost hidden catches in the floor and hinged a section of it back up on itself revealing a way down into cramped crawl spaces.

"In here," he ordered, and dropped down through.

In the underbelly of the shuttle Dezza paused, old memories suddenly coming to the fore. He looked around at the cramped walkways and the electronics lain bare in open cable runs, and remembered the same spaces deep in the *Magellan*'s underbelly. He hung back, but David called out to him.

"Hey buddy, get over here. It takes two people to do this."

Dezza swallowed hurriedly and fought back the nerves as he crawled to David's side. His heart leapt as he saw the glowing chamber of the shuttle's own drive core. In an instant it was like he was back on the *Magellan* getting ready to see the body that had been in the drive core chamber.

The image was still there after all these years, burned on the back of his mind. There were some things that were impossible to forget. He tried to keep moving closer, but could not make himself move.

David rested with one hand on a bank of cable connectors. He looked back at Dezza. "What's up?"

"I... I can't," Dezza heard the frightened words come from him, "It's like all the things that happened before are happening again. I'm stuck in my own personal nightmare and it just keeps on coming around again and again." He pointed to the glowing drive core chamber. "I can't seem to do it. My mind won't let me." He felt the tears welling in his eyes and his heartbeat screaming in his ears.

"I need you're help. Be strong, buddy and we can do this. I can't do this without you."

Dezza nodded. Slowly he managed to coax himself forward.

David pointed to a bank of cable plugs along a console. "Pull these when I give the signal. Take no prisoners, and stop for nothing."

In a blinding flash, something appeared in the air, shimmering like a haze and growing stronger as tendrils extended out from the maze of electronics. A dull moan grew in volume, starting as a bass rumble and growing until it reached a high-pitched banshee squeal. Dezza wanted to cover his ears, to try and shut off the terrible sound. He felt the electrical buzzing creep over him, as the creature fought to take control and to stop them. He heard the shout from the engineer; he was not sure whether it was a shout to pull or a scream of pain, but he pulled the plugs apart, and screamed.

In a flash of brilliant light the whole crawl space seemed to explode. Then the light faded. The silence that it left behind was almost overpowering. For a moment neither spoke. Then Dezza plucked up the courage to ask the question. "Did we do it?" he whispered.

For a few seconds there was no reply, then he heard a sigh and he knew that David was still there too.

"Yes."

In the darkness, Dezza let out a whoop of joy.

"Not so fast," David warned from somewhere in front of him, "We've got to get this thing back up and running. The *Persia*'s still going to drop into the Rösenbridge, with or without us. I'd rather it go it alone. The plugs you've just pulled – push them back in now."

In the darkness Dezza fumbled over the connectors laid out somewhere in front of him. They had seemed so simple when there had been light, but now they seemed like a curious puzzle. Eventually he managed to find the vacant slots the cables had come from and push them home. A low glow came from the drive core, growing steadily stronger. He saw the beaming face of the engineer illuminated in the glow.

"Now get upstairs and get us the hell out of here whilst I plug the rest of the systems back in," David screamed at him, "Go!"

Turning back to the open hatchway he scrambled back up into the passenger compartment above.

*   *   *   *   *

He ignored the sea of faces that looked at him from hiding places, cowering. There was a smell of ozone still lingering in the air and he guessed that the creature had put in an appearance, before the power had spiked and died.

Philipa rushed up to him as he reached the front of the cabin. "David?" She asked, her voice faltering.

"He's okay," he replied. "I need you up in the cockpit with me."

Pushing past the crush of confused passengers he made it back into the cockpit and she followed. He thumped down into the pilot's chair again and she slid into the chair next to him.

"Get everything you can online that we need – air, life support all that sort of thing," he ordered, flicking switches and powering up the console. He was quickly rewarded by the cool flow of air from the life support systems. At least they weren't all going to asphyxiate.

The holographic display buzzed into life in front of him and he smiled a genuine smile of happiness for the first time in a long time.

"What's up?" Philipa asked.

"Back in the saddle!"

The shuttle rocked and the sound of metal on metal grated through the cockpit. The flat view of the inside of the shuttle bay beyond the screens began to move up and away from them. A lip appeared, and then white-painted steel was replaced by the vastness of deep space. He leant forward and saw the huge bulk of the *Persia* rolling away from them until details like portholes and antenna were lost into the distance.

"Do you think she really is going to drop into the Rösenbridge?"

"David thinks so. I believe him."

Before he could say anything else a bank of buzzers wailed across the control desk. The huge expanse of the Starliner appeared to wink and flicker and then the whole vessel disappeared leaving nothing more than the twinkling of stars in its wake. In a feeling of strange calm the shuttle was left alone drifting in the abyss of space.

Dezza activated the radio channels. On most of the bands there was nothing but static, but on one the sound of frantic talking broke through the noise.

Philipa leant closer. "What's that?"

"A beacon from the outer planet fields."

The holographic display in front of them shimmered and changed as the computer calculated the distance and plotted in a new course. It was going to be a long drag for the shuttle, he knew, but the fuel gauges showed full and they could make it within a couple of days.

Looking back out through the Plexiglas screens he saw the stars with a new outlook that he had not had since the day the *Solitude* had first dropped out of the Rösenbridge and picked up the *Cerberus* on the scopes. With a jolt he realised that the memory did not bother him anymore. He thought about Tubs and Zoë, and the military crew that had come back years later with him. It was the first time that the memories did not bother him at all.

"I went to the stars," he murmured, "And the stars came home."

Philipa just shook her head as if unsure what to make of him. "You know," she said, "I always thought you were odd from the moment you stepped onto my shuttle and started acting all weird. I never thought that it would come to me saying 'thanks' to you for saving my life."

But Dezza hardly heard her; he was too busy being happy and at peace with himself for the first time in years.

Also by Jennifer Kirk

Bringing Home the Stars

Dezza is a salvager in a harsh world. Forced to confront an urban myth, he is flung into a nightmare aboard a derelict Starliner in uncharted space. He loses his friends, his career and his reputation. When he returns home, he struggles to come to terms with society's prejudices and the demons that lurk within his own mind fuelled by the memories of his mistakes.

Isolated by society, he is thrown a lifeline by the one person who might believe his story. On one condition: return to the derelict. He is offered the chance of redemption and to confront his demons but in the process he must face the horrors that took his world from him.

Available in paperback and all eBook formats.

Also by Jennifer Kirk

The Orb of Arawaan

Universal holism is in turmoil. A new force has emerged
from the Eastern arm of the central spiral, mystical and
unafraid to embrace new technology. Marching forth
victorious, the mysterious forces of the New Order have
lain waste and conquered a hundred thousand worlds.

Those who have stood their ground against them have
been defeated and cast aside. Those who submit become
the new frontier in an Empire promising to stretch to the
eight corners of the known worlds. Now, perhaps there is
nothing to stand in the way of the advancing forces,
except the power of the lost artefact: The Orb.

Available in all eBook formats now
and paperback in 2012

Also by Jennifer Kirk

Daytrippers

The night before the morning after. Everybody loves a
good after hours party, except for when the Boss has
somehow managed to get himself invited, and the home
brew ginger beer would make a hippy proud...

Available in all eBook formats now

Also by Jennifer Kirk

The Life of Nob T. Mouse

When the universe was born in the chaos of the Big
Bang, a hole was ripped in reality. To prevent the influx of
unreal creatures from other dimensions, the hole was
plugged by an amorphous blob called The Mass.

Reality on the Mass is unstable and affected strongly by
belief, so it's a very good thing that Nob T. Mouse (the 'T'
stands for 'The') lives there. He just wants a quiet life in
his frontier town, where he runs a café.

Unfortunately not everyone who lives around him is so
inclined. Join Nob Mouse as he battles the forces of
chaos and the unreal in his never-ending quest to get
some peace and quiet.

The Life of Nob T. Mouse is Britain's first Internet comic.
You can read it daily, for free, at **www.nobmouse.net**.